"I absolutely loved this roman... loving people and places that c... ...on your terms. If you've ever tried to make yourself smaller for a world that was never meant to contain you, this book will be a balm to your soul."

—DAHLIA ADLER, author of *Home Field Advantage*

"Jenna Voris beautifully explores the high and low notes of fame, showing that there's no shame in wanting people to know your name, but the choices you make to reach that goal are what really matter. A must-read for anyone who loves layered characters, true-to-life personalities, and country music!"

—JASON JUNE, *New York Times* bestselling author

"*Every Time You Hear That Song* is the literary equivalent of hitting the open road with the windows down and the radio blasting. A powerful, moving anthem for anyone who's dared to dream big and grow new roots while discovering the meaning of home. After devouring this book, I'm officially in my Jenna Voris era."

—BRIAN D. KENNEDY, author of *A Little Bit Country* and *My Fair Brady*

"*Every Time You Hear That Song* takes readers on a captivating journey across miles and decades as two young women chase their dreams and discover who they are. With the fast-paced storytelling and lyrical prose of the best country songs, this book made me a Decklee Cassel and Jenna Voris fan for life!"

—KAITLYN HILL, author of *Love from Scratch* and *Not Here to Stay Friends*

"The scavenger-hunt book of my dreams! *Every Time You Hear That Song* is a love letter to the strong hold music has on all of us and the magic that comes with sharing it. I loved following Darren as she hunts down the ultimate prize and finds herself along the way."

—JENNA MILLER, author of *Out of Character*

ALSO BY JENNA VORIS

Made of Stars

Every Time You Hear That Song

Jenna Voris

VIKING

VIKING
An imprint of Penguin Random House LLC, New York

First published in the United States of America by Viking,
an imprint of Penguin Random House LLC, 2024

Visit us online at PenguinRandomHouse.com.

Library of Congress Cataloging-in-Publication Data is available.

ISBN 9780593623398
1st Printing

Printed in the United States of America

LSCC

Edited by Maggie Rosenthal
Design by Kate Renner
Text set in Macklin Text

For the wildfire girls who burn too bright

And for Chelsea,
who's been there for this book (and me)
since the beginning

THE TENNESSEAN

NASHVILLE, TENN.
JULY 16, 2024

Decklee Cassel, Beloved Pioneer of Country-Pop Music, Is Dead at 76

Decklee Cassel, singer, songwriter, producer, and country-pop icon, died Tuesday morning at the age of 76 after a two-year battle with brain cancer. According to her rep, she passed peacefully in the bedroom of her Nashville home.

With 22 No. 1 singles across the US pop and country charts from 1971 to 2011, Cassel earned ten Grammys and 12 CMA awards, along with membership to both the Country Music and Rock & Roll Halls of Fame, respectively. She sold more than 100 million records worldwide, topping international charts with well-loved hits "Times Are Changing," "Little Blue Suitcase," and "Isn't It Trouble?"

Decklee Cassel was born Cleo Elizabeth Patrick on Jan. 28, 1948, in Mayberry, Arkansas. She attended Mayberry County High School for one year before moving to Memphis, Tennessee, to pursue music full-time. Her smooth, smoldering vocals and musical mastery earned the attention of DCR Records executive Richard Grasso, who produced all 42 of her studio albums.

But it wasn't until "Whiskey Red," Cassel's first No. 1 record in 1971, that she became a household name. Cowritten with her longtime collaborator Mickenlee Hooper, the soul-stirring ballad about love and loss sold over two million copies. The duo went on to cowrite 16 more No 1. hits before parting ways in the nineties due to creative differences.

The funeral is being handled by the Nashville Directive Funeral Home and the Decklee Cassel Estate. The Decklee Cassel Memorial Time Capsule, which contains a new album of previously unreleased songs, exclusive photos, and mementos throughout her career, will be opened live at the ceremony and released to the public immediately afterward.

Cassel is survived by her brother, sister-in-law, and three nieces. Although she never married or had children, she always said the fans were enough. Today, we mourn as family.

ONE

Darren

On the morning of Decklee Cassel's funeral, I'm in the employee lounge of Bob's Gas Station, losing a fight with the coffee machine for the second time that day.

To be fair, I never stood a chance. Everything at Bob's is at least a decade older than me, but the fact that this specific machine has started spontaneously leaking boiling water whenever I clock in feels a little personal. Kendall is already behind the register, too busy holding back the bleary-eyed morning crowd to lend me a hand, so this, overall, is not the best way to start my morning.

Oh, and Decklee Cassel is dead.

There's also that.

I slap the OUT OF ORDER sign onto the machine and lug it back into the open. "Sorry, folks. Energy drinks are third cooler on the left."

Kendall finally looks up from the register as the crowd dissipates. "Coffee out again?" he asks. "Weren't you supposed to fix that?"

I roll my eyes. Kendall is *technically* shift lead and *technically* my boss when Bob's not around, but he's barely a year older than me and only marginally better at operating our ancient cash register, so I don't like to think of him as "being in charge." I've known Kendall since the day my second-grade teacher went into labor and left us with the class next door. We've worked together for the last three years and the idea of him telling me what to do is still genuinely laughable.

"No, *Bob* was supposed to fix it," I say, giving the coffee maker one more shove for emphasis. "This thing hates me, remember?"

"It doesn't hate you, it's just Friday." Kendall braces his elbows on the counter. "Right on schedule."

He has this theory that Bob's coffee machines know what day it is. He swears they know what *time* it is, too, because one of them always seems to go out right in the middle of the morning rush. Today, at least, it's summer, so we don't have to break the news to the school crowd. Any other day I might have laughed along with him because this whole thing really *is* getting ridiculous, but today is Decklee Cassel's funeral.

And there's absolutely nothing funny about that.

In a town this small, every change feels like a kick to the gut—swift and sudden and aching with a strange sense of inevitability. You feel it in the air first, and when I came home from work Tuesday to find Mom already waiting by the door, I knew something big had happened. For a second, my mind ran wild with every terrible possibility. She was sick again. She lost her job. They were firing *me* for some reason.

But then Mom took a deep breath, squeezed my hand, and said, "They found Decklee Cassel at home this morning, Darren. It was peaceful, but . . . she's gone."

Her voice had cracked on the last word, and I was so relieved at the momentary confirmation that she herself was fine that I didn't register the news. She had to repeat herself two more times before the reality hit me, and even then, I hadn't really believed it until I checked my phone and found memorial videos and posts already pouring in.

> The world lost a good one today, RIP Decklee Cassel.

> I'll never forget meeting her backstage in Tupelo. Her music changed my life. I'm forever grateful.

> I have *Whiskey Red* on repeat today. Decklee's music was my sanctuary as a kid. Still don't know how to process this.

Most of the comments and tributes I saw were written by people more than twice my age, fans who grew up with Decklee's music and followed her meteoric rise in real time. Maybe that's why I haven't posted anything myself. I don't know many seventeen-year-old girls whose favorite singer is a country artist old enough to be their grandmother. In a town this small, there are some things you keep to yourself.

The familiarity smothers you after a while.

I pull my phone out of my pocket, stealing a glance in Kendall's direction in case he suddenly decides to start enforcing our *no cell phones* policy, before opening Instagram.

I have my private account with a handful of followers from school, but *Mayberry Unpublished* is the one I really care about. The account started as last year's journalism final, a semester-long feature story broken down into individual interviews, clips, and sound bites that my best friend, Emily, said was *very Caroline Calloway* of me. Instead of a single human subject, I wrote about this town—its singular, stifling pull and all the people caught in its orbit. Somewhere along the way, the account developed a decent following of people outside the county line, and even though the school year is long over, I still update as often as I can.

It's not much, but it's something to keep the boredom away, to keep this town from feeling like one long cry for help and to keep me from counting the days until I can pack my bags and leave for good. My post from this morning already has a few hundred likes—a quick interview I'd snagged with Melanie Grauer, a girl a few grades below me. I asked if she'd heard about Decklee Cassel and she just shrugged and said, "Yeah, I saw. I don't really listen to her music, but my dad was really upset about it."

And that was it. No choking back tears, no shake of her head. Decklee could have walked right by us with her baby-blue guitar slung across her back and Melanie wouldn't have noticed.

But her interview contrasts so well with the one next to it that I really can't be mad. I'd found Clayton Sperry's dad loading dog food into the bed of his truck the day the news broke and asked if he wanted to talk about it. That's a little secret I learned about interviewing last year. People in Mayberry don't like questions. They're suspicious of most things—outsiders, CNN, people with too many piercings—but ask them to tell you about someone? Ask if they want to talk? They open right up.

When I asked Clayton's dad about Decklee, the wrinkles on his face deepened and he ran a hand through his graying beard. "Everyone my age has a story about the first time they heard a Decklee Cassel song," he said. "'Losing You' came out the summer of '73 and the first person I thought of was Ellie. I remember getting in my truck, driving all the way to Little Rock to see her, and we've been married fifty years this Friday. That's what those songs did. I think this town is going to miss her a lot."

Even now, I can't help grinning as I scroll past his photo on my grid. It has all the beats of a good story—the lede, the hook, the happy ending. His interview next to Melanie's is a juxtaposition even I couldn't have planned. A generational gap with me somewhere in the middle.

"Heads up!" Kendall tosses a bag of gummy bears in my direction, and I barely reach over in time to catch it. "There's a bunch of inventory in the back. If you ever decide to work today, you can totally restock."

I slide my phone back in my pocket. "I'm sorry, what was that?"

"I said you can totally restock."

"No, the other thing."

Kendall grins and rips the top off another bag, dropping a handful of candy into his mouth. "Nothing."

"That's right." I walk back down the aisle as the door shuts behind our last customer, Instagram momentarily forgotten. "Because it would be pretty bold of you to talk about my work schedule when you're the one who was late this morning."

Kendall laughs, head tipped back enough for the sun falling through the windows to cut warm shadows across his brown skin. "I honestly didn't think you noticed. You've been so quiet."

Something in my chest twists. Of course I'm quiet. I almost tell him why. But our relationship is nothing more than the result of living in the same small town. I know what Kendall eats for lunch every day. I know where his brothers live and what his parents do for work. I know him in the same shallow, superficial way I know everyone in Mayberry, and that's exactly how I want to keep it.

So instead, I snatch the bag of gummy worms from his grasp, dump the rest into my mouth, and say, "I notice everything," before pushing myself off the counter and striding into the back.

We only get a few more customers the rest of the morning, but it doesn't get quiet enough to risk checking my phone again. As far as part-time jobs go, Bob's isn't bad. Working at a gas station wasn't exactly at the top of my vision board, but the pay is decent, there's plenty of air-conditioning, and it'll be easy enough to leave when I go to college next year. There used to be another station up the road, but it closed a few years ago and the raccoons took over before the people could. Now it sits abandoned and unused on the side of State Road 34, a great place to go after football games to drink stolen wine and summon ghosts.

I know because Madison, Emily, and I tried to summon ghosts multiple times last year to varying degrees of success. Madison is still convinced the place is haunted.

But that leaves Bob's as the only viable gas station for thirty miles. And since we're the sole place for people to grab cold drinks and subpar snacks, it also means Kendall and I aren't alone when Decklee Cassel's funeral starts.

I don't know if he means to have this specific channel on. I don't think he knows it's unmuted, but when the first chords of a church processional start, a bag of Moon Pies slips through my fingers. It hits the floor right as Kendall reaches for the remote.

"Wait!" I'm surprised I can speak at all. The sight of people gathered in the pews on-screen feels like a shard in my chest. *Real. This is real.* I swallow as several heads turn in my direction. "Can you leave it?"

Kendall glances from me to the customers, most of whom have stopped shopping to watch. I know them all. There's Ms. Rapisarda, my fourth-grade teacher, Alan Carmichael from across the street, Paul the librarian. They're all watching the screen and I'm watching them so I don't have to look at the casket slowly being marched down the aisle.

I've never been to a funeral, so I'm not sure how much of the ceremony is normal and how much is happening because this is *Decklee Cassel*. I try to place each speaker and musical guest as they come on-screen, but I don't have Mom's encyclopedic knowledge of celebrity names and faces. I recognize Hunter Wallstreet in the first row, but only because that kind of star power is hard to miss. He has to be nearing ninety and his hair is shockingly white on camera, head bowed as an artist I don't know performs a stripped-back cover of the first song Hunter and Decklee recorded together.

Behind him, hand in hand with his husband, is Markell Fansworth. His intricate purple suit stands out in the sea of black and navy, the rhinestones on his sleeves catching the light whenever he moves, and I wonder, briefly, if that's an inside joke. If Decklee would have hated the formal, stifling atmosphere of her own funeral enough to make her oldest friend promise to make it interesting. For a minute, I wonder how she would look among the crowd of mourners, dressed in layers of sequins and glitter, arm in arm with her longtime writing partner, Mickenlee Hooper, and scratching out lyrics for their next number-one song on the back of the offering envelopes.

The thought makes my throat close. Decklee and Mickenlee haven't worked together in decades, but I think part of me expected her to be here despite whatever creative differences drove them apart years ago.

I'm distantly aware of the customers still hovering around me, the cool interior of the gas station, and the fact that I should definitely be working right now. But I can't move. I'm stuck in the aisle, watching the funeral continue as I grip the edge of the freezer, fingers slowly going numb with each passing second.

It's Kennedy Grasso, Decklee's goddaughter, who concludes the ceremony eventually. She's been sitting up front the entire time, wiping her eyes and nodding in time to each musical guest, and as she stands, I wonder if she thinks the eulogies sound genuine. It's hard to capture someone like Decklee Cassel with words. I haven't seen one article get it right. It's always lists of accomplishments and accolades, a character in shoulder pads and sparkly boots; none of the things that make her feel vibrant and rich and real.

I think I could write a story like that one day, if someone let me.

The church quiets as Kennedy looks up from the podium, a smooth copper box clutched in her hands. My fingers curl around the phone in my pocket and I wonder if Mom is watching at home, perched in the middle of our couch, right where the cushions dip down. I should be there with her. We should be experiencing this together. But when I tear my eyes away from the TV, I realize I'm not alone at all.

Ms. Rapisarda blinks back tears as she presses a hand to her chest. Paul the librarian has a bottle of Gatorade clutched in one hand, like he can't quite remember what he came here for in the first place. I swallow over the lump in my throat. *Community.* That's another thing Decklee was always good at creating, and I'm grateful for it now, for how it makes this singular pocket of Mayberry feel a little more like home.

Then Kendall looks up and, because he has this complete inability to read a room, asks, "What's in the box?" so loudly half the gas station jumps.

"Shhh." Ms. Rapisarda swats him with her purse before I have the chance. "It's the time capsule!"

I wipe my palms on my jeans, suddenly sweaty despite the frigid air-conditioning. I picture Mom doing the same, leaning forward on the couch, caught in the spell of Decklee Cassel's legacy.

"Thank you all for being here," Kennedy says, voice crackly on the old gas station TV. "I really think Decklee would have loved this. She loved when she could bring people together. That's what she wanted her music to do and that's what she wanted *this* to do." She taps the box. "For the last fifty years, she's been tucking things away in here. She wrote journals during every tour, kept photographs and ticket stubs, and even recorded an entire brand-new album with the explicit instruction to release it only after she was no longer with us," Kennedy continues. "And even though that day came sooner than any of us would have liked, I'm comforted by the fact she found peace in this project. That she found joy in the music."

I can't stop my toe from tapping a nervous rhythm on the linoleum floor. This time capsule isn't a secret; Decklee talked about it all the time. She called it a mosaic, a scrapbook of her life, and even though I, too, wish the situation was different, the idea of new Decklee music soothes a bit of the ache in my chest.

New songs for me. New songs for Mom.

It's been eight years since the last Decklee Cassel album. She still made music after Mickenlee left and every record was objectively a hit, but it never quite replicated the magic of her old stuff, the songs I knew were born on Tennessee porches, in smoky bars and old church pews.

Kennedy slides a key from the chain around her neck and slips it into the time capsule's lock. When it turns, I swear I hear it click from where I stand, five hundred miles from Nashville. No one in that church breathes as her hands hover over the box. Then she lifts the lid and we all lean forward. Even Kendall cranes his neck to see from behind the counter. The lid falls back, the cameras zoom in, and I suck in a sharp, bewildered breath.

Because there isn't an album at all. There aren't crisp tour journals, piles of black-and-white photographs, or letters penned in Decklee's familiar, looping handwriting.

The time capsule is empty.

TWO

Decklee
Texarkana, 1963

This is how you light the way—with the bridges you burn behind you.

There's a single bulb flickering above the ticket counter in the Texarkana Greyhound station. I watch it pulse and rattle and wonder if it knows me, somehow. If light can still recognize light in different forms. The man behind the counter looks half-asleep, head propped in his hand as he drums his fingers on the table.

He doesn't know about the cash tucked against my hip, stolen from my father's wallet in the dead of night. He doesn't know about my brother's watch around my wrist, under my coat where no one can see. He doesn't know I stole that, too, that sometimes the only things you need to bring are a packed bag, a guitar case, and a dream too big to fit in either.

My mother gave me that guitar on my tenth birthday. She told me it was okay to take it slow, that everyone learns at their own pace, but my pace is wildfire. My pace is lightning and luck and all the desperate longing of the universe. Mayberry eats wildfire girls, though. It's a place of locked doors and limits, such a messy tangle of contradictions that I don't know where to start pulling them apart.

"When's the next bus out of here?"

The man behind the counter looks me up and down and for a second, I wonder what he sees. A fifteen-year-old girl in a dirty coat, skinny and pale with a wild nest of blond curls that never lays flat. I wonder if part of him sees who I'll become, or if he's just looking through me—another nameless passenger on another unremarkable night. He rubs a hand over his face.

"Where do you want to go?"

Everywhere. To Nashville, where the streets pulse with music. To New York, a city on the brink. To Los Angeles, where it's warm and balmy and rich.

"Out," I say without hesitation. And I slide my father's cash across the counter.

Later, I sit in the corner of the station, single ticket clutched in my hand, and close my eyes. My father cooked for us last night, like he had every day for the last month. He ruffled my hair and pulled me close and whispered, "I know you're upset, Cleo. I'm sorry. We'll talk about it next year."

But I know we won't. My father is soft and sentimental and weak. He won't send me to the city, no matter how many times I ask him to let me work. He doesn't care that I still see my mother in every inch of that house because Mayberry got her, too, in the end. It chewed her up and spit her into the ground like she was nothing, and now everywhere I look feels like an open grave.

It feels like I'm next.

My ticket is damp with sweat by the time I hand it over and board the Greyhound. Number seventeen. Express to Memphis, Tennessee. I sit alone toward the back of the bus and slide my bag under the seat. My guitar case stays locked in my arms, though, smooth leather pressed against my chest.

I've never been on a bus before, never ridden in anything but the bed of my father's truck, arms wide, wind in my hair. But now I feel the growl of the engine under my feet, shuddering through me, shaking dust off my bones. The next time I see Mayberry, it's from the road. We're moving, cutting north as the sun breaks over the trees, and I catch a glimpse of the pale church steeple in the distance. Then I blink and it's gone.

I close my eyes and rest my forehead against the window. Leaving is a little bit like learning to breathe, I think. It's like waking up after a long, restless sleep to find the entire world feels vibrant and new. Maybe that's what makes it worth it.

Maybe this is something I'll write into a song one day.

THREE

Darren

¶ 'm still thinking about Decklee's empty time capsule when Madison picks me up from my shift.

"Is that a new polo?" she asks when I slide into her passenger seat. "Did they finally promote you?"

Sometimes I'm convinced Madison is the one destined to be a reporter, not me. She notices everything, like the time Emily accidentally bought a hair dye two shades darker than usual, or the fact that I'm wearing a blue polo now instead of red.

"As if Bob would ever promote me," I mutter. "No, the coffee maker exploded this morning, so I had to borrow one of Kendall's."

"Cute!"

I resist the urge to roll my eyes as Madison pulls out of the parking lot. She's one of the only people my age who has a car—a privilege she says is entirely a result of her parents' divorce guilt. Her younger sister got a puppy and she got a 2001 Ford Taurus named Betsy who occasionally projectile vomits oil onto the road. I personally don't think those two gifts are comparable, but I'm never going to complain about being chauffeured to and from work. I lean my head against the window, letting the cool air wash over me as we pull back onto the road.

"Wow." Madison smirks. "What are you going to do when I leave? Are you mentally prepared to walk tomorrow?"

I groan. "Don't remind me. Any chance you want to skip camp and drive me around forever?"

"Absolutely not." She flashes me a wicked grin. "You could always ask Kendall for a ride."

"I don't know him."

"Yes you do. Everyone knows him."

But that's not what I mean, and she knows it. Of course we all know each other. That's, like, Mayberry's whole thing, but it doesn't mean I want to be trapped in a car with just anyone.

"I'm just saying it's an option," Madison adds as we turn onto my street. "Forced proximity is a really good trope."

"Right," I say. "And which one did you want me to try last week?"

"Fake dating," she answers immediately. "But that usually works best if you're trying to make someone jealous."

Madison pulls into my driveway, shifts the car into park, and looks at me expectantly. I never know what she wants me to do with this kind of information. After she announced that my ex-boyfriend, Benton, and I were "endgame" (we weren't) and that Emily was in a "clear enemies-to-lovers relationship" with her lab partner (she wasn't), I started taking everything she says with a grain of salt. Madison might have a pile of well-worn romance books in her back seat at all times, but I have yet to find a story in this town that truly feels like me.

"Well, on that note." I grab my bag and open the door, squinting as the afternoon sun hits me square in the face. "See you in August. Send me postcards."

"I will!" Madison reaches across the car, pulling me into a brief, rib-crushing hug. "Stay out of trouble!"

Betsy's gears grind back into drive as I shut the door. I wave until Madison disappears around the corner, then turn to find Mom already sitting on Carla's porch next door, magazine in hand.

"Yikes," she says when I drop my bag on the steps. "You look exhausted. What happened?"

My face twists as I remember the events of that morning. "Lost a fight with the coffee machine."

She laughs, sun catching in her soft brown curls, and I collapse into the rocking chair next to her. We don't have a porch of our own, but over the years we've slowly taken over Carla's— sitting outside when the weather's nice, letting her feed us baked goods, talking about everything and nothing with equal enthusiasm. Mom kicks her feet up on the railing and I do the same, savoring our familiar pattern. This is another great thing about summer: she's always home. As soon as June hits and she doesn't have to worry about being a "responsible English teacher," it's all T-shirt Mom and Trying to Garden Mom and Drinking White Claws at Noon Mom. All the versions of her I wish I'd had earlier. All the versions I'm still scared to lose.

"Did you hear back from Doctor Vij?" I ask, tone as casual as I can make it. "About next week?"

She nods, knuckles tightening on her magazine. "It's on the calendar."

I exhale as best I can. Mom's been in remission for years, but the thought of more appointments, more doctors, and more tests always makes my chest tighten.

She got sick for the first time when I was seven, back when we were still getting used to being a family of two. Dad was gone—somewhere in Oregon pretending he hadn't left a wife and daughter alone in a dead-end town with no way out—and I don't think Mom ever told him about her diagnosis. I don't think he asked. It was always just the two of us, in our little house across from the post office, backed up against a soybean field and seven miles from the Oklahoma border. Sometimes, I'm grateful everything happened when I was so young because I don't remember the worst of it. I don't remember the nights it got bad, when my grandparents came in from Texas and we all sat in the waiting room of a strange city hospital two hours away from anything familiar.

But I do remember Carla, our neighbor with the blue eyes and soft, silver hair, who took me in after school and let me play in her flower beds until the damp earth soaked through my jeans. I remember her teaching me to play piano one tremulous note at a time until I forgot all about needles and tubes and hospital walls. I remember my teachers bringing us home-cooked meals, the post office workers sending a gift basket directly to Mom's hospital bed, and I remember thinking that, despite everything wrong with Mayberry, things like this didn't happen just anywhere.

And I absolutely remember the day Mom taught me about Decklee Cassel.

It was one of those rare weeks where she was home—tired but not in pain. We were a year into treatment, and she spent more time in the car and at the hospital than with me, but that day, we were tucked together in her room, sunlight dappled across the worn gray carpet. I was absentmindedly flipping through homework I hadn't started when Mom leaned down, put her face close to mine, and whispered, "Do you want to do something fun, Darren?"

Mom talks about everything like that—like it's the single best, most *amazing* thing to happen in the history of the universe. I used to believe her, but after the third Renaissance Faire and the endless black-and-white movie nights, I learned to view her promises of "fun" with an appropriate level of wariness. I mean, the woman loves Steinbeck novels and the Star Wars prequels. She doesn't exactly have flawless taste.

But that day, I nodded and told myself that no matter what came next, I would pretend to love it because Mom needed a win. She ruffled my hair and reached over to where her ancient iPod sat docked in the speaker, turning the dial until the first notes of a soft guitar solo blared through the house. I sat cross-legged on the bed, enthralled as the opening chords gave way to smooth, pure vocals, and decided that finally—*finally*—this was something I didn't have to pretend to like.

The first album she played me that day was *Whiskey Red.* I

didn't understand the lyrics back then, or hear the deep yearning woven into every bridge, but I loved it from the start. Each
verse was thunder in my veins, the hooks catching me right
in the chest. We played it on repeat that afternoon, just ran
through the tracks again and again until I memorized every
word. I can't sing to save my life, but Mom has this beautiful
voice, and when the doctors declared her cancer-free and she
got to ring the bell on the way out of Little Memorial Hospital
almost five years after her first treatment, we danced around
the kitchen exactly like we had that day in her bedroom and
belted "Times Are Changing" at the top of our lungs. After that,
we sang in the car back and forth from her checkups, on the
way to school when I needed a morale boost, whenever and
wherever we wanted.

Those songs are a shield. They're armor. I wrapped them
around my shoulders back then, held them close, and whispered them into Mom's ear on the bad days. They were magic
and they *worked*. Because she's still here and we're both still
singing.

People never talked about Decklee Cassel being from
Mayberry unless it was to compliment her for getting out, because here's the truth: no one cares about towns like this until
they're behind you. Listening to her music always felt like someone was ripping back the hazy curtain of my life, leaning in and
shouting, *Look at her. She got out. What are you still doing
here?* Because if Decklee could leave, if she could turn herself
into a star, what was stopping me?

Mayberry County High School isn't exactly known for its extracurriculars. Most kids take Newspaper as a blow-off class, or to sneak pictures of themselves into the yearbook. I take it for a way out. We didn't even have an editor in chief until I created the position halfway through my first semester, and I've spent the last three years building a pretty decent staff. We'd be better if the school actually let us cover the beats I want, but I only have one more year of high school left. One more year of being told what to write and how to write it by adults who never pushed the boundaries of this town far enough to see if they would bend.

That's what Decklee Cassel and Mickenlee Hooper did when they wrote together. They *shattered* boundaries, and when a partnership as powerful as theirs ends, I feel like it should leave something behind. It should tear the world apart. Instead we get empty time capsules and unfulfilled promises.

I don't know why I expected this town to give me anything different.

The screen door slams behind me and Carla steps back onto the porch, plate of almond cookies in hand. She's in blue today, a soft linen dress that brings out her eyes and perfectly matches the butterfly brooch on her collar. "Ah, there you are, Darren." She pats my shoulder as she sets the plate next to my chair. "Busy day at work? How's Mr. Wilkinson?"

I grin and take two of the cookies. Only Carla—perfect, polite Carla—calls Kendall *Mr. Wilkinson*, like he's the lead in a Jane Austen novel. "He's fine. How's the garden?"

We all crane our necks to take in her front lawn, following the line of the sprinklers as they pulse back and forth. Carla

Krenik is good at a lot of things. Baking almond cookies, finding vintage jewelry in the back of estate sales, giving advice that's both scathingly blunt and refreshingly honest, but this garden has always been her pride and joy. I used to think she gardened because she was lonely, living by herself in her seventies in a town with no family or visitors, but I think she just genuinely loves it. This summer, she's growing roses.

"They look good," I say, stretching my arms over my head.

"No." She sighs. "They're wilting."

Mom laughs. "It's a hundred degrees, *I'm* wilting!" She looks toward me then, lowering her voice to a conspiratorial whisper as Carla inspects one of the bushes. "Did you watch this morning?"

I immediately know what she means. I remember Decklee's funeral playing over the grainy gas station TV, the plummeting disappointment of finding the time capsule empty. I nod and Mom blows out a breath. "It's a shame, isn't it? I really thought there'd be something."

"There *is* something," I say with more confidence than I feel.

"Oh yeah?" Mom raises an eyebrow. "What makes you so sure?"

I don't have an answer. The simplest one is that Decklee Cassel never actually filled the time capsule in the first place. She was busy or life got in the way or she lost interest. But something about that doesn't feel right. That project was never intended for the press or for celebrity speakers, it was supposed to be for *us*. The fans. I know because every time an interviewer brought up how she never married or had children, Decklee would laugh and say, *I have millions of children. They're all buying my records.*

"You know that lyric from 'Lucky in Love'?" I say, turning back to Mom. *"Everything's a game with you, honey, but there's one thing you forgot—"*

"*—I'm the master, always have been, pity those who think I'm not,*" Mom finishes for me. "That's a good one. You might know more of her songs than I do by now."

"It's a Mickenlee lyric. You can hear it in the rhyme."

"See?" Mom gestures like *told you so.* "Why does it matter?"

I shrug again and lean my head against the wall. The sun is directly overhead now, baking us both into the pale wood of Carla's porch. "Because maybe this is a game. Or maybe it's lost. Someone could have taken it."

Carla snorts, letting the petals of the nearest rosebush slide through her fingers. "It probably never existed."

"That's a good point," Mom says, turning another page in her magazine. "I mean, a new album? After eight years? Feels too good to be true."

I slide down in my chair, watching the bushes bob in the faint breeze. *It probably never existed.* That's the most logical explanation, but it's also the one I refuse to accept. There are a lot of things I've had to come to terms with over the years. That my teachers will never let me write the stories I want. That Bob is never going to give me a raise. That, no matter how often Emily and Madison and I discuss it, the odds of us actually getting out of this town are low.

But those are Mayberry things, normal things. Decklee

Cassel belongs to me and Mom. People like her aren't supposed to have limits.

I run a hand through my hair as Carla settles herself in the chair next to me. She opens the newspaper, flipping back to the half-finished crossword puzzle we started yesterday. "Twenty-four across," she says. "Thirteen letter word for 'regret'?"

"Disappointing," I say immediately.

"Disillusioned," she offers.

Mom sighs and takes another long drink of lemonade. "Decklee Cassel."

I laugh and Carla lifts her own glass in Mom's direction. "Cheers to that."

"Cheers," I echo.

The three of us drink, and for a minute, the only thing I hear is the whistling of the breeze through Carla's roses. *Disappointing.* That's what this whole town is, really.

I wonder why I thought today would be any different.

FOUR

Decklee
Memphis, 1963

¶ meet him in the doorway of a crumbling motel room, caught halfway between my old life and the one I'm stepping into now.

There's a faucet *drip*, *drip*, *drip*ping in the bathroom, and for a minute, the only thing either of us can do is stare. Him, at the dirty, crumpled girl frozen in the door, outlined by heat and sun and wavering humidity. Me, at the boy with the towel thrown across his bare shoulders, toothbrush in hand, standing in the middle of the room I supposedly paid for.

I blink, double-checking the key in my hand, matching it with the number stamped outside the room. "I'm—"

He doesn't let me finish. "This is my room."

The words are all bite, but there's something underneath that makes me hesitate. This boy can't be much older than me, with smooth brown skin and high cheekbones. His eyes are striking, framed by thick, arched brows, and they're currently doing an excellent job of staring me down. I look at my room key again, the same one I traded the rest of my cash for. It only bought me a week and now I'm starting to think that deal might have been a lie, too.

"No," I say. "This room is mine."

The boy crosses the room in two long strides. It's so quick I don't even have time to panic before he plucks the key from my hand. If I was still the small-town girl, raised on practiced manners and polite Southern façades, I might have slunk back into the parking lot and left. I might have let him win. But that girl is long gone, and I did *not* spend seven hours on a Greyhound to give up this fast.

His brow furrows, then he lets out a derisive laugh and chucks my key onto the bed. "That bastard. I knew he'd do it again."

I hesitate, still half expecting a fight. "Do what?"

"The manager likes to double-book this room when he needs extra cash."

The boy picks a shirt off the floor and tugs it over his head. It's only then I notice the rest of the room—the single, half-packed suitcase, the pile of mail on the bedside table, the small candle burning in the corner. All the signs of someone trying to make a temporary place feel more like home.

I step forward, inching onto the stained carpet. "I'll just tell them to give me a different room."

The boy scoffs. "No you won't."

"And why not?"

He tilts his head, looking me up and down, and answers with another question. "How old are you?"

I scowl. "Eighteen."

"Sure. And where's your family?"

"I don't have one."

The boy taps a finger against the smooth dimple in his chin. "No, I suppose you don't. No one who comes off that bus ever does. You got a husband?"

"Do *you*?" I snap.

The boy laughs again, and I wonder if it's because I'm entertaining or if it's out of pity. "My point is that you have something to lose," he says. "We both do. You can ask for your money back if you want, but they won't give you a different room."

I shake my head. "Then what am I supposed to do?"

"I don't know. I'm still deciding."

He sinks onto the bed nearest the door, leaning back on his hands as he considers me. His posture is carefree, casual in a way that scrapes across my nerves, and something hot pools in the pit of my stomach. Most days, I feel like I'm going to burn up, like every sharp, raging desire buried inside my chest will just burst into flames and take me down with it. I know now that the want isn't the problem. It's the staying still that kills you in the end, and right now, I want to move.

"So." The boy levels me with a single, piercing stare. "What brings you to Memphis?"

The handle of my guitar case is sweaty in my palm. "It was the first ticket out."

"Out of where?"

"Doesn't matter."

One of his eyebrows lifts, but I don't care if he thinks I'm rude. I'm done with that town. I don't want to remember our empty house or my mother's casket, and I certainly don't want to acknowledge the sliver of my heart that still aches for the open stretch of road and the back of my father's truck.

"Why are *you* here?" I ask.

The boy doesn't move, doesn't avert his gaze. "I asked you first."

I bite my bottom lip so hard I taste blood. It's coppery on my tongue, steadying somehow, and when the words come again, they feel like they're clawing their way out of my throat. "My mother died last month. And no one will admit it, but I know that town wore her down. I know it killed her and I'm not letting it get me."

Something in the boy's shoulders releases, ever so slightly. "People die here, too, you know."

"Not like that."

We stand there for another second, silence stretching between us until he nods. "I came here for a job, this tailor's apprenticeship over on Madison. I'm learning to sew, make clothes for rich people. You in the market?"

"To be rich? Always," I say. "Does it pay well?"

"Of course not. Nothing pays well. I wait tables in the meantime—you know Top Cat? That music club on Seventeenth with the rainbow bricks out back?"

He says it like I should know what he's talking about, so I nod, because I want to be the kind of person who does. My hand tightens around my guitar. "Do people perform there?

You said it's a music club. Would they let me sing?"

The boy's mouth twists and now I know he's laughing at me. "You know how many people are trying to get through those doors?" he asks. "They had Elvis a few weeks ago, shut down the whole street and everything. So, no. They won't just *let* anyone sing."

Fire licks up the column of my spine. I exhale through my teeth. "They'd let *me.*"

Someone has to. It's the whole reason I'm here, the only thing I'm good at.

The boy watches me a second longer than necessary, fingers tugging at a stray thread on the blanket. I wonder if he's still deciding what to make of me, if perhaps he's lived with one too many strangers and been double-crossed by one too many landlords to ever feel truly comfortable again. His gaze is wary when he stands, but when he extends a hand, his fingers are steady.

"I'm Markell," he says. "Who are you? And think carefully," he adds, drawing his hand back before I can take it. "You only get to tell me once. Who do you want to be in this city?"

Maybe Markell isn't his name at all. Maybe this boy needed to be someone else as much as I do, but I've had a lot of time to think about who I'd turn myself into if I got the chance. Little snippets of sounds, letters stolen off highway signs and soda bottles, scribbled on the back of homework sheets until I found the perfect combination.

"Decklee," I say, gripping his hand. "Decklee Cassel."

It's sweet like strawberry wine, like summer rain and springtime and all the bright, beautiful things I'm trying to become. It's the name of a star.

"Decklee Cassel." Markell grins. He takes my hand and his fingers feel like the first solid thing I've touched in years. "Welcome to Memphis."

And I close the hotel room door behind me.

FIVE

Darren

The rest of the week is pure Arkansas summer—hot and humid and dull.

Mom and I stay inside as much as possible, watching our yard wilt through the front window even as Carla's garden thrives. I work back-to-back double shifts at Bob's, restocking shelves, organizing the breakroom, and even coaxing the coffee machine back to life for three glorious hours. It's dark by the time Kendall and I lock up to head home, and I realize I haven't thought about Decklee Cassel's empty time capsule all day.

We start to clear the summer haze out of the house, Mom unearthing her classroom decorations, me dusting off my backpack and notebooks. School doesn't start for another few weeks, but she's already deep in admin meetings, gone more days than she's home. Dr. Vij calls to confirm her appointment next Monday and I shiver, blasting "Whiskey Red" until the house feels less empty.

When I'm not working, I'm on Carla's porch, twisting a pen between my fingers, trying to brainstorm articles that won't come. As editor in chief and the only reliable member of our school paper, I'm supposed to walk in on the first day of class with a plan. Instead, I'm staring at yet another blank page. I'm about to rip this one from my notebook entirely when my phone buzzes and a text from Emily slides across the screen.

Dude, when did Benton start dating
Mary Kelly?

Beneath is a screenshot from Benton's Instagram, a washed-out selfie of my ex-boyfriend with his arm wrapped around Mary Kelly Hugo from homeroom. The caption says *love of my life*, followed by half a dozen angel emojis, which I think is bold considering the two of us just broke up at the beginning of the summer. I roll my eyes and slip my phone back into my pocket without answering. It's not worth it.

Dating Benton had felt too much like a checklist—the boy next door asking me to winter formal because that's what people do. It was a few months of driving his mom's car to McDonald's and making out in the back seat until curfew hit and it was *fine*. Until the day he casually told me his parents were gifting him the car entirely and he could have it whenever we decided to get married. It was like someone wrapped both hands around my throat and squeezed—a terrible, suffocating reminder that I'm not like people here. I'm not staying in Mayberry and I'm not marrying Benton Hatcher, whose idea of deep conversation consisted of saying "damn, that's crazy" before asking if I wanted to play *Fortnite*.

Maybe I should write an article about that.

"What's wrong?" Carla looks at me over the lip of her teacup.

I shake my head and go back to my nonexistent notes. "Nothing. Benton's dating someone else."

"Hmm." She purses her lips. "I never liked him."

"You don't like anyone."

"That's irrelevant. I don't even think *you* like him."

I slide down in my chair, already annoyed with the entire conversation. "I don't. But he liked me. I think. It was nice."

The corner of Carla's mouth lifts. Her dress is lavender today, her brooch a collection of jeweled lilacs, and her silver hair is perfectly combed despite the heat. She takes another careful sip of tea. It's times like this where I'm convinced she sees right through me, straight down to every complicated thought twisting in my chest. "You're so young, Darren," she says, patting my knee. "You shouldn't have to guess if someone cares about you. Trust me, you'll go to college next year and find someone who *actually* likes you. Someone who doesn't tear up my flowers every time they visit," she adds. "That would be best, I think."

I burst out laughing at the memory of Benton standing in the middle of Carla's garden, petals dripping through his fingers as she glowered from the porch. This isn't the first time Carla has reassured me like this. I don't even know if she means to do it, but I love that she never tells me that I'll meet "a boy." It's always *someone*, a gender-neutral *them* that makes something warm flutter inside my chest.

No one else really talks like that. I barely let *myself* talk like that or imagine what it would be like to not be with a boy at all. I don't think Mom would care. I doubt Emily or Madison would either, but something about this town keeps me stuck. There are moments, of course. The rainbow sticker in the library window that reappears each time someone tries to scrape it off. The pride pin on a random backpack, cleverly placed so you have to know exactly where to look. One of the Laurentis siblings coming back from summer vacation freshman year and telling everyone her name is Joy now.

There might be a place for me here, if I look. There might be a community tucked somewhere between the soybean fields and the gas station, but I don't want it in Mayberry. I'll think about it next year, I've decided, after I leave this place for good. I'll unpack everything in the rush of a busy city and let all the different, questioning pieces of myself get swept away in the noise.

Before I can go back to my notes, Mom turns up Carla's driveway. Her portable radio swings from one hand and the faint sound of Elton John's "Goodbye Yellow Brick Road" drifts across the garden. She always takes it for walks even though I've told her countless times that's what her phone is for.

"It's hot," she says, dropping down to sit on the porch. "It should be illegal to be this hot."

Carla offers her a frosty glass of iced tea and Mom takes it gratefully, leaning back against my legs as she drinks. I rest a hand in her hair and exhale the rest of my unease. I love moments like this, when it's just the three of us, looking out over the sun-drenched road. It feels like something that could be permanent, like something I'll miss when I put Mayberry in my rearview mirror next year.

The song on Mom's radio comes to an end, replaced by the soothing, NPR-style vocals of Mark Raylon. Mark has been the host of the country-hits station as long as I can remember, but he hardly ever speaks unless it's to add some old, exaggerated anecdote about Loretta Lynn or Johnny Cash. That's what I expect him to do now, so I'm only half paying attention when his voice crackles through the speakers.

"Well, here's a new one, folks. I'm interrupting today's broadcast to bring you breaking news from the estate of Ms. Decklee Cassel."

I sit up in my chair, notebook falling to the floor. There's a moment where Mom and I lock eyes, then we both dive for the radio. She gets there first and cranks the volume up as I stumble to my knees beside her.

"Earlier this week, country-pop sensation Decklee Cassel left fans shocked when her famous time capsule, which reportedly contained exclusive photographs, tour journals, personal letters, and most importantly, an entire album of unreleased songs, turned out to be empty. Now, I don't know how many of you watched the funeral, but I've been thinking of nothing else for the last several days. Here to explain to us exactly what happened is . . . well . . . Decklee Cassel."

"What?" Mom gasps. "How?"

But I can't move. Next to me, Carla stands, gaze fixed on the radio as she takes a step back. I grip the edge of the porch with one hand and Mom's wrist with the other as Mark Raylon continues like usual. Like he hasn't just launched a live grenade into the middle of his otherwise uneventful broadcast.

"This next clip, which was recorded in the final days before her death, was leaked to our station via an anonymous source at the Decklee Cassel Estate. No one in our studio has heard it, and I must admit, I'm rather excited. So, for everyone listening at home, here's Decklee Cassel's final message."

The silence that follows feels like it's grating over my bones, every second agonizing until I hear the static shift. When Decklee's voice comes on over the radio, Mom claps a hand over her mouth.

"Well, hi there! If you're listening to this, it's probably because y'all saw what happened earlier this week."

The voice cuts through me, twisting on the way out, and I tighten my grip on Mom. Decklee didn't give many interviews in the months leading up to her death. I don't know how much of that was her team, shielding her from the public, or how much of it was because she simply *couldn't* speak like she used to. But she's here now, voice calm and clear and familiar on the radio. I lean in, not wanting to miss a word.

"I know, I know. This isn't what you were expecting, but I never could resist a little fun. Here's the thing: I really do think of y'all as family. You, who supported me from the beginning, who brought me into your homes, who helped me live out the dreams I had since I was a little girl. It wouldn't be fair if I didn't offer you something in return." There's a sound of rustling paper in the background and Decklee clears her throat.

"The time capsule exists. It's real. The journals, the photos, and—yes—even the new album are all there. It's just waiting for one of you to find it."

I suck in a breath, and next to me, I feel Carla do the same.

"Shit," Mom whispers, and I let out a shaky laugh because that's all I'm thinking, too. *Shit.* I was right. The songs are *real.* And if she just needs someone to find them . . .

"I've also decided to toss in something special of my own." I can practically hear the smile in Decklee's voice now, like she's some sly game show host who's been waiting for the right moment to reveal the big twist. *"It wouldn't be much of a game without a prize, right? How about a check for . . . does three million dollars sound all right? I know it'll never really be enough to repay you for everything, but maybe it'll help someone else out there live their own dream."*

The porch is too hot. My arms are already reddening in the sun, but I can't bring myself to move. *Three million dollars.*

Decklee's voice lowers as she continues. *"Here's how it'll go: Keep this station on, because we'll be revealing the first clue right after this—one for the money. Then it's up to you. Trust yourselves. Trust the music. It has been the greatest honor of my life to play for you all. Let's play together one last time. Happy hunting."*

Her voice fades out. There's a moment of absolute silence and then the faint strains of Judy Garland's "Somewhere Over the Rainbow" drift through the speakers. A deceptively calm way to end that bombshell of an announcement.

Three million dollars.

Everything's still—the heat rising over the black asphalt of the road, the bright outline of Carla's roses, my shadow etched against the grass. I press my hands against the smooth wood of the porch until my palms burn and try to calm my thundering pulse.

Carla's the one who breaks the silence in the end, letting out a short, disbelieving laugh. "Well," she says. "There you go, Darren. Looks like you were right."

I still can't quite believe it. "Mom," I breathe.

She nods. "I know."

"I have to..."

I trail off, trying to remember everything we just heard. I have to *what*? Find Decklee Cassel's missing time capsule? Solve whatever clue comes next? That's big talk for a girl who's hardly left the state. I have a shift at Bob's on Monday, Mom's new appointment to think about, a real life full of real people who I can't just leave.

But what if Dr. Vij gives us bad news? The thought is enough to chill me to the bone. What if it's bad and Mom and I need to slip back into our familiar fortress of banjo chords and drumbeats? Decklee's music made us invincible, but that other prize...

Three million dollars.

There's a folder of college applications sitting on my desk. Dream schools. Journalism schools. Schools in big cities where the monthly rent costs more than Mom's paycheck. Every so often, I flip through the materials, pore over flashy brochures and empty promises from campuses I'll never see.

People always told me that success comes from hard work. Get good grades, Darren, colleges only accept the best. Create a job for yourself at the school paper, prove you're a self-starter. Ace every assignment and pass every test because then, *only* then, do you earn the opportunities you want. No one told me none of that actually matters in the end because I can barely scrape together enough money to cover the application fees.

Three million dollars.

And Mom is still paying her way through a lifetime of medical debt because it turns out the prize for not dying of cancer is a bill with more commas than should be legal.

Three million dollars.

I get to my feet. At some point, Carla slipped back inside. I feel the screen door swinging back and forth behind me, a steady rhythm not at all like the frantic racing of my heart. "Mom."

She holds up a finger before I can finish. "I know what you're thinking, Darren."

It's not a *no*. I can tell she's thinking about it, too, imagining a new Decklee Cassel album in her hands, pulling the armor back over her shoulders. She stands and I follow her across Carla's lawn, back toward our house.

"Let's just listen," I plead. "She said they'd be back with a clue. Maybe the time capsule's close. If it's in Mayberry . . ."

I don't finish the sentence. Decklee isn't planting clues here, in the town she left behind. The last chords of "Somewhere Over the Rainbow" trickle into staticky silence and I pause, caught in this strange, liminal space as I wait for Decklee's voice. But instead of a new announcement or anything that sounds remotely like a clue, another song I don't recognize starts right up in its place. Not even Mark Raylon jumps in to comment. I stumble to a stop, twisting one of the piercings in my ear as I try to make sense of it.

"That's it, then?" Mom taps a nail against the speaker. "There's nothing? It was a mix-up at the estate or a prank?"

I rub a hand over my forehead and wish I wasn't so tired from work so I could think through this like a rational person. That was Decklee's voice we heard just now; it can't be a prank. I start pacing again, trying to remember exactly what she said.

Here's how it'll go: Keep this station on, because we'll be revealing the first clue right after this . . . Then it's up to you. Trust yourselves. Trust the music.

The grass is prickly against my bare feet, and I realize I left my Birkenstocks back on Carla's porch. I turn and start back across the lawn. *Trust yourselves. Trust the music.*

But I'm having a hard time trusting anything right now. I don't know how.

Trust the music.

I stop. "Oh my god."

"What?" Mom looks up, shielding her eyes against the sun.

But I'm already moving. I whip out my phone as the world turns back on. I can hear everything clearly, from the drip of Carla's hose onto the pavement to the pulse in my veins.

"Darren," Mom says. "One more time, honey. For those of us not inside your head."

"Trust the music," I say, still frantically scrolling. "Decklee just said they'd *reveal* the first clue, not that she'd actually tell us. It's the song. 'Somewhere Over the Rainbow.' The song is the clue."

"That feels like a leap."

I roll my eyes. "Just pretend! For a second, pretend I'm right and this is happening. Where would you think it's telling you to go?"

Mom hesitates, forehead creasing, before she decides to play along. "Kansas for the original connection?" she offers. "Or LA, maybe? The lot where they filmed the *Wizard of Oz* movie?"

Both solid guesses. Both answers that make sense, but a third keeps catching in my brain. It's not as obvious as Kansas or LA, but I can't shake the feeling that I'm right. Because if this quest is supposed to be the beginning, wouldn't it start at Decklee's beginning, too?

"I think it's Memphis," I blurt. "Top Cat, specifically. She used to play there all the time—it's where her record label found her, remember?" I hold up my phone so Mom can see the pictures I pulled up of the old iconic music club in its prime. It's been closed for nearly a decade, but the building remains. "There were all these different colored bricks in the alley by the stage door. Decklee called it the 'Rainbow Wall' in one of her memoirs. And I know it's not Kansas and it's not even an official title, but . . ."

I trail off. *But it's what I would do.* I would hide something important at the place where I was discovered as a pointed reminder to everyone who didn't take me seriously.

Mom shakes her head. "No."

"I didn't even say anything!"

"But I know what you're thinking. You're not driving to Tennessee on some wild goose chase."

I groan, head falling back as she folds her arms. Does she not understand that I want this for *us*? That I'd go anywhere if it meant making sure she's okay and we're happy. "You could come with me, you know. It's summer! Let's make it a road trip."

"I have meetings all weekend. I can't just drop everything to chase some fantasy album." She hesitates for a moment before adding, "What about Emily? Or Madison?"

Hope flares briefly in my chest. "Madison just left for camp and Emily is still in Michigan with her grandparents." I turn in a circle, searching for another solution. "What if I took the bus?"

"Absolutely not!"

"Mom, it's *Decklee Cassel*."

"I know. And I'm trying to help you out, sweetie, but I just don't think it's possible."

I turn away, running both hands through my hair. This is the first exciting thing that's happened in this small, sleepy, disappointing town for as long as I can remember. I feel the urgency of it, the adrenaline pushing me forward, telling me to take this chance before it disappears. Nothing good ever stays here for long. Decklee Cassel got out.

I could, too, if people would let me.

The idea creeps in slowly, so obvious I almost miss it. "What if I had a car?" I ask. "And someone to go with me?"

Mom lifts an eyebrow. "You mean a chaperone?"

"What is this, a Regency film?" I wrinkle my nose. "Sure, whatever. What if I had a *chaperone*. Would you let me go?"

Mom chews on her bottom lip, and in that single moment of hesitation, I know she wants this as badly as I do. Because she has that appointment on Monday where Dr. Vij might tell her something we can't handle on our own. She has a water bill to pay, two classrooms to decorate, and she wants the magic of Decklee's songs. She wants the luck. And even though we both know luck is fleeting and fickle and flighty, that doesn't stop me from wanting it, too.

She exhales slowly and I lean in. "I'd . . . consider it," she says.

That's all I need. I open my phone again, already scrolling through my contacts. This isn't a waste of time. This isn't a fairy tale. If there's even a chance I'm right, I have to take it. Three million dollars is enough to pay off Mom's remaining medical bills, enough to put some away for the future. It's enough to get me the hell out of this town.

So before I can talk myself out of it, I take a deep breath, put the phone to my ear, and call the only other person in Mayberry I know with a car.

SIX

Decklee
Memphis, 1966

I learn to climb the same way I learned to fight—one fist at a time.

The back alley of Top Cat is packed, lines of patrons already stretching around the corner. It doesn't usually get this cold in Memphis, but it's biting now. I feel the chill settle on my skin as I weave through the crowd. Pierce is watching the entrance, like he's done every night for the last three years.

"Big crowd tonight," he says, tugging his hat low. "You performing?"

"Of course. Wouldn't miss it." The lie rolls off my tongue, easy as breathing.

Pierce eyes the growing crowd. "You know Ricky Grasso? I just let him in earlier. He's one of those big time execs up in Nashville, and rumor has it he's looking for a new star."

I bite my tongue and resist the urge to tell Pierce that *I know*. I know everything that happens here. Three years of working this club and I'm no longer the bright-eyed girl off the Greyhound. I'm hardened and honed, in a city coming apart in pieces as businesses move on and nightlife dries up. I was supposed to go with them. Instead I'm here, still working, still fighting, still playing this same damn club.

"Well, good luck, kid." Pierce motions me in, ahead of the waiting crowd. "Stay warm."

I don't need luck, but I still run a hand over the wall as I slip inside, just in case. Each brick is a slightly different color, faded from years in the sun and checkered in shades of reds, oranges, and yellows. *Rainbow Wall.* That's what we call it. The bosses call it a problem—something to be fixed when they have the money, but I won't be surprised if they tear this whole place down eventually to make room for something shiny and new. I won't be surprised if they try to bury me with it.

But tonight, my ticket out of town is sitting at table five, drinking an old-fashioned, and I think this is the closest thing I've felt to hope in years.

Markell is already behind the bar, a blur of motion as he takes orders and tops off drinks. He has a tailor's hands, nimble and quick, equally as good with a bottle of bourbon as he is with a needle. I told him once he'd make a good musician. He told me I made a wonderful liar.

"No," he says the second I slide into view. "I know what you want and *no.*"

My mouth falls open. "I didn't say anything!"

"You don't have to." He eyes my guitar pointedly. "Open mic sign-ups closed an hour ago."

"I was playing across town, Markell, you know that!"

"I'm sorry, I don't make the rules."

I grit my teeth, ignoring the sharp ache in my jaw. Maybe he doesn't make the rules, but he could bend them for me now. I try again. "You have to get me on that list. *Ricky Grasso* is here."

"It's flattering you think I have that kind of power." Markell gestures to his uniform for emphasis. I'd be wearing a version of that same starchy white shirt and tie if I was working tonight. Maybe I should have taken the shift instead of the other gig, because I can see the open mic list pinned to the wall over Markell's shoulder.

I can see every spot that doesn't include my name.

"Who's performing, then?" I snap. "Betty? Michelle? Leah? I'm better than all of them and you know it."

Markell exhales, and when he looks at me again, his expression is a careful, patient mask. "No one's saying you aren't talented, you just missed the sign-up. The boss gave the older girls first chance—apparently he wants to impress some big names tonight."

It takes everything in my power not to scream. *I* want to impress the big names. That's the entire reason I came here in the first place. Now that I'm inside, away from the biting wind, I feel the familiar heat pulsing through my veins. I feel the pull, the ache, the wrenching desire to *do something*. I need to be on that stage.

I need to get out of this club.

"Markell." I lean in, forcing him to look at me. There are patrons lined all up and down the bar, but for a minute, it's just the two of us. "That shop is never going to promote you," I say. "You've been there for years. People love your clothes, but we both know they don't want you. I do, though. I want you to design everything for me. Every red carpet, every award show, every performance. But I can't do that until someone signs me and takes us out of here. I need to be on that list."

He could do it. He could cross out someone's name and write mine before anyone notices. I would do it for him if the roles were reversed, if it meant getting out of here. Markell's jaw tightens and for a second, I think I have him. I've lived with this boy for three years. I know how to get under his skin, and I know the idea of that glamorous, intangible future tempts him in the same way it tempts me.

Then his expression clears. He shrugs and steps back, fresh glass already in hand. "Sorry," he says. "I can't. Maybe stick around after the set? The boss likes you—it's not like he wouldn't let you play if there's time. I'm sorry," he says again, reaching across the bar to pat my cheek. "Really. You'll get them another time."

Then he's back to business, handling drinks and taking orders, and I'm sitting alone at the bar. I sink into my seat, watching the hazy outline of Ricky Grasso's profile through the crowd. His head is inclined toward the other men at the table, all three of them watching the stage with a palpable sort of hunger. He could change my life right now, if he wanted. Just snap his fingers and take me away. I dig my nails into my palms until the bite clears my head. This is where I think it finally gets me—not the fight, not the climb, but the waiting. The slow, stagnant drag when all I've ever wanted to do is run.

So when Markell's not looking, I reach behind the bar and snag the first bottle I find. Then I slide out of my seat, into the dark embrace of backstage.

Because sometimes, this is what it takes.

"Good luck tonight, girls!"

I pour the drinks and hand them out one by one, sparkling wine encased in glittering crystal flutes. These are the girls with me at every open mic, playing set after set in the hopes of catching someone's eye. There's Betty, with her gaudy jewelry and sweet soprano, Michelle, with her long pianist fingers. And there's Leah, whose lips fit perfectly under the curve of my jaw, who whispers careless, reckless things to me in the dark when everyone leaves.

Who I might love if this place hadn't twisted us all so thoroughly that I don't remember what honesty looks like.

Michelle grins at me over the top of her glass. "Thanks, Decklee! I'm so glad you came!"

"Of course." I smile back, all teeth. "Wouldn't miss it for the world. Did you hear Ricky Grasso's in tonight?"

Betty nods, heel tapping nervously against the floor. "I hear he's looking for a star."

Leah takes her glass last, fingers lingering over mine, and I don't pull away. I let her think it's her idea for me to set the bottle of wine on Betty's station and wish them all good luck one more time. I let her think it's her decision to lead me back into the dark corner between dressing rooms, fingers brushing between our skirts as we walk. Leah's a few years older than me and she's been here longer. If I were fair, if I were kind, I might feel bad about what I'm about to do. She wants to get out of here almost as badly as I do. I know because she tells me every day. She's poured her heart into my hands more times than I can count and now I know exactly how to break her.

"Full house," Leah murmurs as we pause halfway down the hall. We're far enough from the other girls to whisper, but too close to the stage to do anything reckless. I'm used to this, though—the stolen moments, the borrowed time. I can smell the vanilla perfume dotted beneath Leah's throat, feel her fingers threaded through mine, cool and sweet. I nudge open the supply closet and pull her inside like I have countless times.

"They're all here for you," I say. "They're here because you're brilliant."

Leah blushes, color working up her neck. I can barely see it in the dark, but I feel the heat under my fingers. "It should be you," she whispers. "They should have put you on the list."

I lean in, close enough to hear her breath catch as my lips brush along the shell of her ear. "Oh, Leah." She shivers when I say her name, hand sliding under the hem of my skirt. I grin once, cutting and vicious. "I know."

She stiffens a second too late, but I'm already gone. I shove her away and slip out the door, locking it behind me as Leah throws herself forward.

"Decklee!" Her voice is muffled as she slams against solid wood, the sound almost imperceptible in the bustling frenzy of backstage. "Decklee! Let me out!"

I don't. I just run a hand over the rumpled fabric of my skirt,

smooth my hair, and head back toward the stage, boots clicking over the floorboards with every deliberate step. Leah will
have other chances. I might, too, but this is the one I want. I've
known what I wanted since the day I picked up my first guitar
and I'm not letting it slip through my fingers tonight.

I stay at the bar as the night goes on, performance after performance until the other girls notice they're one name short.
The whispers are slow at first, frantic by the time they reach
me. *Where's Leah? She missed her ten-minute call. Has anyone seen her? Did she leave?* I make sure my expression is
casual, posture relaxed until one of the stage managers lays a
hand on my arm.

"I know this is last minute, but we can't find Leah anywhere.
They're expecting a full show tonight, do you have anything
prepared?"

Only then do I grin, shifting to pull my guitar in front of me.
Of course I have something prepared. I always do.

Markell's mouth tightens as he watches me stand. I'm up
next, performing last in what should have been Leah's spot.
"What did you do?" he asks.

"I don't know what you mean." I drain the rest of my drink
and slam the empty glass back on the bar. "Add that to my tab,
will you?"

I ignore the way Markell's eyes flash, arms crossing tight over
his chest. Sometimes I think he's afraid of me, afraid of what I
might do if he was the one in my way. Sometimes I'm afraid of
that, too, but right now, I'm not afraid of anything.

"Hi there, hope y'all are having a good night."

This stage is as familiar as the guitar in my hand and the whiskey in my stomach. I've been here countless times, performed hundreds of songs, and tonight, I know exactly where Ricky Grasso sits. I tilt my stool in his direction and make sure he can see my face as I fit my fingers over the strings. The song I play now is one of my favorites, and when I strum the first chord, I know I've chosen correctly. The lyrics are like wine on my lips, words I wrote on a Greyhound bus years ago—all that lightning and longing bottled into perfect rhymes.

When I finish, there's a single breath where nothing moves and then the applause is rapturous. I lock eyes with Ricky and I know I did it. I know he's mine.

He finds me after, leaning against the bar and sipping someone else's drink. I'd never order an old-fashioned, but Ricky would, and I want Ricky to like me. I want him to think I'm the kind of girl who orders this for herself, who revels in each bitter sip.

"That was a hell of a performance," he says.

I grin. *I know.* "Thank you."

"What's your name?"

"Decklee Cassel."

"Decklee. I like that. You from here?"

"Might as well be."

Ricky nods, like that's the answer he expects, and slips me a card. His name and information are printed on the front, on the kind of paper that looks like money.

He winks. "Think about it."

There's nothing to think about. Ricky plucked Sylvia Styles

off a street in Mississippi. He found Micky Henningson at a Baton Rouge nightclub, grabbed Ruby Daly from a Dallas high school talent show. If he wants to make you a star, you let him.

"Why don't you stop by tomorrow?" I say with the confidence of a girl already in his office. "I'm here all morning and I might buy you a drink if you ask nice."

He laughs. "How could I say no to that?"

He can't. And that's the point.

SEVEN

Darren

I hear Kendall's truck before he turns the corner—the grumbling roar of the single loudest vehicle in the state of Arkansas. How it's legally allowed on the streets is a mystery I've been trying to solve for the last several years. When he pulls into our driveway and cuts the engine, there's a single second of silence where even the cicadas hold their breath before everything explodes back into summer.

I open the front door as Kendall jumps out of the truck. "Are you sure that thing can make it to Memphis?" I ask.

"Excuse me?" Kendall presses a hand to his chest. "Blue Delia is a national treasure."

I'm not sure that's true, but I'm also not in any position to complain. I'm lucky Kendall is here at all. I'm lucky Bob gave us both the weekend off to enjoy the last bit of summer, and I'm lucky that, for once, there's something to look forward to.

Mom is still wavering in the doorway when I step outside.

She leans against the screen, surveying the truck with a healthy level of wariness as Kendall sweeps his baseball cap off in her direction. "Good morning, ma'am," he says. "I promise my truck can, indeed, make it to Memphis."

The smile she gives him would look casual to anyone else, but I see the way it pinches at the corners. "Hi, Kendall. Nice to see you."

She grabs my backpack from the floor and follows me outside. I didn't pack much, just a phone charger, a notebook, and a sweater in case it gets cold, but I'm not expecting to be gone long. I can't be. Mom and I will just think about her appointment when I get back. We'll order takeout, make a plan, and then we'll do what we always do when things get scary—curl up on the couch and blast "Whiskey Red" as loud as it'll go. Only this time, we'll have a brand-new album of Decklee Cassel songs to get us through. We'll have millions of dollars at our disposal, and that, I think, is enough to let me know I'm making the right decision.

We trail Kendall back down the driveway, away from the house. He's still in his gas station polo from the morning shift and I wonder if he's thought about the fact he'll be wearing it for the rest of the day. "Thanks for doing this," I say. "I know it's probably not how you wanted to start your only weekend off."

"Are you kidding?" Kendall waves a hand. "I would do a lot for a few million dollars. Driving you across state lines is nothing."

He jumps into the driver's seat to unlock my door from the inside. And I mean he literally *jumps*. The truck is so far off the ground that I have to toss my backpack inside. When I turn back to Mom, her expression is still guarded, but something about it feels softer. I get it. Even though this is *Kendall Wilkinson,* who I've known for years, even though everybody in Mayberry knows everybody else, Mom probably wouldn't let me do this if it wasn't about Decklee Cassel.

And I wouldn't leave her if the prize money wasn't enough to change both our lives.

"It's fine," I say, more for myself, as I pull her into a hug. She exhales against my neck, and by the time we break apart, Mom feels steady and solid once more. Then she steps forward and jams a finger into Kendall's chest.

"*Just* to Memphis," she says.

His eyes widen. "Yes ma'am."

"Back by tonight."

"*Mom,*" I hiss through clenched teeth, but Kendall nods solemnly.

"On my honor."

Only then does Mom smile. Just as I've started debating how I'm going to climb into Kendall's monster truck, Carla steps out onto her porch. "Are you really leaving without saying goodbye?"

I turn, watching her pick her way toward us across the garden. "It's just to Memphis," I say. "We'll be back tonight."

She doesn't look like she believes me. "Well, here." She gives Kendall a stiff nod, then hands me a worn canvas tote bag. "It's a long drive. Thought you could use some snacks."

"Oh, Carla." I hadn't even considered that. "Thank you."

I reach out and she tolerates my hug for roughly two seconds before letting out an exasperated sigh. "Okay, that's enough."

I squeeze her harder. "And I would never leave without saying goodbye."

"Get in the car, Darren!"

But she's grinning when I pull back, a light sparking behind her eyes that feels decades younger than she is. I wonder, briefly, if there's a version of Carla Krenik out there who used to throw caution to the wind like this, who would have climbed in a truck with a boy to go on a wild, reckless adventure.

I know, objectively, that things like this aren't supposed to happen to me. Kendall and I are made for quiet roads and sticky summer nights and the few square miles of homes sandwiched between the highway and state roads. There's a reason our high school's "notable graduates" wall is two people. Because a lot of us don't graduate and those who do are hardly notable. Maybe that's why I love Decklee's music so much—something about it makes you think dreams like that are possible. Like right now, for example, it's like I'm on the edge of a verse, teetering into this furious, heart-pounding chorus I have no right to claim.

I squeeze Carla's hand one last time. "Thank you."

Then I grip both edges of the passenger-side door to haul myself into the front seat.

"Call me!" Mom says from the driveway. "I'm serious."

"I will!"

And then my words fade to nothing as Kendall turns the key in the ignition and Blue Delia roars to life.

♫♪♫

WE RUN OUT of things to talk about forty minutes into the drive.

I don't remember the silence between us ever feeling uncomfortable during our long shifts at Bob's, but it's charged now. Maybe because there's nowhere else for me to go unless I want to literally throw myself onto the highway. Maybe because, despite how aware I am of every fleeting second, every passing mile, Kendall doesn't seem to care. He's always like this—content to exist in a space without figuring out what makes it tick.

I pull out my phone and scroll through the hurried research I gathered while waiting for Kendall to show up—Wikipedia articles and fan tributes and tweets. Apparently, every major radio station in the country had received Decklee's message at the same time, and a few minutes after the broadcast, someone dropped a recording online. Now the theories are pouring in. Other people have latched on to the idea of "Somewhere Over the Rainbow" being a clue and they all have different thoughts on where to look.

Ok but have you considered it could be literal?

What if there's something in Kansas?

She wrote a Wizard of Oz movie, y'all! If I lived in LA, I'd go to that lot right now.

They're solid guesses, more substantial than the one I'm

clinging to now, but I still think they're wrong. I can't explain the feeling; I only know it pushes me forward, farther down the highway as Mayberry fades in the rearview mirror. When we finally cross the county line, there's a moment where my breath catches, where I'm convinced the universe is going to yank me right out of the seat and force me to stay. Then I blink and it's gone. I'm out, and Mayberry is falling farther and farther behind me. I let out a breath, relaxing back into my seat as Kendall drums his fingers on the steering wheel.

"So," I say, finally breaking the silence between us. "Did you have any fun weekend plans?"

Kendall's eyebrows lift and I know what he's thinking—Darren Purchase, noted hater of useless small talk, is asking him a question? The irony isn't lost on me, but I can't stand the idea of sitting like this for the next five hours. We're going to *Memphis*. I'm finally leaving and if I don't find something to do, I will combust right here in the front seat of his truck.

"Fun weekend plans?" Kendall pretends to think. "My dad and I usually cook something together on Friday and I'll take my nieces out to the lake if the weather is good. Nothing too exciting."

"No, that sounds nice," I say. "Sorry you're missing out on family time."

"Well, three million dollars would be a hell of a prize to pass up."

Of course it is. That's why we're both here on this empty stretch of highway, barreling toward a city neither of us know anything about. That's why I'm okay leaving Mom, because the promise of what I'll bring back is better than anything we would have found in Mayberry.

"What would you do with it?" I ask. "The money?"

Kendall shrugs. "I don't know."

"Yes, you do! Everyone knows what they would do with a million dollars. It's, like, the most basic dinner party question."

"This may come as a shock, Purchase, but I've never actually been to a dinner party."

Something about his tone is different, a minute shift I almost don't recognize. It's not until I watch his hands tighten around the steering wheel that it hits me—he's deflecting. He knows exactly what he would do with that kind of money, and he doesn't want to tell me.

"You're avoiding the question," I point out.

"Oh, right." Kendall's gaze slides over to me. "I forgot I'm talking to Mayberry's most infamous reporter."

"I'm not a reporter."

"Yes, you are. I've seen your Instagram."

"You've . . ." I cut myself off and shake my head. I will not think about Kendall reading my articles. I will not think about him scrolling through my account or analyzing every sentence. "That's irrelevant. I want to know what you'd do with the money."

I turn so I can study him in the driver's seat. His posture is still the same—relaxed, but he's stopped moving along to the music. I know a lot about Kendall Wilkinson. I know that he takes a pint of cookies-and-cream ice cream home each time we restock. I know he was the best tennis player Mayberry County

High School ever had, got a full ride to Louisiana State and everything. I know he turned it down, got bumped up to full-time at Bob's, and just continued working like he didn't have a one-way ticket out of here dropped in his lap. But I don't know why he's shutting me out now.

"Why don't you want to tell me?" I ask. "It cannot be that bad."

Usually when people close up like this, it means I'm getting close to something personal they don't want to talk about, but this is Kendall. I don't know what he could tell me that I don't already know.

"It's not bad," he says. "I just don't think you'll find it particularly interesting."

"Try me."

Kendall's quiet for so long I think that's the end of it. We're going to ride all the way up to Memphis in deep, uncomfortable silence. Then he sighs and his shoulders slump forward, just a bit. "You know that gas station on Hawthorne that closed a while ago?" I nod. "I would buy it and open a restaurant."

I open my mouth, but nothing comes out. A restaurant? I frantically sort through everything I know about Kendall, trying to figure out if he'd ever told me about his culinary aspirations. Eventually, I settle on "Oh."

"See?" He flashes me a quick, fleeting grin. "Told you it wasn't interesting."

"No, it's not that, it's . . ." I search for the right word. "Surprising. I thought you'd use it to go somewhere and play tennis, or something."

"I don't play tennis anymore."

The answer is abrupt; it catches me off guard. "I know, I just . . . you never told me you wanted to be a chef."

Kendall shrugs. "Yes, well, that would go against the whole dark, cool persona I've been carefully cultivating for the last several years."

I roll my eyes as some of the tension cracks at last. I don't think there's a single person in town who would ever call Kendall cool, but now that I'm thinking about it, his answer does make sense. Of course I can see him running a restaurant. This isn't the first time he's mentioned making dinner with his dad—they do it almost every week. He brings Carla fresh loaves of homemade bread, and he baked me an entire batch of lemon meringue cupcakes for my birthday last year. It's something I've always known about him but also something I never bothered to remember.

Because why would I learn more about the people I was planning to leave?

"I think that's a great idea," I say. "You'd be really good at it."

"Yeah?" Again, I feel Kendall watching me from the driver's seat. I pretend not to notice. "Good thing I already know what you would use the money for."

"Oh really?"

He nods. "You'll use it to apply to some fancy East Coast journalism school and come back with no accent, another piercing, and *lots* of opinions."

I touch my nose ring self-consciously. "I already have lots of opinions."

"Sure," Kendall says. "But these will be, like, fancy and dangerous and sponsored by Harvard."

"I would literally never go to Harvard."

"Really? Not even for the *Legally Blonde* jokes?"

"No." I shake my head. "But thank you for the vote of confidence."

Kendall considers me, fingers resuming their incessant tapping across the steering wheel. "Okay, fine. If you could go anywhere for college, where would you go?"

"I don't know."

The same answer he'd given me earlier. The same one I didn't let him get away with. Kendall doesn't let my answer slide either; he just sits back and waits for me to speak again. This is another interview trick, one I use all the time to make people feel like they need to fill the silence, and even though I know exactly what he's doing, I still break.

"Northwestern," I say eventually. "Or Brown. Those are hard to swing, but they have great journalism programs. Maybe UNC Chapel Hill or Vanderbilt."

Mickenlee Hooper went to Vanderbilt.

"I see," Kendall says. "So you'll come back with lots of money and a high-profile job."

"I don't think I'll come back at all."

That, at least, seems to surprise him. Like Kendall Wilkinson never considered the possibility that someone would leave Mayberry for good. Admitting that I want to makes me feel exposed. Unprepared. Selfish, even, for the ambition clawing inside my chest when Kendall is perfectly content to be here.

Again, I wonder what this town ever did to make him want to stay and why it never treated me with the same care.

"A lot of people say they want to leave," he says eventually. "You're just the first person I actually believe."

I don't think he means it to be an insult, but the words still sting. Maybe I am wrong for trying to get out. Maybe I really am selfish, but Decklee Cassel wasn't Decklee Cassel in Mayberry, and I don't know how to be the person I know I'm meant to be in this town.

I lean my head against the seat and watch the landscape whiz by. It's a lot of forests and farmlands in this part of Arkansas, but now that we have the Oklahoma border at our backs, it's not as flat. Soon we'll pass through the city gridlock of Little Rock and make our way up the northeast highways. Toward Decklee. Toward answers.

Toward a prize that could change our lives.

"Hey, Kendall?" I turn my head so I can watch him out of the corner of my eye.

"Hey, Purchase?"

I bite back a grin. Kendall is literally the only one who calls me by my last name. "Thanks again for doing this."

"Of course." He slings an arm over the back of my seat with so much force the truck momentarily swerves. "Thanks for splitting your three million dollars."

"Look at the road!" I push him away as we steady out. "God, it's bad enough your car is a thousand years old, don't kill us before we get there!" But we're both laughing, finally comfortable in this strange little bubble, and I feel the remaining barriers

between us crumble. "You got any music?" I ask, already opening the glove compartment.

"I think it's a decent selection."

It turns out Kendall's "decent selection" of music con-
sists solely of *Fearless (Taylor's Version)*, the soundtrack to
Mamma Mia! Here We Go Again, and the full movie score of
Cats (2019).

"Seriously?" I hold up the CDs. "What's this?"

"That, Purchase," Kendall says, very seriously, "is what we
call taste."

"No." I shake my head. "It's cursed. Turn up the radio."

"You sure? I do an excellent rendition of 'Skimbleshanks:
The Railway Cat.'"

"I'm positive, thank you."

Kendall cranks the volume and I'm not surprised to hear a
Decklee Cassel song pouring through the speakers. She's been a
popular request over the last few days, but as the chorus kicks
in, I think it feels like actual fate.

"Roll down the windows!" I almost elbow Kendall in the face
in my excitement.

"But we're on the highway," he protests.

"Kendall, I cannot stress to you enough how much I do not
care."

And even though we're driving too fast to really hear with
the windows down, Kendall opens them anyway, just for me. So
I thrust my hand into the sticky summer air and let the roar of
the wind chase every lingering, selfish thought away.

EIGHT

Decklee
Memphis, 1966

¶ write a song on the bus out of town.

Markell is next to me, palm pressed to the window as Memphis fades in the distance, and something about the way he watches it go makes me think of another city from another time. I don't miss Mayberry, but sometimes I'll catch a few notes of a childhood folk song or inhale the scent of warm summer grass and the feeling is so familiar it's like my ribs are cracking apart. I think of my father and wonder if he ever read the letter I sent him my first week in Memphis, if he ever sat awake waiting for me to come home, and even though I don't miss him in the ways I think I'm supposed to, I write a song for him now.

One for the money, two for the show, three to get ready, four to go.

I write a verse for each part of my countdown—one for Markell and his brilliance and all the ways I'm certain he's going to change the world. One for Ricky, how it felt when he smiled at me, when he *chose* me, and about how none of those things would have happened if I'd stayed in Mayberry. One for the girls I left behind. One for the bus out of here.

The fields beyond our window blur into each other as we ride, until it's just me and Markell and the music, pulling away from everything we've known for the last three years. He looks at me as the sun sinks over the horizon, then leans over and presses something into my hand.

"For you," he says. "A Fansworth original."

I open my fingers to find a small jewel-encrusted pin—a silver cat winking up at me from the middle of my palm. It's not exactly the Top Cat logo, but it's close. I grin and fasten it to the inside of my jacket, tucked against my heart.

"I love it," I say, resting my cheek against his shoulder. "Thank you for coming with me."

He squeezes my hand once. "Thank you for asking."

And even though nothing about this is permanent, even though I have no idea where we're heading or what waits for us there, I think this is the closest thing I have to home.

NINE

Darren

I notice the cameras first.

Madison Avenue is packed with them, and Kendall has to circle the block three times before he finds a spot big enough to park the truck. I press a hand to the window as I watch the line of news vans linger on the other side of the street, three blocks from where the old Top Cat building still stands on the corner.

"Wow." Kendall follows my gaze as he cuts the engine. "Looks like a party out there."

My stomach tightens at the idea of more eyes, more people, and more publicity focused on the thing that's supposed to be mine. But people wouldn't be here unless they had a lead. Reporters wouldn't be lining the streets unless there's some chance I'm right. I take a deep breath and open the door.

"Come on," I say. "Let's go find it."

The humidity hits me as soon as I land on the sidewalk. Kendall is already several paces ahead, wandering through the crowd, but it takes me a few seconds to remember how to move. Because here I am, outside of Mayberry, and for the first time in my life, it feels like I'm doing something right.

At first glance, this block of downtown Memphis doesn't feel particularly special. It doesn't feel like rock and roll, or a city of stars, or any of the countless glittering vignettes I'd imagined. It's just a street lined with short brown brick buildings and framed by trees. But then I smell food frying somewhere out of sight, catch snippets of conversation from passing shoppers, and I think *no*, that's not exactly true. This city is loud and wild and dense in a way Mayberry will never be, and I understand exactly how Decklee Cassel became who she was here. I understand why she had to.

When something is this different from everything you've ever known, how can you *not* feel it? How does it not sink into your blood, become part of your very being?

Across the street, a HARD ROCK CAFE sign flashes in my direction. Cars honk, the city sings, and I inhale a long, slow breath. How many times did Decklee walk these streets? To her job at Top Cat? To the gigs she played across town? To the motel room she shared with Markell Fansworth before they were both household names?

Had she known, even then, what they were becoming?

"Hey!" Kendall turns, shielding his eyes against the sun as he peers back at me. "You coming?"

"Yes!" I shake away the city's ghosts and jog to catch up. "Sorry. Let's go."

The crowd thickens the farther we walk, until Kendall and I

are shoulder to shoulder, squeezing our way down the sidewalk. The Top Cat music club doesn't exist anymore, but the original building is still intact, echoes of its old life visible in the worn brick façade. A trendy clothing store now sits in its place, feeding into the strip mall through its side entrance.

"I wish I knew why all these reporters are here," I mutter as we walk. "Like, did they find something? Did they figure out the clue? Are they just here for B-roll?"

Kendall glances at the nearest van. "Want me to find out?"

"Find out? Now?"

"Yeah." Before I can protest, he stops in front of the van and waves at the girl crouched inside. "Hey," he says. "Sorry to interrupt, but can you tell us what's going on?"

She lifts her head and I see she's not much older than me—a pretty Asian girl with short black hair, immaculate winged eyeliner, and a nose ring that looks a million times cooler than mine ever will. She must be an intern or a junior reporter, because it's clear everyone left her to watch the equipment while they hunted for a story. There's a knot of cables slung over one shoulder and a backpack dangling off the other, the latter covered in so many pins and patches I can't tell what it originally looked like.

"What do you mean?" she asks. "You're going to have to be a bit more specific."

Kendall shakes his head. "Right. Sorry, it's just . . . why are you all here? Is there an event? Something happening downtown?"

"No." The girl yawns. "My boss dragged us down here this morning to look at old buildings. Apparently people think

Decklee Cassel's time capsule is here, in Memphis. Did you hear about that?"

"No," I answer automatically.

"Who's Decklee Cassel?" Kendall asks with surprising sincerity.

"Who's—?" The girl stops. "Seriously? The country music star? She used to work here, so it's a whole thing." When neither of us move she goes back to winding her cables. "Whatever, my boss wanted us here early in case something happened, but he and the staff immediately went to brunch. He hasn't even texted me about that whole Mike Fratt situation, so if I miss out on an interview because he wanted to drink two-dollar mimosas, I'm going to scream."

"Who's Mike Fratt?" I ask at the same time Kendall says, "The YouTuber?"

"See!" The girl throws up her hands. "I told them it would be a good story. Yes, he's on his way here right now. Last time I checked he was like an hour out. I'm—"

"Okay, thank you!" I grab Kendall's sleeve and tug him back onto the sidewalk. "We have to get going. Good luck with the story!" Kendall tries to wave over his shoulder, but I'm already moving away from the van. "Who the hell is Mike Fratt?" I mutter.

"He's an influencer, vlogger, Twitch streamer." Kendall hesitates. "Well, I guess he's not on Twitch anymore, he got kicked off for 'accidentally endorsing the insurrection,' but he still sells the merch."

"He sounds terrible."

"Oh, he is. I'd actually like to avoid being in the same state as him if we can help it."

But apparently encouraging a poorly planned coup d'état is great for business, because Mike Fratt has almost a hundred million Instagram followers alone. I click the latest post and find an overly saturated selfie of four college-age guys in an open-top Jeep, each wearing a different colored baseball cap and flashing the camera a thumbs-up. I assume the blond one in the driver's seat is Mike Fratt because the caption reads *Taking a little road trip up to Memphis with the boys. Might fuck around and win three million dollars. #DeckleeCasselTimeCapsule #WeKnowWhereItIs*

My stomach drops, and when I look up, Kendall is staring at the screen over my shoulder. For a minute, neither of us speak. I know this quest isn't really mine. There are plenty of people out there who loved Decklee, who want a part of her legacy, but I've been so convinced this first clue, at least, is for me. That hearing her announcement on the radio had been a sign I was meant for something more. If anyone could solve it, how long of a head start do Kendall and I really have?

How long until this street is swarming with hundreds of people who all know exactly where to look?

"Wow." Kendall looks up, expression grave. "That caption is really bad."

I roll my eyes and quicken my pace. "Let's find the time capsule before he thinks of another hashtag."

The streets in front of the old Top Cat building are packed, but the alley curving around the side of the building is quieter.

Maybe it's the smell of hot garbage that keeps the pedestrians away. Maybe it's the puddles of oily mystery liquid spotting the pavement. Either way, I'm grateful for the cover now. Kendall hesitates as we step into the narrow space between the buildings. "Isn't there supposed to be a rainbow?"

"Shhh!" I seize his arm and steer him into the alley before he can announce our plan to the entire world. "Back when they were constructing the original building, there were so many union disputes that three separate crews ended up working this lot," I whisper, glancing over my shoulder to make sure we're still alone. "Each one used different materials, which meant the bricks all started to fade at different times, so it left the back wall looking something like . . . this."

I sweep out an arm as we round the final corner into the back courtyard. I'm about to continue the story, but the sight of the wall above the old stage door has me stumbling to a halt. I've only seen it in pictures, in newspaper clips and black-and-white images, but there's something different about seeing it in person. It makes this quest real. It makes Decklee real.

"Oh my god." Kendall's eyes widen as he takes in the patches of dusty bricks. "The rainbow was a metaphor."

I let out a choked laugh as he runs a hand over the wall. "Yeah, I guess it was."

"Don't get me wrong," he says. "It's cool. But it's also a little weird to think that this place used to be something, right? Like, it's a mall now, but it used to be history."

The thought sends a chill down my spine. Between the reporters outside and the other people joining this quest, I'd forgotten what drew me here in the first place. "It wasn't just Decklee's history," I say. "So many people performed here. So many people were *discovered* here. I mean, even Markell Fansworth worked at Top Cat before moving to New York."

Kendall's brows lift. "The fashion designer?"

"You know him?"

"Of course, my mom is obsessed. We must have fifty of his bags in storage."

I don't know why the image of Kendall's closets overflowing with designer bags is funny. I don't know why I'm thinking about it now, when time is short and we should be searching, but the gravity of this place makes me pause. I want to soak in every detail, commit each brick to memory in case they tear this part down, too.

Kendall turns in a circle, looking up at the sky. "Somewhere over the rainbow," he says. "You think it's on the roof?"

I snort. "If it is, you're climbing."

I let my hand skim over the bricks, over the dark blocks of red and the deeper streaks of purple. The first line of color arcs right over my head, a dull pink two shades lighter than the bricks below. If I stand on my toes, I can reach the top. Everything is smooth under my fingers, hot from sitting out in the sun. Everything looks normal.

Everything except for a faint splash of red dust smeared on a yellowing brick about ten feet above my head.

Anticipation prickles up the back of my neck and I step back. "Kendall."

"Hmm?"

"Do you see that?"

I point. Objectively, it's nothing—a smear of dust against the bricks, a visible sign of age, but Kendall follows my gaze. "Somewhere over the rainbow?" he asks.

The phrase catches in my throat. Could that really be all it means? A literal translation? A quick drive and we're here, a few feet below Decklee Cassel's missing time capsule? I exhale and shake out my arms. "Okay. I'm going to do something really embarrassing and you're not allowed to make fun of me when we get home."

Kendall puts a hand to his chest. "I would literally *never*—"

I turn and haul myself onto the nearest dumpster before he can launch into a speech. The smell is overwhelming up here, and as my foot slides through something slimy, I know Kendall is *absolutely* going to make fun of me for this later. I brace myself against the wall and run a finger over the bricks again, examining the rust-colored powder I'd seen from the ground. It's gritty on my skin, a tiny imperfection on a wall full of imperfections. But I have this *feeling*, this tug in my gut urging me forward. I dig my fingers into the grooves between the bricks and I'm just about to convince myself this entire plan was wrong when something moves.

I yelp and pull back so suddenly Kendall jumps. "What?" he calls. "What is it?"

"Can you throw me your keys?"

Before, the pedestrians cutting through the alley had ignored us. Now they're slowing down, stopping longer than necessary to watch the girl perched on the dumpster and the boy who has to try three times before he finally throws his keys high enough for her to catch.

I adjust my grip on the wall with one hand and feel for the grooved edge of Kendall's house key with the other. Then, when I'm sure I have a good grip, I slide it against the subtle crack between the bricks. Nic Cage did this in the first *National Treasure* movie. And maybe Nic Cage characters aren't a particularly good set of role models, but it worked for him.

Dust drifts into my eyes as I stab at the wall again and again, sawing at the crack until part of the brick comes loose in my hand. My pulse hammers as I pull back slowly, dropping the brick and Kendall's keys to the top of the dumpster. There's an opening in the wall now, just wide enough to slip my hand inside.

"Wait!" Kendall lurches forward, fingers wrapping around my ankle. "Are you sure you want to do that?"

I look down. "Do what?"

"I don't know, reach your hand inside a *wall*? You don't know what's in there!"

He's shifting back and forth on the pavement, watching me with an expression that's half-worried, half-wondering. "I know," I say. "That's the whole point."

And then I slide my hand inside the rainbow wall.

I know it's not the time capsule instantly. I remember Kennedy Grasso holding that box with two hands at the funeral, struggling to lift it by herself. Whatever's in the wall now is hard and slim, fitting easily into my palm. I let Kendall help me down from the dumpster before uncurling my fingers and taking a closer look.

It's a simple gray flash drive, the kind you can buy at any convenience store. I turn it over in my hands as my heart stutters back to normal and realization creeps in. No time capsule. No prize. No money.

So why am I here?

The flash drive is bare except for the words written along the side in silver sharpie—a single line I don't recognize from Decklee's discography.

Two for the show.

The phrase catches in the back of my head, tugging on something just out of reach. It's familiar somehow, but I don't place it until Kendall peers over my shoulder. His forehead creases.

"Like the nursery rhyme?"

I look up. "What?"

"The rhyme." He points at the flash drive. "You know—*One for the money, two for the show, three to get ready, and four to go.* It's, like, a classic playground thing."

It hits me then why the phrase sounds so familiar—I had heard the first part this morning from Decklee Cassel herself. *Here's how it'll go: Keep this station on, because we'll be revealing the first clue right after this—one for the money.*

Kendall glances back at the wall, like he expects me to pull something else from its depths. "Is that all?"

"I have no idea." I had been expecting the time capsule, but now I'm standing under the façade of a historic building in a city I never thought I'd see, holding a flash drive I didn't know existed, with no idea what to do next.

Is there even a time capsule at all? Or is this all a game Decklee decided to play from beyond the grave?

Kendall's still watching me and something about his steady gaze calms my nerves. I take a breath, fingers curling around the secrets in my palm. I might feel unsure about where we're going, but there's one thing I know.

"We need to find out what's on this flash drive."

TEN

Decklee
Nashville, 1970

Everyone in this town wants something new. They hunt shiny, bright-eyed girls for sport, hoist them up to impossible heights, and shove them straight out into open air. *It's fun*, they say, *it's business*. And if anyone fails to fly, there's already another one waiting to take their place.

Hunter Wallstreet is the star everyone wants: classic and timeless and slow. He's the kind of musician who's never been hungry, who's never felt the weight of every desire scorching him from the inside out, and that's how his music feels, too. Like warm honey. Like he has all the time in the world to make people listen and love him.

Ricky thought Hunter would make me a star, too. Instead, I make Hunter desirable—his pretty duet partner, the girl in the back of his videos, a complacent flower, content to bloom wherever this city will have me.

"I want to leave him, Ricky. Get me out of that contract."

It's the first time I say the words out loud, standing in Ricky's office after another recording session. He's quiet for so long I wonder if he hears me. I wonder if he's going to keep pretending I don't exist. "I don't think that's a good idea," he says eventually. "Hunter's videos have an incredible prime-time placement right now. Everyone loves you. You know how many girls would kill for this kind of publicity?"

Of course I do. I was one of those girls when he found me at Top Cat. He promised me the world, and like a fool, I believed him. "I'm a solo act," I say. "That's how you signed me and that's what I want. I don't need Hunter."

"But look what you've accomplished together." Ricky ticks our achievements off on his fingers, one by one. "Two charting albums. A single in the top twenty. Two Country Music Association award nominations."

I shake my head. "Those aren't mine. They're nominating Hunter, you know that. If this is because of my first record sales—"

"Of course not." Ricky waves a hand. "That's old news. I'm more concerned about your future—how would we get Hunter's fans to listen to your new solo record?"

I clench my fists behind my back. I want to scream, to tell him that's not the point. I don't want Hunter's fans and they certainly don't want me. Ricky's the one who gave up on my first album before it had a chance, and I know if I have to spend the rest of my career playing the girl on Hunter Wallstreet's arm, singing the soprano line in his duets, I'll waste away. Mayberry might eat wildfire girls, but Nashville swallows them whole.

Here, everybody burns until they burn out.

"I'm a solo act," I repeat, louder this time. "I want to make another solo album and I want out of my contract with Hunter."

We stare at each other across the desk, Ricky's gaze steady, mine blazing, and I wonder how much power I really hold here. I have one record before Hunter, a moderate debut no one at this label bothered to push. In Ricky's mind, it's enough to sink me.

"Fine," he says after another minute of consideration. "If that's what you want, I'll think about it. But you'd still need a writer."

"Excuse me?"

"A writer," he repeats. "Musically, your songs are exceptional. I've always thought so, but lyrically, you don't stand out. It doesn't matter with Hunter, people will buy whatever he sings, but if you're serious about this, you need someone else on your team. It doesn't have to be public," he adds. "I'm willing to give you another chance after this contract is done, but I want a writer behind the scenes. No one has to know."

My nails dig into my palms and it's an effort to keep my expression clear. *I'll* know. I'll know that even now Ricky thinks I'm not good enough. I'll know that every potential sale, every future nomination won't just be for me. It'll be for whoever the label assigns.

Seven years. That's how long it's been since I hopped that Greyhound in Texarkana. I think of Markell and his little shop off Jefferson, right on the bank of the river. He likes to say it's nothing, that he's barely getting by, but that's not true. While

I've been busy agreeing with Ricky and smiling at Hunter Wallstreet and forcing this delicate version of myself down everyone's throats, Markell has been doing the work. He's built a life, carved himself a place in this town. He'll design whatever I wear next award season, and now I wonder if he wishes his red-carpet debut had been with someone important, someone better.

He could find bigger stars in this town, people who have dozens of awards and charting records and sold-out crowds. People with label support, who Ricky cares enough to invest in. I want it all. But ambition only sells if you're Hunter Wallstreet. On him, it's inspiring. On me, it's abrasive.

I force myself to nod as I hold Ricky's gaze, to fold my hands and smile like this is the easiest thing in the world. "What do you need me to do?"

Ricky drums his fingers on the table, but something about it feels distant, like he's already checked out of the conversation. "Let's make a few calls. We can start taking meetings and making plans from there. I'll be in touch, all right?"

I'll be in touch. Because he has other careers to launch with clients who are more important than me. Because I don't matter to him the way I used to. It takes him two weeks to find me a single meeting option and by then, I know he's written me off. He's trying to placate me, pretending to care about my career and hoping I'll keep myself busy while he finds himself someone new.

"I'll never understand how this works," I mutter on the afternoon I'm supposed to have my first meeting at the soda shop on Elliston. "Shouldn't they *want* me to succeed? Wouldn't that make Ricky more money? Why are they acting like I don't exist outside of Hunter Wallstreet's music videos?"

I'm in the bathroom of my downtown apartment, trying to comb my hair into something presentable. It's not working and the longer I stand there, scowling at the mirror, the more I don't want to go. Markell laughs, sound muffled as he rummages through my closet.

"There's one of you on every corner, remember? Ricky can hop down to Broadway anytime and find himself a new star. He doesn't need to promote you." He pauses before adding, "They have an estate, you know."

I lean back so I can see him in the mirror. "Who does?"

"That girl you're going to meet. Mickenlee Hooper. Did you know her dad is dean of students at Vanderbilt?"

"And her uncle owns my label," I mutter. It's the only reason Ricky wants me to meet her, I'm sure of it. "She sounds insufferable. Tell me more."

Markell tosses another shirt in my direction. "She graduated from Vanderbilt in two years and went straight to Harvard Law School. I don't know why she didn't finish the program, but she's back now. Maybe she couldn't hack it."

"Maybe." I tug the shirt over my head and step out of the bathroom. "How do you know that?"

"People tell their tailors everything. Turn." Markell motions for me to spin in a circle. I do, and when I get back to the front, he's holding a jacket in each hand. "Denim or leather? Who do you want to look like?"

I want to look like the most important person in this city, like I could tear Mickenlee Hooper's heart out, if I wanted to. I shrug. "Like I'm better than her and hope she knows it."

Markell grins, long and wolfish, and drapes the leather jacket over my shoulders. "Excellent."

I can't tell if Mickenlee's early or I'm late, but I spot her immediately, sitting alone at a corner booth with her arms folded. Her dark hair falls in long waves down her shoulders and her wardrobe is all polished lines, a new-money shine I can see from the door. I hate it already. She looks up as I cross the restaurant and approach the table.

"You're Todd's niece?" I ask, extending a hand.

Because that's how everyone talks about me. *You're Hunter's girl? You're Ricky's client?* It hooks under my skin, just like I watch it hook under hers. Her fingers tighten around mine.

"I'm Mickenlee, yes."

For someone born and raised in Tennessee, there's no trace of an accent. Maybe that's something they train out of you in Boston. Maybe it's something she trained out of herself, too embarrassing for a Harvard girl to keep. We sit in silence, Mickenlee straight-backed and waiting, me on the edge of a razor. I allow myself a single second to breathe. Todd Hooper is important enough that even Ricky Grasso can't refuse a request, but lunch is all I've agreed to. Lunch and a conversation about what a potential partnership could look like. I'll play along if it means Ricky will find me someone else after this is over.

I've been playing the ever-changing game of this city a long time. I can make it another hour.

"I hear you dropped out of Harvard," I say without warning. "I don't like people who give up."

Markell had dropped that piece of information like it was an arsenal and that's how I use it now—just wind it up and launch it across the table. But Mickenlee doesn't flinch. "I heard you left your entire family when you were fifteen," she says. "Just *gave up* on that whole town."

My breath momentarily catches. "That's none of your business."

"I'm just making conversation."

No, she's testing me. Her blue eyes are unreadable, the piercing color of ice, and I realize that's what she feels like. Cold and unshakable. There's a battered leather notebook on the table next to her coffee, no doubt filled with words everyone tells her are good. College-educated words, crafted and refined, but I don't want polished metaphors. I don't want East Coast elitism.

"You're a writer?" I ask.

The corner of Mickenlee's mouth lifts. "That's why I'm here."

"You any good?"

"Better than you."

My fingers ache as they curl in my lap. You don't have to be good at things if you're rich. That's something I learned years ago. "You're not better than me. No one is."

Her eyebrow lifts. "Really? That's why you need a cowriter?"

Something about her little half smile infuriates me. It lacks authenticity, like she's been trained to smile politely at important people her entire life and I'm nothing more than a face at one of her family's dinner parties. I want to crack it open.

"I don't need anyone."

"No, of course not." She hesitates, manicured fingers tapping against the front of her notebook. "I hear you're leaving Hunter Wallstreet next month."

"I am." It's the only thing I'm sure of. "But I'm not singing backup for you or anybody else."

"I'm not a singer."

"I don't care. I don't care who you are or what your family does. I'm not singing someone else's songs. This is just a formality."

I expect her to draw back then, away from the bite. That's what always surprises people in the end—the realization that I'm not the girl from Hunter's albums, content with nothing. The realization that I *want* things, that if Ricky won't give them to me, I'll find a way to take them myself. But Mickenlee just leans forward, elbows braced against the table.

"Do you know why Ricky Grasso set up this meeting?"

I grit my teeth. Of course I do. Because Mickenlee Hooper has money and connections and all the things people in this town take for granted.

"It's because he doesn't care about you," she says before I can answer. "If he was serious about your solo career, he wouldn't make you take these meetings yourself. We'd be in his office right now, nailing down contracts and finalizing recording schedules, because *that's* how they treat the people they care about."

She has her hands pressed against the table, fingers curled like she wants to dig them straight through the wood and into the bones of the city itself. "My uncle thinks this is a phase, you know. He's never read my work and he sure as hell doesn't believe I can write songs. He's doing my father a favor just like Ricky is doing a favor for him, and no one cares if I happen to drag you down with me. You're a write-off. You don't matter."

I catch a hint of her accent then, woven against the back of every word. I feel it like a knife to the gut, but she's going to have to try harder if she thinks that's enough to rile me. "So why are you here?" I ask. "Why don't you leave?"

Mickenlee's gaze is hard, aching with an intensity I can't name. "Because I don't believe them."

I don't know if she's talking about her uncle. I don't know if she's talking about Ricky Grasso or this industry or *me*. All I know is that this isn't what I agreed to. She slides her notebook toward me across the table. "Read this. Take your time if you need to, but read it. I'm good, I can help you." She hesitates before adding, "We could prove everyone wrong."

I eye the battered cover, the places where the leather has worn down under her touch. For a single second, I let her think I'm considering it. I feel her lean in, brimming with quiet anticipation, and that's her mistake. I run a finger down the length of the pages, thumb them between my fingers. Then, when I have Mickenlee right where I want her, in the palm of my hand, I close my fist.

"I'm sorry, Ms. Hooper. I don't think this is going to work out."

Her cheeks flood with color and the ice cracks, just a bit. "I promise it's worth your time."

I have to bite back a grin as I stand. The game is always more fun when someone's begging. "No, I don't think it is."

"You're making a mistake."

I pause. She's glaring up at me, and for a single second, I think I see fire, hot blue flames and burning rage. Then I blink and it's gone. "Is that a threat?"

Mickenlee shakes her head. "No. It's a fact."

I look at the notebook one last time. There's a whisper of curiosity rising in my chest. What makes her think she's better than me? Why does she care so much? I force my face to smooth into a sweet, placating grin. "Tell your uncle I say hello."

And then, without waiting for her reply, I leave.

ELEVEN

Darren

"**D**o we have a plan? Or is this the part where we just kind of wing it?"

Kendall hurries after me as we spill out of the alley, back into the busy flow of afternoon foot traffic. I'm putting a lot of effort into walking fast enough to satisfy the adrenaline pulsing through my veins but not so fast I attract the attention of every news camera on the block. Of course I have a plan. I just have to stall long enough to figure out what it is.

"What would we even say?" Kendall mutters, half to himself, as we sidestep a group of tourists. "Are we just going to waltz into the mall and ask someone to insert a suspicious flash drive into their company computer? Are you going to tell them you vandalized their building?"

"I didn't *vandalize* anything!" I hiss.

"I think we'd all be interested to know how, exactly, you define vandalism."

I roll my eyes, but Kendall's right. We need a computer, something to see what's on this flash drive, and I can't just walk into one of these businesses. I can't stop someone on the street and expect them to understand. I'm sweating by the time I stop under a shaded awning, and that's when the full weight of the situation hits me.

Decklee Cassel.

I'm holding something that was *Decklee Cassel's* in my fist. Hers, mine. This thin gossamer thread connecting us through the years, and I need to know what it means. I can't wait until tomorrow. I can't go home when I'm standing on the brink of something real for the first time in my life.

I run a hand through my hair and turn in a circle, trying to gauge our options. We've stopped next to a news van, one of the local station's, where a reporter is broadcasting live on the other side of the door, a few feet from where we stand. If I lean back, I can see the monitors inside the van, photos flicking by one by one as he narrates. It's a flashback of Decklee Cassel's career—her onstage at Madison Square Garden; standing arm in arm with Markell Fansworth on a red carpet, decked out in matching silver; sitting with Mickenlee Hooper on a smooth, grassy hill.

It takes me a minute to recognize the Memphis skyline behind them, not far from where we stand now. They're tangled together on a picnic blanket, Decklee barefoot and dressed in her classic denim cutoffs. Mickenlee's wearing a perfectly tailored gingham sundress, but it's her face that pulls me in, half-hidden behind an enormous wide-brimmed sun hat. I can just see the curl of her lips as she leans toward Decklee, like the camera caught them inside of a joke, and I think something about the expression feels familiar.

I turn back to Kendall with a renewed sense of urgency. "What if we tell them we're following the clues from the radio?" I ask. "We're obviously not the only ones looking for the time capsule."

"Who's 'them'?"

"I don't know. A shop owner? A kind pedestrian?"

Kendall's eyes light up. "The girl from before!" He grabs my arm. "The reporter who wanted the Mike Fratt interview. She had a computer."

I suck in a breath, remembering her alone in the back of the van. "Do you think that's smart? This flash drive could have the location of the time capsule or something. What if she leaks it?"

Kendall falls silent, chewing on his bottom lip. This fear is the thing that unites us right now—the reminder that we could make it this far, solve this clue, and still have someone snatch the real prize from right under our noses. I think of the reporters lining the sidewalks, of people like Mike Fratt who are turning this search into a spectacle. Maybe that's what this quest was intended to be, a way to keep Decklee's legacy alive a little while longer, but for me, it's something deeper.

A way forward. A way out.

Kendall extends a hand. "Well, there's only one way to find out. Can I see that?" It takes me a minute to realize he means the flash drive. I uncurl my fist, fingers aching as I drop it into his palm. "Thanks." He taps it against the end of my nose once. "Let's finish this."

Then he's gone, ducking behind the reporter still giving his on-air monologue before looking both ways and blatantly jaywalking across the street. By the time I catch up, he's half-way down the road, crouched next to the van from before. The girl is still by herself, sorting through the same boxes of cables.

"You," she says, barely looking up as I skid to a stop next to Kendall. "What now?"

Kendall flashes her a brilliant smile and holds out a hand. "I don't think we introduced ourselves before," he says. "I'm Kendall, this is Darren."

The girl takes his hand with what I consider to be a healthy dose of wariness. "Dani."

Her backpack slides down her arm as she moves, and I catch a glimpse of one of the pins hanging off the strap—a pink enamel square that says BI AF.

"Dani." Kendall nods. "Perfect. Earlier you said you wanted an interview with Mike Fratt but your boss wasn't responding."

Dani rolls her eyes. "Yeah, it's really obnoxious." Then she hesitates, fingers momentarily stilling on the strap of her bag. "Wait, do you know him? Is he here?"

"Oh, no." Kendall shakes his head. "I would not be caught dead anywhere near that guy. But I might be able to give you something better."

I'm still looking at Dani's backpack, trying to pick apart her array of pins, but I notice her eyes flash at that. She leans forward and it's an expression I'm all too familiar with. Hunger. Ambition. The thrill of a story waiting to be uncovered. She looks from Kendall to me. "I'm listening."

"Right." Kendall inhales. "This is going to sound weird, but please know that I'm not trying to hack your computer."

"That's exactly what someone trying to hack my computer would say."

"Okay, good point." Kendall looks at me for backup and I step forward into the space between them.

"What he's trying to say is that we have a lead for you."

Dani lifts an eyebrow. "Better than Mike Fratt?"

"Okay, *what* is your deal with him?" Kendall asks. "He's a University of Alabama senior whose biggest claim to fame is a protein-powder sponsorship. Are you really missing out on that much?"

"He's also one of the most popular people on the internet," Dani says. "I don't like him either, but if I got an interview, my boss would have to hire me next year. That's, like, a guaranteed promotion." She glances over her shoulder, and I get the feeling she's still waiting for her boss now, wondering if she should call someone. Eventually, her curiosity wins out. "What do you have?"

Kendall opens his hand and holds up the flash drive. "If you're looking for something on Decklee Cassel's time capsule, I'd start here. We found it around back by the old Top Cat building. We think it's a clue."

He conveniently leaves out how, exactly, we found the flash drive, and Dani doesn't ask. There's a moment where the three of us stand there, unmoving, caught in the orbit of this single piece of plastic. I know the street behind me is teeming and bustling, but it's muted now. Dani's eyes are wide and something in her expression reminds me of Carla's right before we left. It reminds me of the way I felt driving on the open highway with Kendall—like promise and purpose and pure, unbridled possibility.

"Somewhere over the rainbow," Dani mutters. She plucks the flash drive from Kendall's hand. "So it *was* Rainbow Wall."

The knot in my stomach relaxes. "You know about that?"

"My dad's from here. Apparently, everyone called it that back in the day."

"And you really didn't know it was here?" I ask. "Your boss didn't send anyone to check?"

Dani rolls her eyes. "My boss couldn't care less about Decklee Cassel. He just wanted to be the first on the story. But I heard the announcement this morning. We're so close to the city, I wondered if it was connected."

I shake my head. *Unbelievable.* Of all the reporters Kendall could have stopped, he managed to pick one who might actually help us. "We just need a computer," I say. "I think it's a clue to the time capsule's location. Coordinates or directions or something."

The three of us look down at the laptop sitting on the floor of the van. It's probably a work computer. Dani's probably not supposed to use it for anything personal, and there are probably consequences if she does. But sometimes, I think, there are perks to being the insignificant, underestimated intern. Dani hesitates a second longer and I see the exact moment where her resolve fails. She takes a deep breath and jams a finger into Kendall's chest. "If you're actually hacking my computer, I'm going to sue you so hard."

She picks up the laptop and sits in the back of the van, legs dangling into open space. She inserts the flash drive and there's a tense second where we stand, frozen, on the sidewalk. *Please*, I think. *Please be something.*

"It's an audio file," Dani whispers.

"Audio?" I lean in. "That's all?"

Dani nods and Kendall cranes his neck to see the screen over my shoulder. I rub a hand over my face and try to think. I wanted a map to the time capsule, something clear-cut and easy.

"Can you play it?" I ask. "Please?"

Dani wavers a second longer, like she's still thinking of all the ways this could go horribly wrong. She takes a deep breath, turns up the volume, and clicks play.

I brace myself for another announcement, for Decklee's voice to come through the speakers like it did on the radio this morning and give us another cryptic clue. Instead, we're greeted with a single, silky-smooth chord that lingers briefly in the air before falling into a lilting melody. I inhale, hand closing instinctively around Kendall's wrist. Because it's a song. It's *her*.

It's not the voice of Decklee Cassel from the seventies, young and flashy and full of hope, but it's the Decklee from *now*, how she would have sounded if she was still alive today. This Decklee hadn't put out new music in years, but her voice is clear and strong. There's no evidence of her declining health in this song. I close my eyes, sinking into the lyrics, and we're halfway into the chorus before another realization hits me.

This is a Mickenlee Hooper song.

Mickenlee, who didn't attend Decklee's funeral, who hasn't made a public appearance in decades, who even now is a woman lost to time. But there's no mistaking her clever rhymes and intricate verses. It's the kind of song that deserves to be sung in a smoky bar, low and throaty, lips pressed close to a microphone. It's haunting, this melody from beyond the grave, and it sings of home—an old porch swing; a wide, muddy river; and the kind of hope that's quick and catching.

It's a love song.

My hand finds its way into Kendall's instinctively. I don't notice until the last chorus fades and for a single second, the song feels like it's for me. For us. Then he looks down, outlined in the midafternoon sun, and I pull away, dropping my hand back into the empty space between us.

Dani's blinking back tears, even though she's doing a pretty convincing job of pretending otherwise. We all look at each other then, caught in this strange new world of secret music and lost love, and she whispers, "That's a new Decklee Cassel song."

It is. It feels impossible, like trying to grab smoke. I want to seize the flash drive and tuck it against my chest. I want to listen to this song over and over. I want to call Mom and play it for her over the phone, just to let her know that we're going to be okay.

"God." Dani shakes her head. "My boss would kill for this story. I mean, *shit*, anyone would kill for this. It's the whole reason they brought us here and you just found it."

The hunger is back, deep and consuming in her gaze, and I step forward instinctively. Dani isn't wrong. This is the story of a lifetime—a time capsule that's not actually a time capsule. A quest that doesn't end with a single prize but continues on with a series of clues dotted through Decklee's life. If Dani premiered a new Decklee Cassel song, one cowritten by Mickenlee Hooper no less, it would make her career.

Forget her boss, even *I* would kill for that scoop.

If I take the flash drive back now, no one else will hear that song. It'll stay safe in the cocoon of my chest as long as I want, in that same warm, inviting place that feels like Kendall's hand in mine. The thought is like fire in my veins. And then it makes me unspeakably sad.

Decklee Cassel has never been mine to keep.

"You should have that," I say, nodding to the drive in Dani's hand. "You should give everyone a good story."

Kendall's eyes widen. "Wait, no. I think that's a clue, you—"

"I'm serious," I say. "Everyone should get to hear this. A new Decklee Cassel song after years of nothing? It doesn't belong to me."

Dani shakes her head. "I'm their summer intern, you know," she says. "I'm not even a real reporter."

For some reason, that makes me like her more. I shrug. "Well, you are now."

The corner of her mouth lifts and my skin heats at the intensity of it. "You know where the next clue is?" she asks.

Yes. The answer is immediate. Of course I do. I knew as soon as I heard the first chorus. I nod and Dani's grin widens.

"Good," she says. "You go, I'm going to give you two a head start. My boss isn't coming back from brunch anytime soon. I'm not in a rush."

"Thank you."

"Of course." She pauses, looking between me and Kendall, then adds, "I really hope you find it."

I almost linger, just to hear that new song again. I want to sink into its layers, wrap myself in the melodies. Kendall is still looking at me wide-eyed, incredulous, like he can't quite believe we're leaving the flash drive here. I can't believe it either, but again I think that I know who this quest is for. People like us. People like Dani, on the brink of something.

"Come on," I say, pulling Kendall away from the van and back toward the truck. "I told you—I know where we need to go next."

TWELVE

Decklee
Nashville, 1970

The first time Mickenlee Hooper calls me at home, I answer without knowing it's her.

"Meet me again," she says before I can get a word out. "This afternoon, at the soda shop. I think we got off on the wrong foot and I want to—"

"I'm sorry, I'm busy this afternoon," I say, knowing full well I haven't been busy in months. "I doubt I can make it."

"Tomorrow, then. Or this weekend."

"I'm afraid I'm booked."

The second time she calls, I slam the receiver down when I hear her voice on the other end of the line. The third time, I tear the entire phone out of the wall and fling it onto my bed, where it lies in a tangled heap.

Who does she think she is? I did my part. I met her, I played along with her uncle's whims, I told Ricky it wasn't going to work and to find me someone else. We're done. But the messages start piling up then—on my answering machine, on the phone in Ricky's office. When I check my PO Box later that week, it's stuffed to the brim.

"Fascinating," Markell says as he watches me shred the latest letter. "You're going to kill each other."

I'm starting to think we just might.

I call Ricky at the beginning of the next week and tell him to give me more names, actual, serious writers whose family doesn't pay his salary. I play gigs in bars, in basements, in drive-ins to handfuls of people who barely glance my way when they realize I'm not with Hunter. I write dozens of songs on the floor of my apartment, the best I've ever done, and still there's a part of me that remembers the creased edges of Mickenlee's notebook.

Better than you.

That's what she said. I don't know if it's true, but it's still going to haunt me, another *what if* to add to my ever-growing list. Every day the end of my contract with Hunter draws closer with no sign of a replacement writer. It's like Ricky has forgotten about me entirely, attention turned toward newer, brighter, fresher stars.

Because this is how they get rid of me, apparently. This is how they drive me out. I won't explode at all, I'll simply fizzle. Some end to a career that never was.

It's raining the day my contract with Hunter ends, and as I sit alone in my apartment, sorting through stacks of old sheet music, I think there has to be something more than this. I have to be meant for more. I'm still sitting there when the knocking starts, loud and insistent at the front door. I sigh and push myself up.

"You're early, Markell. I'm not even—"

I pull the door open and freeze, momentarily speechless because it's like someone pulled her right out of my head. Mickenlee Hooper on my doorstep, soaking wet and shivering, blinking rain out of her eyes. I lift a hand to shield my face. "What the—?"

"Read this," she snaps with no introduction. "Read this and stop ignoring my calls."

Again, she thrusts the notebook in my direction. It's the same one as before, soft and splattered with rain, dark wet spots that only deepen the longer we stand there. Her dress clings to her pale shoulders, but her eyes are still frosty.

"What . . . ?" I shake my head. "How did you get my address?"

She just lifts her chin. "Read it."

It's not an answer, but I think I like it better. *It'll be your loss.* That's what she's really saying. *If you let me go, you'll regret it for the rest of your life.* I let Mickenlee stand in the rain a second longer before stepping back and motioning her inside.

The first thought I have as she trails me back down the hall is about the size of my apartment. Even with two charting albums and Hunter Wallstreet's star power, I don't have the room to show for it. I brace myself for the judgment, for Mickenlee to start hurling poison-tipped insults like I'd done at the soda shop, but she just looks around once before kicking off her pumps and hopping onto my bed.

"They should be paying you more," she says.

"Excuse me?"

"Your label." She glances around the apartment. "They should be paying you more. I've seen the kind of money Hunter Wallstreet makes. What does your contract say?" She shakes her head. "Never mind. I'll negotiate."

I bark out a laugh, because even now, with her sitting in front of me, I'm not entirely convinced she's real. "You're not negotiating for me."

"Yet." Mickenlee thrusts her notebook under my nose for the second time. "Here, read this. I promise it's worth your time."

Her mouth is set, like she's already preparing what to say when I turn her down. I almost do, just to hear it, just to watch her fight, but curiosity wins out in the end. I don't want another *what if*.

The next time I turn Mickenlee Hooper away, it'll be because I was right.

"One page," I say, taking the notebook from her. "That's all you get."

She grins, leaning back on her elbows despite the wet clothes. "That's all you need."

I don't know if I believe her, but I sit down on the floor anyway. I open the cover and start to read.

There are a few things I've learned from almost four years in this city. That country music is, at its core, a boys' club. That I'll always be expected to look as pretty as I sing. That no matter how many chart-topping records I make or how many nominations I get, there will always be a part of me that longs for more.

But as I leaf through that notebook, cross-legged on the floor with my back pressed against the foot of the bed, I learn something else: that Mickenlee Hooper is the best damn writer I've ever seen.

I don't just read one page. I read them all, practically fly through it. There's a melody to the words, this pulsing rhythm I can already picture weaving into verses. I thought her work would be contrived, coated in East Coast shine, too bright to have much meaning. And even though it's different than anything I have, I feel the same passion hidden in every clever rhyme, the same relentless drive that brought me here in the first place.

When I finish, it takes me a full minute to remember where I am. My room comes into focus slowly and my vision narrows on Mickenlee, still sprawled against my pillows, picking at a spot on her nail. "This is all yours?"

She smiles, and this time, I think it's genuine. "Every word."

I open the front cover again, flipping back to the first page. My favorite. There's a line right there in the middle that I want to weave into a bridge. I want to sing it to an arena of thousands and hear every single person sing it back.

"Why did you leave Harvard?"

I don't need to know, not really, but there's a part of me that wonders if something about it was too much for her. I'm too much most days. If she's looking for easy, she won't find it here.

"It wasn't for any dramatic reason," Mickenlee says. "I would have been an exceptional lawyer. I still could be, if I went back, but I was mostly doing it for my father. To prove something."

I hesitate, tracing the line of her words over and over again with my finger. "And now you don't have anything to prove?"

"No." She shakes her head and crawls across the bed until she's perched right above me, face hovering over mine in the rain-soaked afternoon light. "I have *everything* to prove. But I'm going to do it my way and it's going to be better than anything my father would have made me."

Her breath tickles my ear, trails down the side of my face. I shiver. "Why . . ." I hesitate. I don't want to sound unsure. "Why me? I'm sure Ricky has a bunch of clients he doesn't mind throwing out on a limb. Why did you agree to meet with me?"

Mickenlee considers me a long time, teeth sliding across her lower lip as she thinks. I can't decide if her steady expression makes me feel reassured or on edge. She's open and unreadable all at once, someone who hasn't had to spend the last several years hiding their rough edges just to get noticed. Eventually she shrugs. "Because I like you."

"You don't know me."

No one who knows me likes me very much.

"No, I don't." Mickenlee runs a hand through her still-damp hair. "But you wrote all the songs on your first record, didn't you?"

My face heats and it's an effort to make myself nod. Sometimes I wish that album didn't exist, that I burned it before it burned me, but Mickenlee doesn't laugh.

"I can tell," she says. "Those songs are so different from what you do with Hunter. He's boring. He makes *you* boring."

"I don't really have a choice."

"Oh, no, that's not what I meant. It was a really good record and Ricky screwed you over. But you've always been better than Hunter Wallstreet. He should have been singing backup for you since the day you rode into town, and I want to be here to see his face when he realizes letting you go was the worst mistake of his career."

I turn to look at her, head tipped back against the mattress. This isn't new information to me. I've known I was better than Hunter since we first stepped into the recording studio. I've thought it every day since, but no one has ever said it out loud. Ricky certainly won't, not when he's put all his money into making sure Hunter succeeds, and I realize, for the first time, that I don't remember what it's like to have someone else believe in me like this.

I swallow, throat aching. "What do you want to do about it?"

Mickenlee slides down from the bed so she's right next to me on the floor. There's no concern for her wrinkled dress or rapidly frizzing hair, and when she meets my gaze, it feels like she's been waiting years to say the words that come next. "I want to hear you play."

And so I do.

We write half an album that afternoon, Mickenlee's words, my music, and somewhere along the way I realize this is what I've been missing. Here's someone who burns with the same relentless desire, different than mine, deeper, colder, but just as dangerous. Here's someone who clawed her way out of a different kind of cage, one that was gilded and jeweled and stuffed with arbitrary rules of success.

Here's what I've been looking for since the day I left Mayberry.

Ricky jumps when I barge into his office the next morning. "I like her," I say before he can tell me to leave. "Mickenlee Hooper. I want her to write with me."

His bushy eyebrows draw together, and he leans back in his chair, worn leather creaking under his weight. "I thought you turned her down?"

"Well, I changed my mind."

"What . . . ?" Ricky rubs a hand over his forehead. "She was more of a suggestion, Decklee. I mean, the girl has no credits, no experience."

That's exactly what Mickenlee told me he would say. It's what we prepared for. I fold my arms. "Then why did you waste my time?"

He winces. "It was more of a formality, a favor for—"

"For Todd, I know. I'm not an idiot, Ricky, but you said I needed a writer if I wanted to go solo. That was the deal and I want her."

"She's . . ." Ricky hesitates again, and I see him working through how best to proceed. "She's not exactly what I had in mind."

"And what did you have in mind?"

I want him to say it out loud, to tell me to my face that he didn't mean I needed a cowriter. He meant I needed a man. Another Hunter to write my songs and parade me around like some sort of trophy.

Ricky sighs. "People love your dynamic with Hunter. I know

you're done with him, but there's a certain level of expectation now. People love you."

"They love *him*," I snap. "They love the idea of me as his girl because you never let me be anything else."

"That's not fair." Ricky holds out a hand. "Your debut—"

"Was *good*. It was a damn good record, and you didn't care. You never pushed it. You never put it on the radio, and you gave me to Hunter before it got the chance."

"You and Hunter sell fine. You're steady. You're reliable."

"I don't want to sell fine! I want—"

I break off. *I want everything.* But I can't say that here; he'll call me unreasonable. He'll call me ungrateful when he's the only reason I have any of this in the first place. He could send me back right now, if he wanted. Maybe that's what makes men like him so powerful—not the things they give, but how easily they can take everything away.

"I want Mickenlee," I say. "Please, Ricky, I've been here for years. I've done everything you've asked me to, and I'll keep doing it. I want to work, I want to make things, but I need you to trust me."

Ricky doesn't know what it's like to be desperate. He doesn't know what it's like to have everything to lose. He watches me carefully, finger running over his mustache, before he sighs. "One year," he says. "I'll give you a year, and I swear, Decklee, you better have something to show for it or I'm putting you back with Hunter."

I open my mouth, ready for another fight, but the words don't come. "Really?"

"Really. I'll draw up the contract this week, but I'm serious. You need to give me results."

If the desk hadn't been in the way, I might have hugged him. I debate doing it anyway, but I'm afraid to move. I'm afraid to break this second chance. "Yes! Yes, of course!"

It's all I can say, over and over, until Ricky shoos me out of his office. But I don't care when he shuts the door in my face. I don't even care that he's dismissing me, because I'm going to give him more than results. As I walk back down the hallway, I feel the certainty of it in my bones with every step. I'm going to give him a number-one record.

THIRTEEN

Darren

¶call Mom the minute we're back in the truck. She picks up on the second ring.

"Darren Purchase," she says after I explain the situation. "That boy said you'd be home *tonight*."

I wince and desperately hope her voice doesn't carry to Kendall sitting beside me in the driver's seat. "I know, I know. I'm sorry. We didn't realize this would be a whole thing."

"It better not be. Where are you staying?"

That, I realize, isn't a question I know the answer to. "We're getting a hotel," I blurt. "Seriously, Mom, it's fine. There's just one more stop we need to make and then we'll be home, I promise."

In reality, I have no idea how long this trail of clues spreads. I thought it would end in Memphis, with a time capsule box tucked conveniently into Top Cat's old wall. Now I'm wondering if that was always just wishful thinking.

"A hotel," Mom says. "Separate rooms, I'm assuming?"

"Oh my god." I slide down in my seat, face burning at the implication. "Of course. Obviously."

There's a long stretch of silence before I feel Mom soften. "You really found that song?" she asks. "The one they're playing everywhere?"

I nod and swallow over the sudden lump in my throat. "Yeah, we did."

"It sounds like both of them, doesn't it?"

She hears it, too, I think. Mickenlee woven into every bridge, every measure, every note. "Yeah," I say. "It does."

"Do you think the next clue is another flash drive? Another song?"

"I'm not sure."

I really don't know what to expect anymore. I don't even know what I want to find. I feel like I'm flipping through a scrapbook of Decklee's life on fast-forward, told through people and places instead of words. Dani, breaking open her career with a story that'll change the world. All the people in Memphis who remember Top Cat as it was. The faded photos flashing across news monitors.

If I was in charge of telling Decklee Cassel's story, I think I'd start there—with all the ordinary people caught in her current.

"Are you doing okay?" I ask when I realize Mom's been silent as long as I have.

I regret the question immediately. We both know the answer. Me leaving was supposed to give her comfort, peace, a thing to look forward to. I don't know if I'm achieving any of that right now. All I know is that I miss her.

"Of course," she says. "I'm fine. Give me a call tomorrow morning, all right? Let me know when you're on your way home."

I tighten my grip on my phone, like she'll somehow feel it despite the miles of space between us. "I will. I love you."

"I love you, too."

The call ends, and by the time I look up, it's dark outside. Kendall is relaxed behind the wheel, one arm leaning casually against the window. "Is she doing okay?" he asks. I nod, but he doesn't look convinced. "She's going to hate me for not having you home. She's never going to let us hang out again. You'll have to quit your job."

"Oh no," I deadpan. "You mean I won't be able to stack boxes in the back of Bob's Gas? How *will* I go on?"

But I can tell Kendall still feels bad. I study his profile in the passing glow of the highway lights—the set of his jaw, the way his hands curl and uncurl around the steering wheel. He does that when he's nervous, I realize, twists his hands together in his lap, tugs at his fingers, picks at the skin around his nails. I didn't know I knew that about him.

I can still feel those same fingers laced through mine, the memory so intense it makes my mouth go dry. And I know I'm only thinking about that, about *him*, because the new Decklee song is still playing on the radio, like it has been every hour on our drive north. It was made for moments like this— fleeting glances and soft touches, and it's not Decklee's fault I'm mid-crisis.

"How far out are we?" I ask, suddenly desperate to change the subject.

Kendall glances down at his phone, at the single blue line we've been tracing since Memphis. "About twenty minutes. We should be able to see the city soon." He hesitates before adding, "I don't really have money for a hotel."

Right. The hotel I conveniently told my mother we were staying at. I wonder if there's a Decklee Cassel song about breaking into Nashville motels or sleeping in your car at a rest stop. I sigh and pull Carla's bag of road trip snacks into my lap.

"We'll figure something out," I say. "I can break out my emergency credit card if we need to, but—"

I stop as my hand brushes something strange in the bottom of the bag.

"What?" Kendall glances into the passenger seat as I pull a thick wad of twenty-dollar bills from beneath a peanut butter sandwich. We both stare so long Kendall almost veers into the next lane of traffic.

"Shit!" he gasps. "Is that yours?"

I shake my head, momentarily unable to speak. "It's from Carla."

"Do you think it's, like, legit?"

"Kendall."

"What?" He glances down at the money again. "Maybe she has roomfuls of counterfeit bills at home, I don't know her life."

I roll my eyes, but he's right. This isn't nothing. This isn't a crisp bill tucked inside a birthday card, this is four hundred dollars dropped right in my lap. For a second, I'm thrust back to when Kendall told me he wanted to open a restaurant, how it felt like a contradiction to the person I thought I knew. Carla is as much a part of my family as Mom, and there are still things I don't know about her.

Maybe that's my fault, for treating my time in Mayberry like a temporary rest stop.

"I'm willing to risk it if you are," I say eventually. "I mean, what choice do we have?"

"Famous last words, Purchase." Then Kendall leans forward, pointing at something in the distance. "Hey! Look!"

We round a corner of the highway and I see it—the Nashville skyline silhouetted against an enormous full moon. It cuts through the dark like a dagger, the sight of it driving straight into my chest. It looks, I think, like something out of a song. The mythic city that gave Decklee Cassel everything.

Stars in my eyes, feet on the ground, I was gonna make it in this town.

The lyric echoes in the back of my mind as we approach. Stars in my eyes, feet on the ground. I would finish what Decklee started. Maybe it'll end here, with a time capsule buried under layers of crooning country songs, dark whiskey, and sun-bleached memories.

"Wow," I breathe. "It . . . it doesn't look real."

Kendall nods, mouth half-open as he watches the city expand on the horizon. I press my lips together to keep from smiling. We're such stereotypes—two country kids who have never been farther north than the state line. We're looking at the skyline like it's something extraordinary, and maybe it is. There's so much of this world I don't know anything about, so many things I've never even dared to dream.

This, I realize, is one of them. Driving with Kendall on an unfamiliar highway toward a city that feels very much like it's been waiting for me. It makes me feel reckless, high on the sheer number of possibilities.

"Hey, Kendall?" I run a finger over the crisp, clean edge of the twenty-dollar bills. "Can I ask you something?"

A muscle tenses in his jaw. "Sure."

"Why did you turn down that tennis scholarship? Why didn't you leave Mayberry when you had the chance?"

He hesitates and I hold my breath. We're on the precipice of something here, I feel it. I want to peel back his layers. I want to *know* him. Eventually, he lets out a breath, shoulders slumping, as the shadows thicken outside the window.

"I was really good at tennis," he says. "Everyone treated it like some sort of gift, like it would get me out of that town, and I didn't mind because I genuinely loved it. I loved playing, I loved the game."

He pauses again and I lean in. "So what happened?"

"I don't know. It was all people talked to me about. It was all they cared about, so I didn't care about anything else either. Then, even though I was winning, even though I was really good, it didn't feel like me anymore. It wasn't fun."

I don't understand. "But you could have gotten out. You could have left."

"I told you, I don't want to leave," Kendall says simply. "I never have. Everyone just assumes I should because I'm young and full of potential or whatever, but I really love Mayberry. I like knowing everyone in town. I like driving the roads at night and taking my nieces to the lake and playing cards with my friends. That's why I want my restaurant there instead of Little Rock or another city. I want people to come to Mayberry and see what I see."

"And what's that?"

The words feel stuck in my throat, but he answers without hesitation this time.

"That there's something there most people overlook. That it can be a place worth staying, if you let it."

I look down at my hands and the stack of bills pressed between them. I've never once thought of Mayberry as a place to stay, but Kendall said no to a life-changing opportunity because he wasn't happy. Because for some reason, he loves that town.

"Do you regret it?" I ask.

He shakes his head. "No."

Again, I wonder what it's like to feel that confident about something, to know without a shadow of a doubt that you are making the right choice. That's how Decklee Cassel walked through life, and now that I'm here, speeding toward something I don't quite understand, I have no idea how she did it.

There's this clip of her from the Academy Awards the year she won Best Original Song. One of the red-carpet reporters asks if she thinks her date will finally give her a ring to take home. Everyone laughs because they know he means a proposal, and Decklee laughs because she doesn't care and says, *What I'm taking home is a gold statue.*

Then she turns and walks away.

I still think that's my favorite thing she's ever said. *What I'm taking home is a gold statue.* Because that's what everyone thinks when they walk the red carpet at the Academy Awards. They all want it, even the ones with shocked expressions and hastily written speeches. Even the bright-eyed Nashville country singer with her first nomination.

They all think it's going to be them. No one ever says it out loud.

How many times have I asked myself what I want? How many times have I avoided my own question because saying it out loud would mean voicing dreams that have no right to exist in the first place? How many times have I closed my eyes and let those fantasies play out in the dark behind my eyelids?

Me, getting out of Mayberry for good, writing a story that blows the lid off the world. Me, sought after and recognized and praised. Me, a *force.*

I'd give anything for an ounce of that courage, to say exactly what I want the way Decklee did, live on the red carpet at the fucking *Oscars.* I'd give anything to be like Kendall right now.

Somewhere in the last few miles, we've stopped driving toward Nashville and started driving through it. I straighten as the towering buildings close in, lights popping against the darkening sky. The highway curves west, right above the rush of traffic, and maybe it's because we're here at night, in the beating heart of the city, but the sight stops my breath. I don't notice we're slowing until Kendall parks along the side of the road, and I'm still half-dazed when I look up. "Are we stopping?"

"For a bit." He cuts the engine. "You didn't think we'd come to Nashville without seeing the sights, did you?"

"I . . ."

He nods toward the bustling sidewalk. It's busy despite the late hour, painted in the buzzing glow of a dozen neon signs. "Come on. There's a bar up the street I think you'll really like."

"Kendall, I'm seventeen."

"Technicalities. Just walk in like you own the place, no one's going to say no." He holds out a hand. "Do you trust me, Purchase?"

I nod slowly, carefully. Because I do. Because he's Kendall Wilkinson and because I don't have to be Darren from Mayberry tonight if I don't want to be. I trust him even though I'm tired and sweaty, even though I have no idea where he's leading me, because this is *Nashville* and sometimes you say yes.

"Walk in like I own the place?" I ask.

He grins. "Like you already belong."

"Fine." I take his hand, let the warmth of his fingers slip through mine again. "Here goes nothing."

FOURTEEN

Decklee
Nashville, 1971

There's a magic to Nashville music clubs—something older and deeper than the city itself. There's a pull to it, a swelling when the lights fade and the first drink slides down your throat. Tonight, standing around a table at The Bridge, watching open mic hopefuls clamor for a spot onstage, I think there's also a promise.

"To Decklee Cassel and Mickenlee Hooper, the two most talented award-show snubs this city has ever seen." Markell loops an arm around my waist and pulls me in until I'm pressed against the silky fabric of his shirt, some new trend from New York that hasn't quite trickled this far south. He throws the other arm over Mickenlee's shoulders and plants a kiss on our foreheads, one after the other.

Mickenlee laughs and hugs him back, but I can't bring myself to do the same. I know Markell's joking, trying to make us feel better about our lack of recognition this season, but the words still sting. A reminder of all the things that still hover right out of reach. I shrug out of his grip and turn toward the stage.

The Bridge reminds me of Top Cat, if Top Cat had been a little more polished and a little less desperate. There's the same energy—performers coming in night after night to play, to be seen. It's why Ricky's here, sitting several tables away with a few other label executives. He wants to find a new star. I know because he ordered me an old-fashioned at the beginning of the night, a drink I still pretend to like because it makes him like me, and when he smiled at me over the top of his glass, it felt like a consolation prize.

We both know this industry doesn't want you, but here, have a drink.

I wonder if he still remembers that first open mic—me on-stage, stars in my eyes, feet on the ground. I wonder if he thinks he can find someone better.

Mickenlee's hand brushes mine under the table, but I don't look at her. *It's fine, Decklee. It's just a trophy.* That's what she said after the nomination lists went live, first for the CMAs and then for the Grammys, and we were nowhere to be found. But I know better. It's never *just* anything in this town. *Times Are Changing* was a better record than anything I made with Hunter Wallstreet. It charted for weeks, I sold out shows across the state, and still, there's nothing to show for it. Last month, Hunter brought home three more Grammy Awards, and I'm here, nursing a drink I don't even like.

Across the room, Ricky leans forward as the next performer takes the stage and I decide that's enough. He's not finding someone new tonight, not when I'm right here. I reach up and unwrap the scarf from around my head, shaking out my curls. People know who I am now; I'll get stopped on the street if I'm not careful. They recognize my blond hair and sequined jackets and every time it's a little bit more of a thrill.

Mickenlee's fingers tighten on mine, under the table where no one else can see. "Careful," she murmurs. "Someone will recognize you."

"I know." I shake her off and pick up my drink. "Happy birthday, Mick."

I drain the old-fashioned in one burning gulp. Mickenlee's mouth twists as her hand drops back into her lap. I feel the absence like cold water. We're locked in this strange dance, her and I, one that began the day she showed up on my doorstep in the rain. I still don't know quite where to step.

"Another drink for you, ma'am?" Our waiter stops at the table, eyeing my empty glass. Then he falters, and I watch the recognition flash across his face, watch his throat bob as he fights to regain his composure. "Just let me know how I can help," he adds, voice half an octave higher.

"No," Mickenlee answers for me. "Thank you, we're fine."

But I bite back a grin, flashing the waiter a wink as he walks away. He looks over his shoulder twice, like he's confirming it's me. *Good.* He'll be in the kitchens soon, backstage telling everyone Decklee Cassel is in his section.

"Cleo . . ." Mickenlee's voice is barely more than a whisper.

I turn back to the stage. "Don't call me that."

She's the only one who does, the only one who knows my

real name at all. I hadn't even meant to tell her, but the story slipped out. We were both in the studio sometime last summer, perched shoulder to shoulder on the piano bench. Mickenlee had just come from Ricky's office; I could tell because she was wearing her glasses and a soft flush painted her cheeks. She was still a year short of a law degree, but our label didn't know that. All they knew was that she was ruthless.

"I told you I would negotiate." She grinned, hair falling down her back like liquid smoke. "Those contracts were shit. You're finally getting paid what you're worth, Decklee Cassel."

I raised an eyebrow. "And what do you think I'm worth?"

She smiled a little half smile, the kind that always felt like springtime. "More than this."

We went back to the piano, Mickenlee trying to sound out chords as I scribbled over our sheet music. I remember watching her fingers slide across the keys, searching for the right notes. I remember laughing. For all her lyrical brilliance, she'd never been able to master this.

"It's here," I said, fitting my hand over hers. "Like this."

We moved together down the piano until the chords made sense. *C major, G major, A minor, F major.* Her skin was cool under mine, then it was hot. And then I was floating, lost in the feel of her beneath my fingers.

"You know," I said as we repeated the scales again. "Decklee Cassel isn't my real name."

She grinned and I almost forgot to breathe. "Mickenlee Hooper isn't mine."

And that's how we wrote the second half of *Times Are*

Changing. Because they were. Because we wanted them to. But now, in this club, my old name feels like a burden.

"Excuse me."

Mickenlee and I both jump. There's a woman at my elbow, all bony limbs and sharp features. She's dressed like Ricky, in the way that implies casual, disposable wealth. "Miss Cassel?"

I lift a brow. "Yes?"

"I'm Carmen Brown, I own The Bridge. It's a pleasure to have you with us." She holds out a hand and I take it, resisting the urge to look over my shoulder to make sure Ricky's watching.

See? They love me.

See? You don't need anyone else.

"Were you looking to perform tonight?" Carmen asks. "I'm sure it's nothing like what you're used to, but I also know I speak for everyone here when I say we'd be honored."

"That's all right, actually." Mickenlee puts an arm between me and Carmen before I can answer. "We're actually here for—"

I stand, cutting her off mid-sentence. "I'd love to."

Mickenlee's smile never dims, but something cold flickers behind her eyes. "Really?" she says, voice barely audible above the noise of the crowd. "It's my birthday."

"Relax, it's one song."

She and Markell lock eyes across the table, a silent expression I don't understand, but I'm already moving. I'm not wasting time pretending to be modest or squandering an opportunity to perform. I'm not Hunter Wallstreet's girl and I'm *not* the award-show throwaway.

I borrow a guitar on the way to the stage, just take it from the hands of the performer on deck. He's more than happy to let it go. That'll be the story tomorrow, I think. *Decklee Cassel Wows Open Mic.* For once it won't mention the *what ifs.* It'll just be me and the stage and the music. I touch the small silver cat still pinned inside my jacket once, and then I play.

I pick the lead single from *Times Are Changing,* and from the minute I play the first chord, I really feel like they are. Mickenlee's words, my music. That's the magic combination—all the lightning and the luck, everything I'd been chasing for years. It still doesn't feel like enough, but this audience loves it. They love me. They're clapping before I even finish the song, and as I sit back in my stool, I think *this* is the reason I'm still here.

"That one was for the Recording Academy, actually," I say, and everyone laughs, in on the joke. "Y'all want another?"

I want them to say yes. I want to live on this stage.

I sing an old song, straight off my debut, and then I start taking requests. Someone wants to hear a Hunter duet, but most want to hear me. My music, my songs, this new era Mickenlee and I are starting. Halfway through the next song, I look up to catch Ricky's profile in the dark. He's taken my spot at the table, leaning over to whisper something to Markell that makes them both laugh. It soothes something in me, the idea that for tonight, at least, neither of them are going anywhere. I look for Mickenlee, too, searching for her face in the dark, but she's not at our table anymore.

I squint into the shadowed corners of the club until I see her, walking straight toward the door. *She's leaving.*

"All right," I say, strumming a lazy hand down the strings.

"I've got one more for you tonight. This is a little something we wrote last week, so it's still a work in progress, but I need y'all to tell me if you think it's good for the new album, deal?"

The crowd nods, eager and waiting, but I'm still watching Mickenlee. She pauses by the door, limbs tense as she turns back toward me. She knows what I'm about to play. She knows it's for her. I have to close my eyes before I start, centering myself under the spotlight. I've performed countless songs in countless venues over the years, but this one is different.

"Whiskey Red" is ours.

It's not the typical song of open mics and crowded bars. It doesn't have the drumming beat or wild rhythm, but there's this magic hush that falls over the room when I start singing. People stop moving, every eye turned toward me, and I know with absolute certainty that I have them. When I finish, there's a single second of silence. *Love me*, I think as the crowd inhales. *You have to love me.* The room explodes in wild applause. There's a flash of a camera, quick and bright to my left, and I release my temporary hold.

"Whiskey Red" is the best song we've ever written. There's no doubt about it. I look for Mickenlee again, certain I'll see her back at the table, laughing with Ricky and Markell. Instead, she wavers in the doorway a second longer before shaking her head and slipping out into the night.

"Good night, y'all!" I say. "Hope you had fun!"

I get offstage as quickly as I can, handing the guitar back to the next performer as I pass. "How am I supposed to follow that?" he jokes.

You aren't. That's the point.

I find Mickenlee outside, leaning against the wall with one ankle crossed over the other. Behind her, Broadway flickers and gleams, making her glow in a pale, otherworldly light. "What are you doing?" I ask.

"Calling a taxi." The words are clipped, frosty as the star-flecked sky. "I'm going home."

I shake my head. "But we're here for you. To celebrate your birthday."

She rounds on me, eyes flashing along with the neon signs. "I *was* celebrating. With you and Markell. With my *friends*, not two hundred of your biggest fans."

The fire comes out when she's angry. She's usually so poised and stoic, so unfazed that sometimes I'll poke at her until I find it. But tonight it feels uncalled for, especially when I'm still riding the high of that crowd.

"That was our song, Mick," I say. "I sang it for you."

"Did you?"

I step back, surprised at the intensity of the accusation. Mickenlee knows me. She knows who I am and what I do. She knows I need the stage like some people need air, and I don't understand what's different about tonight. "Are you asking me to stop?"

"No." She rubs a hand across her face. "God, no, I'd never ask you to do that. But I wish you didn't feel like you have to prove yourself all the time."

I open my mouth to tell her no, that's not true, but nothing comes out. I do have to prove myself. I have to do it every day, over and over again. I'm not good enough for the Recording Academy or Ricky Grasso, and there are days I'm convinced I'm not good enough for her.

Mickenlee takes my hand and I tense, looking over both shoulders to make sure we're alone. "What did I tell you after the Grammys?" she asks.

I huff out a laugh. "That the Recording Academy has terrible taste and it's only a matter of time before they die out."

"And I stand by that. I love our record, Decklee. Don't you?"

"I . . ." I hesitate. Do I love it? Or do I love the things I think it could do for me? I shake my head, forcing the thought away. "Yes. Of course I love it."

"Then why does it matter?" Mickenlee's fingers tighten around mine, thumb skating over my knuckles. "I would still write with you if no one was buying our music. I'd still want to be here, on your team, and there's nothing you have to prove to me."

I wish it was that simple. I wish I could be content with what we have, but I've been here too long. I've sat in the middle of every chart, watching the people around me get everything I want, and I know if I have to spend the rest of my career being mediocre, I'm going to combust.

I'm going to bring this whole city down with me.

"It's not like that," I say. "I'm not—"

"Do you want me here, Decklee?" Mickenlee looks up at me through her eyelashes. "Do you want me to stay?"

Even now, I know what she's really asking. *Do you want me, or them?* The crowd. The lights. The fame. It's not a question.

The wind cuts through my jacket, too cold for Nashville in April, and I know which I'd choose.

I think Mickenlee does, too.

"Of course I do." I nod toward the door, back toward the warmth of The Bridge. "Come on. I promise I'm done for now."

A ghost of a smile tugs at the corner of Mickenlee's mouth. "I don't think you'll ever be done."

"Maybe not," I tease. "I guess you'll just have to trust me."

But as we walk back into The Bridge together, I want to lean over and tell her not to do that either. I want to apologize for all the times I'm sure I'll let her down, over and over again.

What I really want to do is tell her to run.

FIFTEEN

Darren

I owe Kendall for a lot of things I'll never be able to repay. Driving me across the South on a moment's notice. Putting up with me at work for the last three years. Not telling Bob about the time I kept a stray cat in the bathroom. But mostly, I owe him for bringing me here, to The Bridge on a Friday night, where the air is hot, the music is loud, and I can practically taste the electricity crackling on my tongue.

The Bridge used to be a music club, a place of sophistication and stardom, and even though it's been modernized into a karaoke bar, there's no ignoring the history. It's plastered all over the walls in photographs, in signatures, in signed programs. Johnny Cash. Linda Ronstadt. Billy Joel.

Decklee Cassel.

Kendall and I sit under her picture now, passing a towering plate of nachos back and forth as a group of girls belt a Carrie Underwood song into the crackly mics.

"They're not bad," Kendall says, nodding toward the stage.

I bite back a laugh. "I think everyone's good here."

The spotlights catch on Decklee's glossy photo, illuminating the faded sepia tones. They've captured her young, perched on this very stage. She's singing something special. I can tell by the way her face turns down, away from the cameras, almost like she's forgotten they exist. Rare for someone like her.

"How did you know about this place?" I ask.

"It's not exactly an underground club, Purchase. It's pretty famous."

"Right, but did you know about Decklee? This is where she performed 'Whiskey Red' for the first time, before anyone knew about the album or before she swept the Grammys. I mean . . ."

I trail off. It's hard to put into words what this place is. What it *was*. All I know is that Mom would absolutely kill to be here, and when I find the time capsule and win the prize money, this will be the first place I take her.

Before Kendall can answer, a short, steel-haired woman appears at our table, clipboard in hand. "Either of you doing karaoke?" she asks, rapping her pen against the sheet. "Sign-ups close in ten."

"No," I say at the same time Kendall lunges for the clipboard. "Absolutely!"

He scrawls his name across the first line and the woman makes a little mark next to it. "Perfect. You're on deck."

I'll have to add *enthusiastic karaoke participant* to the list of things I didn't know about Kendall Wilkinson. I look at him over the pile of nachos. "I didn't know you could sing."

"Oh, no." He shakes his head. "I absolutely cannot, but you don't have to be able to sing at bar karaoke. It's part of the experience."

I settle back in my seat as the girls onstage swing into the final chorus and try to imagine Kendall up there, standing on the same stage as Decklee Cassel. I certainly didn't have that on my summer bucket list. I glance up at her photo again, studying it in the light. The way it's angled, I can't see much of the crowd, and I wonder if anyone else was here with her that night. Ricky Grasso, with his bushy mustache and tailored suits, or Markell Fansworth, maybe, wearing clothes that were always a little too wild and a little too fashionable for the Nashville social scene. Maybe Mickenlee Hooper was in this room at some point long ago, a faded memory of photographs and lyrical metaphors.

I used to wonder a lot about what happened to the two of them, where Mickenlee went and why she disappeared. It wasn't until last summer that I finally thought I figured it out.

Emily and Madison and I had been out at the lake for Fourth of July, sitting cross-legged on the dock and passing a wine cooler back and forth. The sun was sinking behind the trees, and everything had gone still, the heat of the day faded to a warm whisper. I reached over to take the bottle from Emily and froze when I found her outlined against the setting sun, hair illuminated in its golden glow.

For a second, my brain forgot everything it knew about subtlety. *Kiss her.* The thought had been a sudden ache, clanging through my skull. I almost did. I almost put a hand on her bare thigh, almost leaned in close enough to smell the wet grass clinging to her shoulders. She turned toward me before I could, bottle still clutched in one hand, and I practically jumped away from her. The three of us laughed as I fell back against the dock, blaming the wine coolers for my poor balance, and I played along.

As Emily turned to watch the fireflies flicker across the water, I pushed myself back into a seated position and swallowed the voice that had been so loud before. I already knew what it was like to want someone who didn't want me back. It wasn't worth the heartache. *This*, I thought, slamming a lid back on that part of myself. *This is something that would ruin me.*

I wonder if it ruined Decklee and Mickenlee, too, because here's what I know: You don't write a song like "Whiskey Red" about a one-night stand. You don't write it about a man who didn't stick around long enough for the papers to learn his name, and even though the pronouns are traditionally male, I think you write a song like that for a partner. An equal. Someone who shows up in the rain and dares you to turn her away.

The sound of raucous applause pulls me back to the present and Kendall slides out of his seat as the woman with the clipboard motions him toward the stage. "Don't worry," he whispers, pointing back at me with both fingers. "I won't forget you when I'm famous."

I roll my eyes and wave him forward. "Good luck!"

But he doesn't need it. Kendall already has the audience on his side by the time he grabs the microphone. "Hey, everyone, it's my first time in Nashville!" They all cheer and he waits for them to die down before continuing. "I know, I know. But this song is actually for my friend Darren." He points in my direction and my skin heats as everyone turns to look at me. I give them a nervous wave.

"Anyway. She loves this song and, not going to lie, I've only heard it once, but I couldn't let her come here without hearing it in person, so if anyone out there knows the tune, feel free to sing along. Please," he adds. "I really don't know it at all."

The first crackly, instrumental notes of "Whiskey Red" bleed through the speakers and I suck in a breath. Of course I want to hear this song. Of course I want to sing it here, in this bar, and I suppose everyone else does, too. Or maybe we've all just been thinking about Decklee Cassel a lot lately, because the entire bar is nodding and swaying along by the time Kendall starts singing.

He's off-key the whole time but so enthusiastic no one actually cares. And then everyone is singing because when it's a song like "Whiskey Red" in a place like this, there's no way you can't. Even I join in, mouthing the words under my breath. I don't think this song was ever meant for crowded bars and karaoke nights. It's too personal, too subtle, but it works right now. It works with us.

When it comes to an end, the place erupts and Kendall pumps both fists in the air on his way back to our table.

"Hey!" I give his shoulder a playful shove "That wasn't bad!"

He looks momentarily wounded. "Did you think it would be?"

The next song starts, an upbeat cover that pumps through the room like a pulse. I remember my uncertainty in the truck earlier, my desire to feel confident and secure in my own decisions. There might not ever be a life where I'm that girl on the stage, but I think, right now, I could try.

I stand before I can second-guess myself and extend a hand in Kendall's direction. "Dance with me?"

To my surprise, he hesitates. "I don't really dance."

"Seriously? You'll do karaoke but you won't dance?"

"I know my strengths."

But I don't back down. If this is what being brave feels like, I might like it. Kendall wavers a second longer before exhaling a long breath. "Fine." He takes my hand. "But I would only do this for you, Purchase."

I grin. I don't know if that's true, but as Kendall pulls me onto the dance floor, I decide to believe it anyway. I decide I like it too much to ask him to stop.

♫ ♪ ♫

THERE ARE ONLY three other cars in the motel parking lot when we arrive. Our door sticks when I scan the key and Kendall has to shoulder it open. I catch myself on the wall as we both stumble inside.

"Nice place," he mutters as he slides the dead bolt into place. "Really cozy."

"The options were limited, okay?" I peer through the curtains toward the parking lot below, where Blue Delia sits in the glow of a streetlamp. Now that we're out of downtown, away from the neon signs and loud music, this stretch of road doesn't feel much different than Mayberry.

"Do you care if I take the bathroom first?" Kendall asks. "I need to get out of this polo."

I shake my head. "Better you than me."

He shuts the door behind him, and I collapse on one of the beds. As soon as I lean back against the understuffed pillows, I realize this is the first time I've stopped moving since hearing Decklee's radio broadcast. I'm ready to sink into the mattress, but I'm still not done. I need to nail down a plan for tomorrow, one that gets us to the second clue as quickly as we did in Memphis. I know it's here.

Decklee had this old house south of the city—the Brentwood House, everyone called it. It's where she lived after the success of *Whiskey Red*, after she started winning Grammys and selling out arenas. It's a museum now, filled with old costumes, awards, and trinkets. It's also where I think we need to go next. The song on that flash drive talked of porch swings and home with Decklee's music and Mickenlee's words. Memphis might have been where Decklee started, but the Brentwood House was theirs.

It's been closed since the funeral, but according to the website, it reopens tomorrow morning. Just in time for me and Kendall to find the next clue.

I pull out my phone, swiping over to the first few sentences of a new feature story I'd typed on the drive. Dani's business card is still tucked inside my phone case. She slipped it to me as we left, with instructions to update her as we continue the quest. I will, of course. There's so much I want to ask. Like how she found her way to that internship and if she likes working in news. If this is what she wants to do with the rest of her life, if it fulfills her, somehow.

When she knew, exactly, that the BI AF pin on her backpack was hers to claim.

But those are problems for future Darren. Right now, I feel like I'm on the edge of a breakthrough. There's a story forming in the back of my mind and it's about Decklee, yes, but it's also about Mickenlee Hooper's disappearance. It's about their new song tucked behind the bricks of Top Cat and the rhyme scribbled on the side of the flash drive and what that means for them. Everyone's writing about Decklee this week—feature stories and interviews and documentaries that chronicle her life. I want to write those, too, but now I'm thinking the real story starts somewhere different.

I'm thinking it might not be about Decklee Cassel at all.

Kendall opens the bathroom door, hair still damp from the shower. He's changed into a worn Mayberry High School wrestling T-shirt and his eyebrows lift when he sees me sprawled against the pillows. "What are you working on?"

I sit up, hastily tucking my phone away. "Nothing."

"Liar. That's the face you make when you're working on something." He sits down on the other end of the bed. "Is it your big Decklee Cassel Time Capsule story?"

"No. Maybe? I don't know. It could be nothing."

"Well, what do you want it to be?"

I rub a hand over my face. "I'm just thinking about Mickenlee Hooper. I know she wrote that new song, but she and Decklee haven't worked together in decades. She wasn't even at the funeral, so why would she come back to make an album? Did she and Decklee always stay in touch? Where is she now? I'm—" I realize I'm rambling and break off. "Sorry. That's not the point. I just need to write something good."

Kendall nods, leaning forward so his elbows rest on his knees. "For college," he says, and it's not a question. "You want to write something good enough to get out of Mayberry."

Of course I do. That's always been the goal, but admitting it now feels wrong. *Selfish.*

"Yes." I nod. "That's why I'm here. I want to win that prize money for my mom, of course, but I also can't afford to leave without some sort of scholarship. So it's either win a bunch of cash or write something good enough for people to notice."

For the first time since I've known him, Kendall's expression is unreadable. "You and your mom are really close, aren't you?"

I answer without hesitation. "She's my best friend."

"And would she go with you when you leave?"

The question catches me off guard. In all the times I've thought about leaving or brought up college, Mom has never implied she would come, but the thought of leaving her alone in Mayberry is crushing. "I don't know," I say. "I guess I could always just do what Decklee Cassel did—leave in the middle of the night and not tell anyone where I was going."

I mean it as a joke, something to lighten the mood, but Kendall's brows draw together. "She didn't even tell her family?"

"I think she wrote to them eventually, but she never came back."

"That's kind of shitty. Leaving everyone with no explanation? That's a terrible thing to do."

Something about the way he says it heats my skin, like he thinks *I'm* terrible, too. I stand, suddenly unable to sit still on the edge of the bed. "I'd do it."

"Really?" Kendall looks skeptical. "You'd just leave your mom?"

No, of course not. I shake my head. "Well, maybe I wouldn't do it like that, but I'd still leave."

"Why?" he asks. "You've never told me why, Purchase. What's so bad about Mayberry?" I start to turn away, but Kendall stands and catches my arm, so I have no choice but to look at him. "No, seriously. Why do you hate us so much?"

There's real, genuine hurt behind his eyes, and for the first time I wonder if that's what he really thinks. If that's what everyone thinks.

"I don't hate you." The words come out a ragged whisper. "I just . . . I can't stay there, Kendall. I feel like I'll burn up. My father left, you know. He left as soon as he could, and I don't even blame him."

"But why?"

"*Because!*" I snap. "Because if it wasn't that town that drove him away, then it was—"

I stop, teetering on the edge of some dangerous, unspoken truth. *Because if it wasn't that town that drove him away, then it was me.* It was me and Mom and all the things we couldn't be for him.

Kendall's fingers are warm on my arm and I'm suddenly

aware of how close we are, standing together in this too-small hotel room with his hand on my wrist and mine clutching the front of his shirt.

"I want so many things," I whisper, untangling my fingers one at a time. "I don't think it's possible to have them all in Mayberry. But I don't hate you. I need you to know that I don't hate you."

He exhales and I feel his chest rise and fall under my hand. When he speaks again, most of the tension is gone. "Your father's an asshole."

I laugh and it sounds too high-pitched, tinny in my ears. My father did the same thing as Decklee Cassel, just left Mayberry without a word. So why don't I hate her the same way I hate him?

"I'm sorry," Kendall says. "I just want to understand."

So do I. I want to understand why Kendall Wilkinson loves Mayberry so much and why he's content to let the world move around him. I want to know if that makes us too different, too incompatible.

"There's a lot I don't understand," I admit. "About any of this, but I'm glad you're here. I'm glad *we're* here."

The corner of Kendall's mouth lifts, a suggestion of his usual grin, and something deep in my chest warms. I don't wait for him to respond. I can't. Instead, I duck into the bathroom and shut the door with trembling fingers, sliding the lock into place. It takes several seconds to remember how to breathe. It takes several minutes to think about anything other than Kendall on the other side of the door.

SIXTEEN

Decklee
New York City, 1972

I've always belonged on a red carpet. As I stand here now in front of hundreds of photographers, all smiling and waving and calling my name, I think, *This is how it should have been from the beginning.*

Manhattan at night is a wild, untamable creature, different from the warm Memphis streets and electric Nashville glow. I used to think of New York as a city on the brink, always seconds away from falling into something wonderful. Tonight, I think I'm right. I think it's about to fall into me.

I was usually on Hunter's arm for award shows—pretty and harmless, dressed to complement whatever look his team wanted, but this year, I'm on my own. Song of the Year. Album of the Year. Best Country Vocal Performance. Best New Artist. Gone is last season's snub. There are four Grammy nominations with my name on them and I'm here to win.

We all knew *Whiskey Red* was special, but it's one thing to believe something behind closed doors or backstage in the dark. It's quite another to see the evidence of its success laid at your feet. Last year, the only thing people asked me was how it felt to get nothing. I laughed and smiled and said careful niceties through clenched teeth about how this is a competitive industry, how I was lucky to be making music at all, how I was just happy to be here. They were all lies.

I've never been happy to be where I am. I've spent my entire career waiting for more, and tonight, I think I have it.

"Don't forget the train."

Markell's voice is a passing whisper in my ear. When I glance over my shoulder, he's motioning at my dress, showing me the best way to fluff it for pictures. I flick my wrist to the side so it catches in the fabric, and all around us, cameras flash. For once, I know exactly what they see. Markell with one hand outstretched, me grinning at him over my shoulder, ten years of history floating in the space between our fingers.

"Told you I'd let you dress me," I said back at the hotel. He picked pearls instead of diamonds tonight, accented by a jeweled butterfly clip in my hair. Another Fansworth original I want to keep forever.

"People tell me a lot of things," Markell said, smoothing a hand over my skirt. "I don't usually believe them."

When he hugged me, it was fierce and tight, years of wishes in the making.

He's playing up the girl-next-door angle tonight with a voluptuous pink gown. It falls to the floor in a cascade of gold embroidery and soft tulle. Tonight, I'm the new talent, fresh out of Nashville, and I'm the furthest thing from a threat.

Markell blows me one last kiss before ducking into the theater, and it's James who takes my elbow next. The only thing I know about this man is that he's some sort of producer my entire team has deemed worthy of being seen with me tonight. He's very rich, very eligible, and judging by the way his hand keeps sliding to my waist, *very* interested. I couldn't care less.

We pose for every photographer and speak to every reporter on our way inside. Every question is about us—how we met, how long we've been together, and it takes every ounce of willpower not to snap that I barely know this man's name. He's not the reason I'm here, and I'm a hundred times more interesting than anything he could ever say. By the time we break away and make it inside, my smile feels more like a grimace, permanently stretched in place.

I'm not the only one who came here tonight to win. Roman Michaels has won Entertainer of the Year for the last three awards seasons. Hunter Wallstreet is nominated for his newest solo album, and Ruby Daly, another of Ricky's clients, is up for Single of the Year. Big names. Names with power and money and label support. I might have taken home a few CMAs in the fall, but this is different.

Ricky catches us in the aisle and leads us down to our seats. Everyone congratulates him as we pass, praising him for every nomination without glancing my way. Everyone greets James, too, and it's not until I find my seat that I realize why. *They don't think you'll win.*

"I was wondering when you'd get in."

I hear Mickenlee before I see her. She's standing over my shoulder, a vision in burgundy and cream, and in that moment, I don't care about James or Ricky or the red-carpet reporters. I pull her into a hug, exhaling all my earlier frustrations as she holds me tight.

"Sorry," I whisper. "Long line outside."

"Of course. Everyone wants to see you."

We sit side by side in the theater, James on my left, Mickenlee on my right. I don't care that James has to switch seats with Ricky to make it happen, I need her here for me now. Mickenlee's date sits at her other side, a family friend I don't recognize, and Markell winks at me from the end of the row. Some of the other label executives nod as they pass. Some ignore us completely and I make a game of it, wondering which ones even know my name. I find Mickenlee's hand under my skirts as the ceremony starts and give it a quick squeeze.

Here we go.

I win Song of the Year first and the audience erupts at the sound of a new name, the sight of a new face. I remember Mickenlee's nails digging into my arm, Ricky hugging me tight, Markell reaching across four different people to grab my hand. Then I'm walking down the aisle, toward the stage, and I feel every eye on me.

I've known what my inevitable acceptance speech would sound like since I was ten years old with my first guitar. I knew on the Greyhound bus, leaving that dead-end town. I repeated it every day I worked behind the bar at Top Cat, each time I took the stage for an open mic, so when I open my mouth now, it comes naturally.

"I'm just so incredibly grateful to be here. This is one of those things you dream about, right? It isn't supposed to really happen."

I know what people want from me, so I make it their reality. I make sure my steps are shaky, my speech is flustered but coherent. I thank all the right people and make all the right jokes, because I'm grateful and lovely and not at all the threat they believe me to be.

"I told you," Mickenlee whispers when I sit back down. There's a single strand of hair working itself loose from her bun. I want to reach out and wind it around my finger. I want to tuck it back into place, but then Ricky's hand is on my arm. James is smiling too close to my face, there's another executive reaching over to look at my award, and the chaos pulls us apart.

When they announce Album of the Year, the cameras linger on Hunter Wallstreet a little too long, which means the entire theater gets to watch his expression fall and his eyes widen in shock when they say my name instead of his. Markell bursts out laughing, almost tripping down the row in his effort to hug me. "Look at his face!" he gasps. "Who is his stylist? He looks *terrible!*"

I'm still laughing about it when I stumble onstage for the second time. "I didn't think I'd get to do this again," I lie. "You know when you think of a really good joke right after leaving the party? Well, now I'm back and y'all get to hear all my good jokes!"

I'll do this a hundred more times, with a hundred different speeches over the course of my career. I know that, but this one feels important. It feels like one people will remember. On the way back to my seat, I can't resist giving Hunter a little wave and lifting my award in his direction.

Your loss, I think as his expression darkens.

I have the audience in my hand by the time I win Best Country Vocal Performance. I feel them rooting for me, excited for something new, and I tuck their support close to my chest along with my growing pile of awards. If people ignored me earlier, they sure aren't now. They're all whispering behind their hands about the pretty new girl in the pink dress.

Who is she? Where did she come from?

Nobody. Nothing. But I'm here now and I'm not going anywhere. There are other wildfire girls, I'm sure, ones in the audience who'll burn like me one day, but tonight it's my turn.

Everyone's pleasantly drunk by the time the final award rolls around. Even Ricky starts loosening his tie, already preparing for the end of the show. Markell switches seats so he and Mickenlee can whisper together behind cupped hands, and I feel every eye turn toward me as they read the last set of nominees. For a single, blistering second, I wonder if anyone back home will see this.

It's not often I think about Mayberry like this. *Home.* But that's how I feel now. Maybe they will all see me here tonight, onstage where I belong, and forgive me for leaving when I had the chance. I think of my brother, alone in that house, and my father, who died not long after I left. I think of my mother, who never got the chance to see what I'm becoming, and I think I'd give them all up a hundred more times if it means having this.

Mickenlee reaches for me one last time, and that's how I know she's properly drunk, because she does it right here, in front of everyone. She looks me straight in the eye, squeezes my hand, and says, "You're going to win."

And when I do, she's the only one in the entire theater who doesn't look surprised.

SEVENTEEN

Darren

"**¶** cannot believe you're drinking that."

Kendall watches me with thinly veiled disgust, eyebrows lifted as I drain the last of the watery motel coffee. It's not bad. It's not good either, but the last three years at Bob's haven't exactly made me picky. "I forgot that you have a weird vendetta against caffeine," I say. "You never drink it at work either."

"It's not a vendetta, it's disgusting."

I shove the cup under his nose. "Here. Try it."

Kendall makes a face and leans back as far as the seat belt allows. "I literally have a rash from those sheets, forgive me if I don't want to experiment with the coffee."

We're about half an hour from Brentwood, flying up a mostly empty highway, but I'm still nervous. Finding the flash drive in Memphis was a surprise, and I'm not entirely sure what I'm looking for here. Another song tucked in some long-forgotten corner of the house? The time capsule itself, buried out in the yard? There are too many variables and too many eyes on us. I know because I woke up to seventeen new texts from Emily, who cannot believe I didn't tell her I was doing this, and even more from Madison, who thinks Kendall driving me to Memphis is the most romantic thing to ever happen in the history of our lives and possibly the universe.

I don't have time to unpack all that right now, I just want to be ready. The Nashville skyline is fading in the distance, subdued and pale after the glamour of last night. That's how I feel after the conversation Kendall and I had in the motel room, too. Muted. Dull. Like it never actually happened.

"Decklee lived in this house for thirty years, you know," I say, searching for a safe topic of conversation. "Everyone called it the Brentwood House."

"I thought her Brentwood House was where she . . . you know . . ." Kendall trails off, waving a hand in a way that is not at all clear. "Died?"

I shake my head. "That wasn't the original. She moved after turning this one into a museum, but we're going to *the* Brentwood House. It's where everything started. I mean, she wrote *Tides* here. It's where she wrote *Monochrome Heart* and developed the variety show and wrote the *Wizard of Oz* remake. It's where all those pictures of her and Mickenlee Hooper come from."

I suddenly realize how much I'm talking and clamp my mouth shut. *No one cares.*

I don't usually talk like this in Mayberry because I can literally see people losing interest the longer I speak. Even my friends, who are used to my long tangents and winding stories, don't care about Decklee or old country music award shows the way I do. The only person who really truly cares like me is Mom. Kendall barely knew who Decklee Cassel was before yesterday, so I'm kind of surprised when he tugs his Cubs hat down over his eyes and asks, "Were they, like, *together* together? Her and Mickenlee?"

I bite the inside of my cheek. I have my theories, obviously, but it's never something I let myself think about. Despite all the differences between me and Decklee Cassel, this particular question still feels too personal. But Kendall always has a knack for cutting straight to the point.

"I did some research," he says when I don't answer right away. "Last night when you said you wanted to write about Mickenlee. I couldn't find many pictures of the two of them together, but the ones I found look . . . happy."

I nod. It's why I wish there were more pictures for me to analyze. Instead, there's only the subtle curve of Mickenlee's smile, the casual way Decklee's hand occasionally rested on her knee, her shoulder, the small of her back. Nothing but dead ends and more questions.

"I don't know," I say. "If they were together, it was never public. I know a lot of change happened in the seventies, but I don't think it was ever safe or easy to be openly queer in the South, especially for someone as famous as Decklee Cassel. I mean, it's still not particularly easy now, if you live somewhere like Mayberry."

The second it's out of my mouth, I wish I could take it back. Here, on the quiet morning road, it feels too much like a confession.

"Anyway," I say, moving on before Kendall can notice my pause. "Maybe. I don't know. They stopped working together in the late eighties. Decklee went on tour alone and then Mickenlee just disappeared. They never wrote another album together. And Decklee was a great writer," I add. "She was incredibly talented, but it always felt like something was missing."

Not just something, I realize. Someone.

Until yesterday, I had accepted the fact that I'd never know exactly what happened between Decklee Cassel and Mickenlee Hooper. But now there's the quest. Now we have that song and every time I hear it, I think, *what if?*

The radio stations have been playing nothing but old Decklee songs all morning. By now, most people have caught on to the bigger picture: this isn't just a hunt for the time capsule, it's a trail of songs, the one we uncovered yesterday simply another clue. No one knows exactly how many there are, but social media is already buzzing with theories and hints.

I feel like she'd hide something in Nashville, right?
If they found the first clue in Memphis, Nashville has to be next.

Maybe at the Country Music Hall of Fame?

Is nobody listening to the lyrics? She literally talks
about a porch swing. It's totally at the Brentwood
House!

I try to ignore that last one. Of course I'm not the only one
looking. Mike Fratt went live on YouTube last night to work out
where to go next and already has hundreds of fans pointing him
in the right direction. Maybe I made a bad call yesterday, letting
Dani air that song. It felt like the right thing to do at the time,
but maybe it's another example of how unprepared I am for the
real world. Mike Fratt isn't going to give up his clue if he finds
it first. No one's going to give me three million dollars for being
a nice person.

I let my emotions put the prize money at risk, and as we
head south, I swear to myself it won't happen again. From
now on, everything is rational. Everything is smart. I will not
risk any more of this quest by thinking about the origin of the
new songs, or about Decklee Cassel's alleged muse, or about the
toned lines of Kendall's chest when he held me last night.

I won't.

We run into a decent amount of traffic as we head south, and
when Kendall turns up the driveway of the Brentwood House,
something inside me deflates. This isn't like Memphis, where
it was just us and Dani and the music. This isn't like last night
either.

Camera crews and news vans pack the grassy lot in front of
the house, already setting up equipment to film on the lawn.
The museum hasn't even opened yet and most of the park-

ing spots are full, the line to buy tickets stretching around the corner.

"Wow." Kendall cranes his neck to watch the crowd. "There are more of you. *Fans.*"

Unfortunately. I have unwittingly turned this into a spectacle.

Kendall is about to pull into one of the last empty parking spots when a giant green pickup truck flies around the corner and cuts us off, horn blaring the entire time. Kendall has to slam on the brakes to avoid a collision, and I swear under my breath as the internet's own Mike Fratt slides from the driver's seat. He's shorter than he looks on camera, blond hair and classically square jaw the only real defining features. He flashes us a peace sign like he didn't actively steal our parking spot, grabs his camera equipment from the back seat, and proceeds to use Kendall's hood as a tripod as the rest of his group piles out of the car.

"Is he serious?" Kendall lays on the horn. "Hello? I am literally trying to drive?"

Mike has the audacity to look annoyed as he snatches his camera back, like the fact he can't use our car for his vlog is the height of human injustice. He motions for the rest of his group to follow, and they all start toward the museum.

"Oh my god." I slide down in my seat, burying my face in my hands as Kendall circles the lot again. "I did that. He's only here because I released the song."

"No," Kendall says. "He's here because he wants a viral video. He would have found this place with or without you."

By the time we park and make our way toward the house,

the line to get inside wraps all the way down to the sidewalk. It's a nice morning for late July, humidity surprisingly low, but I can't bring myself to enjoy it or shake the ominous feeling that something is about to go horribly wrong. Everyone around us buzzes with anticipation, discussing the last clue, the song, the missing time capsule, and it's my fault. I basically invited them to join me, practically begged everyone to come along.

"You good?" Kendall leans over so no one can hear the whispered question. Not that they'd care. They're too wrapped up in their own fantasies of finding Decklee Cassel's hidden treasures.

I shake the thought away and force myself to smile. "Of course. I'm fine."

Carla's wad of cash covers our museum entrance passes. By the time we make our way through the front doors, the first level is already crowded. I turn toward Kendall to run through my plan. "We need to get outside. If we're following the lyrics of that last song, it should be on the porch. I want—"

Whatever I'd been about to say next dies in my throat. The Brentwood House looks exactly like the pictures on the outside, a sweeping three-story Southern mansion, but the inside has been completely transformed. Glass displays of costumes, instruments, and memorabilia line the perimeter of the first floor and I hear the faint strains of "Times Are Changing" playing overhead.

It feels like standing in front of the Top Cat wall or sitting in The Bridge. Like these aren't simply places, they're memories, too. I know we're here for a reason; I know the time capsule is our priority—the money, the music—but that goal suddenly feels very far away. It's like the house is pulsing with a quiet, waiting energy. Decklee's music in every corner, Mickenlee's words overflowing from the walls.

I wonder how many secret stolen moments they had here, safe in the knowledge that this house would always be theirs.

"Excuse me!"

I stumble as someone pushes in front of me, and Kendall grabs my arm before I trip into the information desk. It snaps me back to my body. Decklee and Mickenlee might have been alone in this house, but we are most certainly not.

"Sorry," I mutter as Kendall pulls me out of the flow of traffic.

"You sure you're okay?"

It's the second time he's had to ask me that. I ignore the hot flush spreading over my chest, the implication that maybe I can't do this the way I thought I could. "I'm fine. Let's just get outside."

I grab his arm and together we start weaving through the crowd. I catch glimpses of displays as I walk—shiny awards and sheet music and rows of sequined cowboy boots all begging for my attention. I've spent the last decade of my life wanting to visit this place, but now that I'm here, I can't enjoy it.

"Wait!" Kendall has to jog to keep up as we march through the sprawling kitchen. "Do you maybe want to slow down? Look around? Isn't this—?"

"No." I keep my gaze fixed ahead, on the sliding glass doors leading out to the back. "Come on, we're almost there."

By the time we burst into the yard, I'm out of breath. It's already warmer than it was this morning and the crowd of visitors is no less overwhelming. I can barely see the porch, let alone the swing, through the tangled mess of limbs. When a woman next to me turns to her friend and says, "I don't think they found it yet," panic starts to close around me.

"Here." I motion Kendall forward. "Let's go."

He hesitates for a second, hand hovering in the space just above my shoulder. Then he seems to remember the urgency and turns toward the porch. He tries to use his height to our advantage in the crowd, but it's not working. There are too many people, too many voices, too many hands reaching for the things I want. Yesterday felt fun, a celebration of everything that made Decklee Cassel special, but now there's a fierce, underlying current of competition. Something to win and something to lose. It claws across my nerves, and again, I wonder if this is really what Decklee wanted.

The porch comes into view slowly, a two-story, open-air wraparound. It's serene against the white columns of the house, somewhere I'd want to stop and sit any other day. But I don't know what I'm looking for, and unlike yesterday, I don't have the luxury of time to figure it out. I'm just working through how best to get near the swing when the crowd takes a collective breath. Kendall and I break through a circle of bystanders, and I don't even have a chance to open my mouth before the cheering starts.

Mike Fratt kneels on the porch, one hand patting around the base of the swing. One of his friends is perched on the railing filming the entire thing, camera held aloft to capture every terrible detail. As I watch, Mike stands, brushes off his cargo shorts, and thrusts his fist toward the sky. There's something shiny between his fingers—a flash drive.

My stomach drops before my brain catches up. *No.*

There's a flurry of movement and the crowd shoves us back. Kendall's hands are viselike on my arms, like he thinks I'm going to fall. Maybe I am. Maybe I should. Cameras whir, every single one of them pointing over my head, and Mike smiles as everyone swarms in to snap his picture.

It feels like I'm watching through a fuzzy TV, edged with static and very far away, because that was supposed to be mine. Because I was *right*.

"That's a clue in the hunt for Decklee Cassel's missing time capsule!" A reporter a few steps away flips to a new page in her notebook. "How did you know where to look?"

Mike shrugs, his head barely visible over the crowd. "The boys and I put together a few leads from the fan forums and went from there."

He sounds exactly like his videos—smug and satisfied and dripping with Southern drawl. Like if a backward hat and muscle tee could talk. I want to rip that grin off his face. I want to rip the flash drive out of his hand, because it's not supposed to be for him. It's supposed to be for me and Mom and Kendall and everyone who doesn't have millions of subscribers unwinding clues for them.

"Play the song!"

I don't hear who makes the suggestion. It's someone in the crowd, over to my left, but the words carry. *Play the song.* My head snaps up. They're right. That's how we should do this—

together on the porch of the Brentwood House. It's not like Mike found the time capsule. He didn't win the prize and we're not out of the race.

But as I watch, he laughs and slips the flash drive into his pocket. "Sure," he says. "You can hear the song. Right after I win."

Kendall's voice is low in my ear, but I can't hear him over the crowd of spectators and reporters pushing in on all sides. It really is over, then. I really did lose. I'm nobody and nothing, and this time, Mom and Kendall are the collateral damage. Kendall's grip tightens on my arm, pulling me toward him, but I can't face him now.

Instead, I yank my arm out of his grip and push him away. I finally do what I should have done from the beginning—I run.

EIGHTEEN

Decklee
New York City, 1972

I throw a party in the elegant suites of the most expensive hotel in Manhattan.

There are too many rooms and too many guests and too many people I don't know handing me drinks. I take them all. If I close my eyes, I can still see the Mayberry girl climbing out her window and disappearing into the night. I can still see the Memphis girl, digging her nails into that city until it came apart. Then I open my eyes, take another drink, and decide I'm better than anything those girls could have imagined.

At one point, Markell lifts me off the ground and twirls me through the living room yelling, "You star! You absolute star!"

I kiss him between bottles of champagne and he actually lets me, which is how I know he's drunk, too, high on the success of finally getting everything we're owed. We hold hands on the balcony under a sky thick with city lights, and even though I make it a habit to never look back, I'm glad Markell is still here with me now.

James finds me next, slips an arm around my shoulders, and tries to lean in for a kiss. I push him away. We aren't in public anymore. We aren't on the red carpet and I have no reason to pretend. "No, thank you."

For a minute, he looks genuinely wounded. "But you'll kiss *him*?" He gestures over his shoulder, to where Markell still stands on the balcony.

"I actually like him, James." I roll my eyes and snatch another glass of champagne from the table. "Now get out of my hotel room."

Ricky makes me pose for pictures with him and the other label executives, with everyone who's ever told me no. They all smile and pat me on the back.

"That's my girl," Ricky says, like he hasn't actively tried to sink me. "That's my star."

"I'm not *your* anything," I say through clenched teeth, and they all laugh, like it's a joke. I clutch my statues so hard my knuckles ache and force myself to laugh along because *I won*.

They all know it.

I don't know when exactly I stumble over to my own room. It's almost dawn, I can tell by the way the air tastes cool and sweet on my lips, but the party still rages around me. Maybe they'll stay all night. Maybe this is my life now—a wild mosaic of celebrations and award-show sweeps. I let out a breathy giggle as I open the door, then stumble to a halt when I see it's already occupied.

Mickenlee sits on my bed in the dark, elbows resting on her knees. Her expression is distant, guarded, but she jumps up when I enter. "I'm sorry," she says. "I'm not . . . I just needed somewhere quiet."

No, this is fate, I think. This must be what fate feels like.

"It's okay." I step into the room and close the door behind me. "I've been looking for you."

Something flickers behind her expression, too quick for me to read. She's always just out of reach, never quite where I want her to be. She tries to slip past me, back toward the party, but I catch her arm.

"Decklee . . ."

It sounds like the beginning of a warning. I don't let go. "I never got the chance to say thank you."

She blinks, and for a second, every city light outside the window catches in the deep blue of her eyes. I'd throw myself into them if I could, drown in the feeling of her. "Thank me for what?"

"Everything. I wouldn't be here without you."

The corner of Mickenlee's mouth lifts. "Yes, you would. You would have gotten here one way or another."

"Maybe," I say. "But I wouldn't want to be here with anyone else."

I don't know how long we stand like that, in front of the door with my fingers wrapped around her wrist. It could be a second. It could be several years. Then Mickenlee's throat bobs and I watch the ice in her gaze solidify. She grabs my face in both hands and kisses me fast and reckless, like she's already counting the seconds until someone tells us to stop. I'm still holding a Grammy. I still hear the sounds of the party outside, the faint conversations of every celebrity, every executive, every powerful person who would burn me for this, and I do not care. I lean into her, mouth opening into the kiss, and Mickenlee practically shoves me away.

"Oh my god!" She stumbles back, out of my grip, and presses a trembling hand to her mouth. "I'm so sorry. That wasn't . . . I'm not trying to . . . I should go—"

"Wait!" The word sticks in my throat. I can't breathe around it, can't breathe around the lingering feeling of her on my lips. "Don't."

I set the award on the bedside table and reach for her again. Mickenlee shivers as my hands slide up her bare arms and for a minute, I think she's still going to leave. I think she's going to turn her back like this isn't something I've thought about doing for months, for *years*. Since the day she showed up at my door in the rain.

"Don't go," I repeat, softer this time, and when I kiss her again, I think I finally know what it's like to truly burn.

There's lightning, yes, but then there's electricity. There's Mickenlee's hands on my waist, bunching in the fabric of my dress. There's her mouth under mine, lip caught between my teeth, and there's this frantic, desperate urgency between us I'm beginning to think has always been there. I plunge my fingers into her hair, tearing out pins as I go.

"Cleo." She breathes my name into the underside of my jaw, and for once, I don't care that she uses it. "Just . . . wait."

She pulls back, eyes wild, lips red. I want to devour her. *"What?"*

"Have you done this before?"

I let out a rough, breathless laugh. "Of course."

"No, I mean . . ." Mickenlee looks up at the ceiling, running a hand through her tangled hair. "Have you done *this*? Because I'm not—"

"Yes." I kiss her again, softer this time, less urgent, and I wonder if she feels the weight of all the things I can't say out loud. How I want her more than I've ever wanted anyone. How I've only ever felt this way about other women, but I will never, ever admit that to anyone, because I have worked too hard to let this be the thing that breaks me.

She laughs, sagging against me, and the sound of her relief is palpable in the dark. "I wrote all those songs for you, you know."

I grin. "I know."

And then Mickenlee is kissing me again, messy and aching, and I wonder how we spent so long pretending.

Markell is a genius with fabric; his zippers are always so cleverly disguised. I have to find my own and Mickenlee laughs into my throat as I unfasten the clasps one by one. The dress pools around my feet, a pile of pink tulle for the sweet, innocent country girl, but the way Mickenlee is kissing me now is not innocent and the way I want her is not sweet.

There are two freckles at the corner of her mouth, another at the base of her throat, three more clustered on her left hip bone. I kiss them all, reveling in the way her hair spills across the pillows. I love her when she's buttoned-up and fearless, but I adore her like this—soft and eager and vulnerable, coming undone in my hands. Her nails dig into my thigh, a devastating contrast with the soft press of her lips, and I think there's a void here I didn't know existed. A feeling I've pushed down and stamped out for years because I don't need anyone. I never have. But when Mickenlee leans over me, hair falling around us in a dark, silky curtain, I think I might be wrong.

I do need this. I need her.

So when she kisses me again, mouth hot and yearning, I don't think anything at all. I just close my eyes and hold her close and pray that when the world catches up, when all my ambition and drive and want unravels into something too messy for either of us to handle, it comes quick.

That neither of us will notice the end until it's too late.

NINETEEN

Darren

Kendall finds me around the side of the house, wedged between the smooth exterior and the row of pine trees that block the rest of the yard from prying eyes. I don't think I'm supposed to be here, but right now, I just need quiet.

I hear him before he comes into view, footsteps soft on the layer of pine needles. "Hey." His voice is gentle, barely audible above the rustling branches. "Why don't we—?"

"My mom has a tumor, Kendall," I blurt. His feet falter and I cross my arms over my chest, forcing myself to continue. "They found it last week. She's going in on Monday to get it biopsied and see if it's . . ." I can't bring myself to say the word out loud. *Cancer.* "She's just been okay for so long. I . . . I don't know what to do."

My voice cracks and I duck my head, suddenly embarrassed Kendall is here, watching me break. I haven't told anyone about

Mom's appointment, not Emily, not Madison, not even Carla. If we don't talk about it, it doesn't exist.

"I wanted to win that prize money for her, you know," I whisper. "God, it's so fucking expensive to be sick like that. And I wanted those songs, too. We listened to Decklee's music last time and it felt lucky. I don't know if we would have made it without those albums, and I can't go through that again."

I can't go through that *alone*. That's the real fear, I think. That this is the place where our luck finally runs out.

Kendall comes forward, hands steady as he gently turns me to face him. He's so close I have to tilt my head back to maintain eye contact and I have a sudden, unwelcome flashback to last night in the motel. I told myself I wouldn't let him get this close again, but now that he's here, one arm wrapped firmly around my waist, all I can think about is how much I hope he never lets go.

"You know Decklee Cassel didn't beat your mom's cancer, right?" he asks, voice low in my ear. "*She* did that."

His gaze is so intense I have to look away. I can still hear people talking, laughing, clamoring over one another in the backyard, but right now, it's muted. If I close my eyes, Kendall and I could be the only two people in the world. "I know."

"It's okay to be scared. This isn't something you can control."

"But I thought it could be," I say. "I thought I knew how this quest worked and what to do. I thought I had a chance, Kendall, but now . . ."

I trail off, unsure of how to finish the sentence. I don't know what to do now. I have no idea where to go from here.

The corner of Kendall's mouth lifts. "We could slash Mike Fratt's tires. Seriously," he adds when I roll my eyes. "You know he calls his followers 'Fratt Babies'? Why would he do that when 'Fratt-ernity Bros' is right there? It's so embarrassing, we could easily rob him on the way out."

I let out a watery laugh and Kendall lifts a hand, brushing away a stray tear with his thumb. Heat pulses through me, spreading from my face down into the pit of my stomach. "I'm sorry I ruined your restaurant," I whisper.

"You didn't ruin anything."

"I released that first clue back in Memphis. We should have just kept it to ourselves."

Kendall shakes his head. "You said it yourself—that's not what Decklee would have wanted."

"Yeah, well." I dig the toe of my sneaker into the mulch. "Decklee Cassel is dead."

There's a moment of tense, sticky silence when Kendall looks on the verge of saying something else. Then he steps back and finally lets me go. "Come on. We never did get to see the museum."

"The—?" I look up. "You don't want to go home?"

He shrugs. "Eventually. What I really want is for you to explain to me why one person owns so many pairs of sequined cowboy boots. I mean, what is the point?"

"Fashion, Kendall," I say automatically. "The point is fashion."

As I follow him back across the yard and into the house, I don't know if I feel *good*, exactly, but the world is solid under my feet once again. Earlier, I had been so focused on finding the next clue that I hadn't bothered to look at the exhibits we passed. The thought of the lost flash drive still hurts, but Kendall is right. Why would we go home now when there's so much to see? We might not have the clue, but I've wanted to come here my entire life. Might as well make the trip worth it.

The lower levels are still crowded when we slip back inside, but it's nothing like before. Most of the reporters have left, no doubt following Mike and his friends back to their car, trying to find out where they'll go next. I push the thought from my mind and focus on Kendall, who's currently standing in front of a display of sequined costumes with his eyebrows lifted.

"See?" he says. "There's no reason for one person to use this much glitter. It's excessive."

"No," I correct. "It's *dramatic*."

"That's for sure. And these are all from that same designer? The guy my mom likes?"

I nod, running a finger over the shiny plaque next to the display. TUPELO, 1976, it reads, COSTUMES FROM THE OPENING NIGHT OF THE SOUNDS LIKE THUNDER WORLD TOUR DESIGNED BY MARKELL FANSWORTH.

"She never used anyone else," I say. "Even when she was going on world tours and he was flying to Paris for Fashion Week. They always worked together."

"Is that surprising?" Kendall asks.

"I don't know. A lot of people think they had a falling-out around the same time Mickenlee Hooper left. They were inseparable for years and then they just sort of . . . stopped. No one really knows why."

Kendall turns in a circle, slowly taking in the rest of the

display—rows of cowboy boots, hats hanging from the wall, fringe jackets dripping with sequins. "Interesting," he says. "For two people who had a falling out, he sure is everywhere."

I shiver, rubbing my hands up and down my arms, but I'm thinking the same thing. There's evidence of Decklee and Markell's friendship in every corner of this room, which only makes Mickenlee's absence stranger. She's hardly mentioned on the plaques, noticeably missing from all the photos, and again I wonder if it's because their relationship was something deeper.

"Anyway," I say, moving down the next aisle. "To answer your question, Markell is the reason she has all the boots. A lot of people wanted Decklee to relate to the old Southern crowd, but she thought that was boring. So she showed up to her first festival with the rainbow sequins and no one had an extra pair of shoes, so they had to let her perform in them. After that, there was no going back."

The pair of boots in front of us now is purple. I imagine Decklee wearing them onstage, throwing them aside for a quick change, slipping them on to dance around the house for fun.

"Cool." Kendall leans down to squint at another plaque. "Wait, did you see this one?"

He's pointing toward the wall, where four photos of Decklee beam down at us. They were clearly taken at different points throughout her life, and she wears a single, distinctive piece of jewelry in each. A small cat-shaped pin. A jeweled butterfly clip. An intricate ring carved to look like her signature baby-blue guitar. A brooch in the shape of a single, blooming rose. Below the photos, the pieces themselves sit against a dark velvet background in a domed jewelry case—three distinct items with an empty spot where the last brooch should be. The plaque next to the display reads THE "ONE FOR THE MONEY" COLLECTION BY MARKELL FANSWORTH, 1966–1978.

I reread it twice before I'm certain I'm not making a mistake. "One for the money," I say. "Like the rhyme."

Kendall nods. "Like the flash drive."

But I don't think it's just a rhyme anymore. There's something more here, another layer to the puzzle I hadn't noticed before. *One for the money.* A clue tucked behind the bricks in Memphis and a pin that looks eerily similar to the Top Cat logo. *Two for the show.* Another clue here, in the house where Decklee wrote her award-winning albums next to the same butterfly clip she wore to the Grammys.

"There are four," I whisper, almost to myself.

Kendall looks up. "What?"

"There are four clues," I say. "That's the rhyme, isn't it? *One for the money, two for the show, three to get ready, and four to go.* This quest doesn't go on forever. There are four songs. 'Somewhere Over the Rainbow' was first. The one we found in Memphis was the second, and now . . ."

I trail off at the prickling reminder that I don't have the third song. I don't have the next clue or a way to find the fourth. It doesn't matter how many layers of this quest I dig up, how badly I want to *know*, I'm not finding the time capsule. I have to let it go. I shake my head and turn my back on the display, forcing myself to smile.

"Never mind, it doesn't matter." Kendall looks like he wants to protest, but I ignore him, already sliding over to the next display. "Come on. I want to see the rest of the house."

The longing ache still lingers, but as Kendall and I walk from room to room, I feel it settle. Every floor is something new, and I can't help but point it all out. The studded shoulder pads, the tight leather pants, the jeweled microphone that always matched her shoes. He asks questions like he's genuinely interested, and for a second, I let myself believe he could be. That he's not just pretending for me. I know this distraction won't last. Sooner or later, we'll climb back in the truck to head home and the true weight of everything I've lost will return, but I don't think about that now. I just think about the history and Decklee Cassel's legacy and all the ways we're now a part of both.

I tell him about the 1972 Grammys where she swept the show and the photo-famous afterparty in the Plaza Hotel suites where Hunter Wallstreet was turned away at the door. I tell him about Decklee kicking off her first national tour in Tupelo, about the time she won an Oscar, about how there's supposedly a recording out there of her telling Ronald Reagan to go fuck himself. ("The context is unclear," I say. "But honestly, she's so real for that.")

I tell him about Markell Fansworth's charity work, how he used the 1982 New York Fashion Week runway to call out the country's dismissal of the AIDS crisis and was abruptly banned for life. I tell Kendall how no celebrity wanted him after that, how Decklee still wore his clothes, and how Markell is still the only designer to ever be awarded the Presidential Medal of Freedom.

And of course I talk about Mickenlee Hooper and her magic pen, all the arbitrarily restrictive industry lines she and Decklee crossed before she disappeared.

I don't know when it happens, exactly, but there's a moment where I stop for breath, watching Kendall lean over a display of vintage records. Maybe it's the glint of sun off the glass case. Maybe it's the way he's genuinely listening to everything I say, but the sight of him next to me tightens something in my chest. It's sudden, and it feels like that moment with Emily on the docks, like every cell in my body sparks and whispers, *Oh*.

"What are you looking at?"

It takes me a second to realize Kendall's talking to me. I blink. "What?"

The corner of his mouth lifts. "You're staring at me."

I suppose I am. I suppose I should look away, but something about this place makes me brave. It's the same feeling I had last night in The Bridge, like I don't have to be the ordinary girl I am back home. I hadn't been brave enough to kiss Emily that night at the lake, but I had wanted to. I want to kiss Kendall now. I want to wrap my arms around his neck and drink in the feeling of him against me and—

There's a sharp burst of static overhead, a speaker system crackling to life. *"Attention, museum attendees, this is a special announcement from the Decklee Cassel Estate."*

I stumble back and Kendall jumps, almost colliding with the

record display. My heart slams against my ribs, so fast I almost miss the rest of the announcement.

"Earlier this morning, another clue to what most are calling the Time Capsule Treasure Hunt was found right here in our backyard. While the finders chose not to release it to the public, I'm pleased to announce that the Decklee Cassel Estate has elected to make that second clue available now, for everyone to hear. The song is now live on all streaming platforms, but we'll be playing it over our systems as well. We hope you enjoy!"

Kendall's eyes widen. I let out a choked gasp as the people around us reach for their phones. "Oh my god."

"Someone from the estate is monitoring the quest," Kendall says. "They have to be. They're keeping it fair."

I shake my head, still trying to make sense of what I'm hearing. I just assumed Dani had been the one to release the first song publicly, but maybe the estate had pushed it wide. Maybe they were waiting to see what would happen with the second clue before doing the same. I brace a hand against the smooth glass of the nearest display as all the fractured facts add up to one intoxicating solution—*we're not done.*

There's another second of silence before Decklee's voice pours from the speakers overhead. This new song is nothing like yesterday's ballad. I tip my head back, not wanting to miss a single word, and think it feels more like an anthem, something meant to be listened to on the open highway. It feels like freedom, like the first sip of watery beer or sneaking into abandoned gas stations to do tarot readings in the middle of the night. It feels like a fight song, an ode to all the dreams too big for a town like Mayberry and every girl who wears ambition on her sleeve.

The song is almost halfway over before I remember it's supposed to be a clue. I whip out my phone to find it online, to write down any lyrics I remember, but it clicks before the final hook.

"I know—" I start, but I look over and Kendall is grinning, intensely beautiful.

"You know where to go," he says. "I can tell. You're glowing."

I laugh because *he's* the one who's glowing—lit from the outside by the morning sun. He's the one who looks like the chorus of this song come to life. Decklee is still singing overhead and I move before I fully know what I'm doing, closing the distance between me and Kendall and throwing both arms around his neck.

He grunts in surprise as I crash into him, a tiny exhale against my ear. Then he's hugging me back, smiling into my hair as he twirls me in a circle. I don't care that we're in the middle of a museum. I don't care that there are people around us, still trying to view the exhibits. For the first time in years, I feel alive.

And I don't think Mickenlee Hooper could have written a better song if she tried.

TWENTY

Decklee
Nashville, 1973

¶ write a song on the porch swing.

Mickenlee is next to me, the curve of her hip tucked against mine like a secret, and Markell is perched on the railing next to us. "Don't move." He aims his camera in our direction. "The lighting is *perfect*."

He's always doing this, always begging Mickenlee to let him take just one picture. If the two of us are unexpected, Mickenlee and Markell's friendship feels inevitable. She always tells him to leave her alone and find another subject, but today she just pulls the brim of her hat down and smiles.

"He's never going to let you say no again," I whisper, right as the camera clicks. Mickenlee laughs through her fingers, and I lean over to watch the image develop. I already know what I'll see—the two of us pressed too close on the swing, Mickenlee's ankle crossed casually over mine as she laughs at a joke no one else will understand. I love it, the idea of us together like this. I hate that an idea is all we'll ever be.

Markell hands me the rest of the photos and I spread them across my lap. "You putting them with the others?" he asks.

I shrug. "Might as well."

He wedges himself onto the swing, right on Mickenlee's other side. She laughs as the wood groans under his weight, and I slide over so the three of us can wind together. No way to tell where one ends and the other begins. Markell throws an arm around Mickenlee's shoulders, reaching over to tug one of my curls. "I should have known," he says. "You keep everything. What are you planning to do with it all?"

I'm not entirely sure. My collection grows all the time—photos and notes and press clippings I can't bear to let go. It feels like proof—like when the world stops loving me one day and everyone moves on, I'll still have something to remember this by.

The song I finish that day sits like a pit in my stomach. I meant it to be fun, something shallow and upbeat to stick on the newest record. But when I put my pen down and sit back, I realize it's an ode to the people I've lost instead and everything I've sacrificed to get here. It's for my family, my old friends, for Leah, who might still be working behind the bar at Top Cat for all I know.

Hearts are fragile. They break like glass if you drop them.

But maybe there's something beautiful about knowing the truth and holding on anyway. Maybe that's what love is. I've always known I would shatter eventually; there's no other way for someone like me to go out. One day, someone will look too close. They'll pull back the curtain, find a list of every terrible, selfish thing I've ever done, and it will ruin me. They'll turn on me eventually, I think, and it'll be my fault for wanting too much.

But now, sitting together on the porch under a sky that's too blue and a sun too perfect to be real, I think the only thing I've ever really wanted was more time.

TWENTY-ONE

Darren

The thing about having a weirdly intimate moment in a dead celebrity's house with a boy you previously only thought of as a friend is that, sometimes, you have to climb back into his truck and pretend that moment never happened as you drive toward the next clue on your mysterious quest.

Speaking from experience, I do not recommend.

We're pulling away from the museum, leaving the crowds behind. There's no sign of Mike Fratt or his truck full of amateur vloggers, but I'm sure he's around here somewhere. I wonder how annoyed he is that the estate released the song before his fans could crack it. He probably would have shared it with his paid subscribers eventually, unable to follow its coded message alone, but he doesn't have the luxury of privacy now. We're back on the road together, all heading toward the same inevitable end.

An image of the museum jewelry case flashes through my

mind again—each piece laid out with an empty spot at the end for the fourth. Maybe that one was too special for Decklee to lock behind glass. Maybe it's buried with her now, lost forever beneath the Tennessee dirt. Either way, it feels important to this quest, somehow, like something about our drive is connected to that missing brooch.

"So," Kendall says, voice too loud in the shadowed confines of the truck. "Where are we going next?"

"Tupelo," I say with more confidence than I feel. "We're going to Tupelo."

Kendall hesitates. "Mississippi?"

"Yeah." I type the location into my phone to confirm. "I'm sorry, I know it's far."

"Don't apologize." We turn back onto the highway and Blue Delia's engine whines as we merge into traffic. Kendall flashes me a quick, agonizing grin. "I would only do this for you, Purchase."

Then we're driving south, away from the Brentwood House, away from Nashville. I turn in my seat to get a better look at the fading skyline. *You're coming back.* I don't know where the thought comes from, but I feel the certainty radiate through my bones. This isn't my last time here. Something about this city calls to me, urges me back with open arms. I pick up my phone, swiping over to the list of questions I started last night.

Who organized the Time Capsule Treasure Hunt?

What's the point—why not open it at the funeral

when everyone was already watching?

Where is Mickenlee Hooper?

Now I type two more:

Who's releasing each new song? And are the clues
related to the jewelry collection in the museum?

Too many questions. Too many unknowns. We're driving straight into another, and I barely know how we got here.

"Does your mom know where we are?" Kendall asks. "I'm really trying to not have her hate me, but Decklee Cassel is making that unexpectedly difficult."

I laugh and swipe out of my notes. "Yeah, I texted her when we left the museum. And she doesn't hate you," I add. "That's, like, actually impossible."

"Hmm." Kendall doesn't sound like he believes me. "I think she would come around eventually, if she got to know me. Even Carla likes me."

"That one's impressive, actually," I say. "Carla doesn't usually like people."

"She likes you enough to drop four hundred dollars in your bag of road trip snacks."

I can't argue with that. I glance at the tote bag wedged between my feet and realize I didn't even text Carla to thank her for saving us from sleeping in the truck. I pick up my phone and scroll until I find her number.

"Are you calling?" Kendall glances into the passenger seat. "Ask her if she robs banks. That's my guess for where she got the money."

I shake my head. "I'm not asking her that."

"Come on, it's just a question."

I ignore him, keeping my phone on speaker and propping it on my knee as it rings. Carla picks up almost immediately. "Darren," she says. "Perfect timing. What's a four-letter word for 'love deity'?"

"Oh." I'm usually good at puzzles, but between the drive and my ever-growing list of questions, I can't think of a single word. "Um..."

"It's 'Eros,'" Kendall calls from the driver's seat. "By the way, Carla, do you rob banks?"

I swat Kendall's arm with my free hand as I pick up the phone. "Ignore him. We were just calling to say thank you. We had to get a hotel last night and you really saved us. I'll pay you back when I get home."

"It was a gift, Darren." I can practically hear Carla's eye roll through the phone. "Most people would just say thank you and move on."

"Right. Well, thank you."

There's a moment of silence broken only by the sound of Carla's pencil on the other end of the line. "So you're on your way home?" she asks.

"No, actually. We're going to Tupelo."

"Why on earth would you do that?"

"Because of the clue," I say. "There's a new song—the Fratt

Baby guy found it in Nashville and we thought we were done, but then the estate released the song to the public. And there's the jewelry collection at the museum that matches the lyrics on the flash drive and I feel like that's significant somehow, so ..." I trail off, just now realizing how little sense this makes, even to me.

"Well," Kendall says, saving me from my own incessant thought spiral. "I, for one, love an open-ended road trip. But I'm also curious why you think the last song is in Tupelo. Not that you've been wrong," he adds. "But going to Tennessee made sense. Why would there be something in Mississippi?"

"Because of her tour," I say. "I'm assuming that new flash drive continued the rhyme—*three to get ready*. Decklee always said she spent years wanting to tour, but her label wouldn't let her. She said she felt like she was 'always getting ready' for something that never happened, and that tour was the first time they let her go. And then the new song—do you remember the guitar solo in the second verse?"

"Honestly?" Kendall shakes his head. "No. I was a little distracted."

"Distracted by what?"

His gaze slides over the console, lingering on me a bit too long, and I suddenly know exactly what he was distracted by. My face warms as I try very hard not to think about hugging him in the middle of a sun-soaked museum, his arms around my waist as he twirled me around. "Right," I say. "Anyway. The song. That guitar solo is the same as the one on *Sounds Like Thunder*, which was the first album Decklee toured with back in ..."

I close my eyes, trying to remember the year, but my brain is swimming with lyrics and stories and half-formed sentences.

Carla saves me from answering. "It was 1976."

"Yes!" I nod. "Thank you. That tour kicked off at the Tupelo Fairgrounds and there was this huge after-party at one of the hotels downtown. It feels right to me."

Kendall nods slowly, like he's still putting the pieces together himself. "Well, I don't know if I trust Decklee Cassel, but I do trust you, Purchase. Which historic landmark are you going to vandalize in Tupelo?"

"Nothing," I groan. "I didn't vandalize Top Cat."

"Well, it didn't look like that before you got there."

"All right," Carla says. "I'm going to hang up before either of you accidentally make me an accessory to whatever road trip crimes you've been committing. Be careful, drive safe, don't call me again."

I laugh. "Okay. Tell Mom I'll talk to her soon. I miss you both."

The call ends and I drop my phone back in my lap. Outside the window, the flat suburban neighborhoods have given way to rolling hills and scraggly forest as we head south. I lean back in the seat, settling in for another long drive, and Kendall tugs his cap down to shield his eyes from the sun.

"She's cool," he says. "I've always thought so. I liked that post you did on her garden last year. It was a good profile."

There's that warmth again, pooling under my skin. "You read that?"

"Of course. I'm a huge supporter of local journalism."

"I wouldn't exactly call that journalism."

Kendall shakes his head, eyes still fixed on the road. "Why do you do that?"

"Do what?"

"Downplay everything that's important to you. You did it last night, too, when I asked you about the Mickenlee Hooper story."

"I don't—" I stop as Kendall arches an eyebrow as if to say, *See?* I take another breath and try again. "I'm not downplaying anything, I'm just trying to be realistic. It doesn't matter if I want to find Mickenlee or figure out her story. The reality is that I'm probably never going to know. And even if I did figure it out, I'm definitely not the person who'll get to write it."

Kendall tugs on his cap. "I don't buy that. You're literally guiding us from state to state based on nothing but a few random lyrics and a good vibe. You haven't been wrong once, Purchase. You're incredibly impressive and more than capable."

I open my mouth, but nothing comes out. I want to agree with him. I want to believe he's telling the truth, but what have I done, really? Started a social media account? Solved a few clues? I can't even tell Kendall the real reason I want to find Mickenlee Hooper, or why I can't think too much about her relationship with Decklee without feeling raw and exposed. That's not impressive. That's not brave.

I look down at my hands, still clenched around my phone in my lap. "I don't know about that."

He laughs, soft and low, dropping a hand onto my knee. "One day, Purchase, I'm going to give you a compliment and you're going to believe me."

Outside, clouds gather on the horizon, a hazy smudge in an

otherwise perfect day, but I'm suddenly very focused on the feeling of Kendall's thumb tracing slow circles against the outside of my thigh. Again, in this moment, I have the strangest feeling that we are the only two people in the world.

In that world, I almost want to believe him.

♫ ♪ ♫

"PUCHASE, WAKE UP."

I jolt upright in the front seat, wincing as my head knocks into the window. We're in a hotel parking lot in the middle of an unfamiliar city. Heat drifts from the asphalt around us in wavering lines, and I have to crane my neck to see the hotel entrance—a soft curve of red bricks against a shockingly green background of trees.

"Are we here?" The question comes out thick and raspy.

Kendall nods. "I think. I just kind of followed the directions on your phone after you fell asleep."

I straighten and peer out the window. We're not alone by any means, but I don't see the influx of news reporters and cameras that crowded the Brentwood House, and I don't see Mike Fratt anywhere. *Good.* Jealously still curls in my stomach at the thought of him holding that second flash drive inscribed with Decklee's handwriting.

Kendall and I slide out of the truck. It's hotter here, muggier than it was in Tennessee. It only takes a second for my hair to start sticking to the back of my neck.

"Where are we going?" Kendall asks.

I open my mouth, then hesitate. "I'm not sure, exactly. I know we're supposed to be in Tupelo. The fairgrounds was where they held the concert, but they had the after-party at this hotel. It's where she got ready for tour."

Kendall glances over his shoulder at the hotel entrance. "*Three to get ready*," he says. "That makes sense. It's a big hotel, though." He hesitates, running a hand through his hair. "Why don't we split up? I'll go inside and pretend to use the bathroom or something and you check out the courtyard. See if anything clicks. If nothing makes sense, we'll try another location."

I look up, surprised at the easy way the plan comes together. "You'd do that? Just keep driving around town until we find something?"

"If the 'something' is three million dollars, yes," Kendall says. "I would drive almost anywhere." He starts walking toward the entrance, then stops, turning back to look at me still standing next to his truck.

"What?" I ask.

"Nothing." He shrugs. "I'm just glad I'm here. I'm glad you called me."

He says it casually, like it's no big deal. Like those words don't ignite a storm of electricity in my stomach and thrust me back to that moment in Nashville, where I was so certain I wanted to kiss him.

"Yeah," I say. "I'm glad, too."

I sag against the truck as he heads into the hotel. *What the hell am I supposed to do with this?* Prize money or not, I know this road leads me back to Mayberry eventually, back to Mom and the unknown and all the restless, ordinary nights. Are Kendall and I supposed to go back to being coworkers? Am I supposed to come into work every day and pretend I'm not still thinking about the tender way he held me when I cried or the steady weight of his hand on my knee? Do I write stories I don't care about and fill out college applications and settle back into a routine, with this weekend nothing more than a small, blissful summer blip?

Sometimes I think Mayberry has its claws in me too deep to ever truly be free, like I could twist and fight my entire life and still wake up in its clutches. Some days it feels like it's going to devour me.

Some days I feel like I should let it.

As if on cue, the first few bars of the new Decklee Cassel song drift out the open window of the car next to me, and I close my eyes, tilting my head back toward the sun. The light paints brilliant colors through my eyelids, uncomfortably hot against my skin. I let it burn anyway, sinking into the lyrics.

> *Cut through leaves, say my name, take me far*
> *away from this place.*

I love that lyric. It's a subtle beauty, mixed with the insistent rhythm of the drums. I open my eyes again. The trees in the hotel courtyard dip in time to the music, swaying in a nonexistent breeze, and my breath catches. *Cut through leaves . . .*

My vision sharpens on the sun-dappled hotel courtyard. It's

an idea that feels too simple, the kind I would immediately talk myself out of in Mayberry. But I'm not in Mayberry right now. I'm standing in a Tupelo parking lot hundreds of miles from home, and I can be whoever I want to be. I walk toward the courtyard, pulled along by a force I don't quite understand. The next lyric is already ringing through my head as I step onto the grass.

> *Faraway love, see you soon, meet me at the lakes*
> *at half past noon.*

The sun cutting through the trees makes the tiny, secluded space feel like it was made for this song. Or, more accurately, like the song was made from this hotel, crafted from the movement and magic of that night in 1976. There's a garden to my left, a sundial to my right, and the long grass brushes my ankles with every careful step I take.

> *Cut through leaves, say my name, take me far*
> *away from this place.*

Maybe the sun isn't actually cutting through the leaves as much as I think. Maybe I'm so desperate for a way out that I'm seeing clues in places they don't exist. But the way the dappled light falls across the courtyard feels purposeful, too much of a lyrical coincidence.

> *Faraway love, see you soon, meet me at the lakes*
> *at half past noon.*

That's a very specific time, I think, to include without reason.

I pull out my phone and squint down at the screen. It's 12:45 now, too late to know if I missed something important. Still, I run a hand over the sundial, feeling for any loose parts or hidden hinges. Everything I touch is solid and smooth, even when I kneel in the grass to examine the base. Its shadow cuts a dark splash across the garden and I tilt my head, following the line of shade to where it stops on one of the large rocks lining the sidewalk. It's only a few inches off from being dead center.

It was probably center at half past noon.

The thought makes goose bumps erupt on my arms. I straighten, still caught in a trance, and cross the garden. When I touch the stone, it's warm under my palm, baking in the sun for who knows how long. It'll be here long after I leave and maybe that's why everything about this moment feels still and heavy. I have to use both hands to tug the rock free. When I finally roll it away, the only thing I see is a pocket of damp earth.

Then, buried in the corner—a soft-gray flash drive.

I scoop it up, turning it over with trembling fingers. Dirt falls away in little clumps as I brush it off. This shouldn't be possible, especially not with the number of people who use this hotel, who no doubt got here before us.

The handwriting on this drive is the same as the first one: neat, curling script. *Four to go.*

I laugh, a choked sound that bubbles up from somewhere deep inside me. Why did I ever doubt myself? Why did I feel unworthy? This quest has always been made for me, for Kendall, for all the people who dream of something more. The sound of the wind through the trees feels like applause. I stand, blinking back tears, and squeeze the flash drive between my fingers. "Thank you," I whisper.

Somewhere out there, the trees whisper back.

TWENTY-TWO

Decklee
Tupelo, 1976

The night we start to unravel, I'm in the back of a car driving through downtown Tupelo.

My hand is on Mickenlee's thigh, hers is knotted in my hair, and we're both a little drunk—her on a very expensive bottle of champagne and me on the thrill of performing, on the press and the cameras and *yes*, drunk on the way Mickenlee looked at me when I came offstage.

There aren't many places I can kiss her like this, but in the back of a tinted car, with the divider up and a driver who's learned discretion, she's *mine*. We know every step of this dance now, have endured the back-and-forth, on-and-off rhythm for years. She might only be mine in the dark, only backstage and out of sight, but for me, it's enough.

"Wait." I can hardly get the words out as we pull into the crowded parking lot. "Stop. We're here."

Mickenlee makes a low, frustrated sound in the back of her

throat as I pull away. It's almost enough to make me forget the after-party, to keep me right here in the back of this car with her for the rest of the night. But I disentangle myself anyway, rebuttoning my shirt as our car stops in front of the hotel. The parking lot swarms with reporters, security officers, and fans, and I feel Mickenlee stiffen as the first camera flashes. She's never liked the attention. I know this, but I'm not afraid. I feel every heartbeat in my throat, and I don't know if it's the thrill of performing or the echo of Mickenlee's lips on my neck that makes me brave. I've always been this way, haven't I? Bottled lightning. Easily consumable.

I roll down the window and wave to the crowd, begging them with every smile, every motion, every breath, to *love me.* I know they do. We belong to each other in a deep, intimate way Mickenlee and I will never replicate. "Go find Markell," I tell her, gaze still fixed on the crowd. "I'll be right in."

A lie. I'll stay out here as long as they want me. I might feel dangerous when I'm with Mickenlee, but out here I feel powerful. Something cool and distant settles behind her eyes and I know she's thinking the same thing. "Don't take too long. He leaves first thing in the morning, remember?"

She slides out the door and walks toward the hotel with her head low, heels clicking across the damp, shadowed cobblestones. When I open my own door, it's into the welcoming roar of the crowd. The questions are immediate, rapid-fire pulses in the night.

"Are you excited for your first tour?"

"How did it feel coming offstage tonight, Decklee?"

"Why did you choose Tupelo?"

I answer them all one by one—I'm more excited than I've ever been; it felt like flying; because I love this city.

Some are practiced lies, sound bites written by Mickenlee and Ricky to make me look good on TV. Others are laced with truth. In between photos I scan the lot for Markell's car. It's been months since I've seen him. He's busy now—opening a shop in New York, designing for celebrity clients who aren't me—and I know it's selfish, but I miss the days when it was just us.

Ricky takes my elbow as I wave to the last reporter, subtly steering me toward the hotel.

"Excellent," he mutters. "That's exactly the kind of impression we wanted." Because everything's calculated with him. Like now, for example, he pauses for half a second before asking, "Have you given any thought to the proposal I sent you?"

"For the movie?" I nod. "It's too small. I want to write music that will win me an Oscar. Get me a better project."

Ricky laughs. "That's bold."

But that's the point. That's how you move the line, one intangible dream at a time. I hold Ricky's gaze long enough for him to know I'm serious, and after another second, he nods.

"All right. I'll make some calls. Oh—one more thing." He catches my arm. "Call James tonight, will you? Get him to come to a show."

"James who?"

"James Brody. From the label. Your award-show date."

"Oh." I can't hide my momentary flash of disgust. "No, thank you."

Ricky's grip tightens ever so slightly. "It wasn't a suggestion."

"Ricky," I groan. "You know what people say when we're together? They say I'm an opportunistic, gold-digging social climber because he *happens* to work at the label."

"Would you rather them say you're a lesbian?"

My head snaps up. I know someone's still taking pictures because the flash lingers in my peripheral vision, crisp and violent, but in that moment the only thing I hear is my own pulse and the echo of Ricky's voice in my ears. "I'm not—"

"I don't care what you do at home, Decklee." Ricky's pleasant smile is still locked in place, a cold, hollow echo of my previous enthusiasm. "I really don't, but when you're on this tour, representing this label, you will not give them a reason to say you're anything other than a star. Do you understand? We've worked too hard for that."

I've never been sure how much Ricky knows, or how much he pretends *not* to know for deniability's sake. But as his gaze slides toward the hotel, tracing the exact path Mickenlee took out of the car, I think I understand. I swallow around the cold fist at my throat.

"Of course," I say, voice too bright. "I'll call him."

Another concession. Another piece of myself filed away and scraped down. I wonder if they'll still love me when there's nothing left.

"That's my girl." Ricky releases me at last, giving me one final pat on the shoulder. "Go have fun. I'll see you inside."

I walk the rest of the way into the hotel alone, chin up, face relaxed in case there are any stray cameras. If they catch me like this, they'll just think I'm heading to the party. They'll think I'm happy, relieved, maybe a little tired, but they won't guess I'm still stuck on the way Ricky looked at me. Like no matter what I've accomplished, no matter how successful I've become, he could still take everything away because of a kiss.

I don't stop until I catch sight of Mickenlee tucked against a wall in the hotel courtyard. She's standing shoulder to shoulder with Markell, just around the corner from the main hotel entrance but still in sight of the watching crowd, which means the reporters behind me also have a clear view of the three uniformed security officers blocking their path. I glance over my shoulder, aware of every lingering camera, and quicken my pace until I hear Mickenlee's voice.

"I'm sorry, are we being detained? It's a yes or no question, officer." She's agitated, I can tell by the way she's talking with her hands, jamming her finger into the officers' chests. "I don't know what's so funny, but I promise you do *not* want to get into an argument with me about reasonable suspicion. You won't win."

"Mick!" I reach them right as the first officer steps forward. "What the hell?"

Relief flashes across her face at the sight of me. She reaches out, nails digging into my forearm, but I pull away. I'm still thinking about Ricky's warning, about the cameras in the parking lot and all the different things people could say if they saw us together now.

"See?" Mickenlee says. "We're with her. Let us in."

The first officer has eyes like dark coffee. They don't soften as they skim over Markell and Mickenlee before coming to rest on me. "This is a closed party, ma'am. I've told you multiple times that you can go in as soon as I see some identification."

"Oh my god." Mickenlee rolls her eyes. "And we've told *you* multiple times that Markell's license is in his room. Because he's staying here with us. With her," she adds, pointing back at me. "I gave you mine ten minutes ago, so what, exactly, is the issue?"

Her cheeks are flushed, and I can't tell if it's from anger or the lingering effects of the champagne. It doesn't matter. We are standing outside one of the busiest hotels in downtown Tupelo, and if she doesn't stop, I know exactly what tomorrow's headline will be.

"I'm so sorry, officer. This feels like a misunderstanding." I step forward, flashing what I hope is a generally believable grin. "They're with me. This is my party."

The officer doesn't move. "They aren't on the list."

"An oversight, probably." I wave a hand. "It'll be fixed next time, but for now do you think you can let it slide?"

I know they will. People always let things slide for me because I'm Decklee Cassel and I've never done anything wrong in my life. I don't have terrible, ruinous secrets lurking in the dark.

It's another second before the officer gives a stiff nod and motions us toward the hotel. "Just this once," he says. "Don't let it happen again."

I exhale and take Markell's arm. "Thank you."

Mickenlee is still furious. I can see the fire burning behind her eyes, but I don't care. Ricky is still on the sidewalk behind us, and I know the cameras are, too. I think of the film proposals and the albums I want to make and how it doesn't take much to bring someone down. A crack in an unshakeable foundation. A single word leaked to the papers.

I don't stop until we're alone in my suite. Then I slam the door and turn to face them. "What the hell were you thinking?"

Mickenlee blinks. "What were *we* thinking?"

"You had to cause a scene tonight of all nights?" I pace across the carpet, unable to keep still. "I'm trying to launch a tour. I'm trying to build something here, but you know what people are going to write tomorrow? *Decklee Cassel Argues with Police.* Nothing about the music, nothing about the show. *That's* going to be the story."

"If that's the worst thing that happens tonight, I think we're fine."

But we're not. This could be the beginning of the end, the thread that unravels everything. "I'm trying to have a career," I say. "Did you even think about that?"

Markell lets out a low, cold laugh. "Sorry, I'll try to remember that next time I'm cornered by three officers in the dark. How would it make *you* look? How would *you* feel?"

"That's not what I meant."

"Then what *do* you mean?"

"Just that it's not a big deal, Markell! Let it go!"

I know it's not true the minute I say it. Markell has lived through vicious landlords and musty motel rooms because he had nowhere else to go. He worked his way through every cruel person in Nashville because Memphis slammed the door in his face, and none of that is something he can just *let go*. It's not something he should have to. But I watch his dark eyes widen, listen to Mickenlee inhale a sharp breath, and I don't take it back.

"You think I did that on purpose?" he asks.

No, of course not, but it doesn't matter. "It's what they'll write."

"Let them write what they want."

"I *can't.*"

I don't know how to make him understand that there's not a choice here. I want him and the music, I want Mickenlee and the fame, but I didn't come this far to lose.

"No." Markell shakes his head. "You can do anything you want, Decklee, you just won't. There's a difference."

We stand there for a strained, agonizing minute, watching each other in heavy silence. I'm the one who breaks first. "Go down to the party, okay?" I say. "I'll fix this."

I don't want to fight with them, not tonight, but Markell shakes his head. "I have an early flight tomorrow. I'm going to get some sleep."

"Markell, wait—"

"It was good seeing you." He pulls a box from the inside of his jacket and hands it to me. "This is for tomorrow. A new Fansworth original for tour."

And then he's gone, a faint trail of citrus perfume the only indicator he was ever here at all. I exhale and look down at the box in my hands, unsure of how we got here. I open the lid, sorting through layers of tissue paper until I find it—an enormous turquoise ring carved in a stunning resemblance to my favorite guitar. It's perfect, of course; every piece he makes is. It's exactly the kind of glamorous, flashy thing I want with me onstage, and I wish, for the hundredth time, that Markell wasn't so much better than everything I deserve.

"Is it worth it?"

I don't look up at Mickenlee's voice. I pretend not to notice her step toward me as I slip the ring on my finger. "Is what worth it?"

"This." She gestures around the suite. "Is all of this really worth it if you lose him? If you lose us?"

I know what she wants me to say. She wants me to deny it, to admit I'm wrong, but fame has always come with a price. If Markell is the next sacrifice, the thing that keeps me in the spotlight, I'll make it right here.

I swallow hard and force myself to meet Mickenlee's gaze. "Yes," I say. "It's always been worth it."

Then, before she can respond, I open the door and walk back into my party.

TWENTY-THREE

Darren

Kendall is mid-conversation with the front desk concierge when I find him in the lobby. I duck past a bellhop, sidestep a group of tourists, and I'm about to tap him on the shoulder when I catch the last half of what he's saying.

"No, I *totally* understand. Why would people think the towels are free?" His elbows rest on the desk, chin propped in his hands like he's talking to an old friend. "I work at a gas station—you'd be surprised at the number of things people think they can get away with taking."

The concierge smiles up at him from under her enormous, blue-lensed glasses. It's meaningless small talk. I can tell that much from where I stand, but it doesn't matter, because this is Kendall and he has this strange, wonderful knack for making you feel like you're the most important person in the world.

I've spent the last several years of my life trying to understand the people around me, figuring out where I fit. That's why I love journalism so much, I think. Because at its core, it's a connection. That's why I launched *Mayberry Unpublished*, so I could learn more about Carla's roses or how Bob bought the gas station or how Emily's dad worked in Guatemala for ten years before moving back to the States. I learned about Madison's love of romance novels and Mom's affinity for Cajun food and how much everyone loves Mayberry County High School football games. I learned everything about everyone in that town so that when I finally put it in my rearview mirror, it will feel like closing a book.

Except now, for the first time, I'm realizing I forgot to learn about Kendall Wilkinson.

I didn't know he wanted to open a restaurant before this weekend. I didn't know he was this charming and kind with strangers, and I definitely didn't know he would ever be willing to drop his plans to drive me across the South.

I didn't know how much I wanted to kiss him.

"Can I help you?"

I jump at the sound of the concierge's voice and nearly drop the flash drive. I realize I've been standing in the middle of the hotel lobby for the last several minutes, staring wordlessly at Kendall. "Sorry." I shake my head. "Kendall?"

He turns, and when I hold up the third flash drive, his face explodes into a wild, unabashed grin.

"Darren Purchase!" He says my name like he can't quite believe I'm real. "You're a witch, you know that, right? It's been five minutes!"

I shrug, biting back a grin as he pulls me toward the desk. "I got lucky."

The concierge leans forward, and I see the name CANDY stamped on her tag. She's older than I thought, her white hair wispy and thinning, but she's wearing a dark smear of lipstick and blue eyeliner that's a hundred times cooler than anything I could ever pull off.

"You're here for that time capsule hunt, aren't you?" she asks. "We've had people in and out all morning, pretending they weren't searching the lobby, filming the entire thing, asking *very* pointed questions to get up to the suites. Do you know Mike Fratt?"

I roll my eyes. "Unfortunately."

"His whole crew just left, but they didn't find anything. I was beginning to think there was nothing here."

"They just didn't have Darren." Kendall shakes his head. "She's a genius."

I blush, heat spreading over the collar of my shirt. I remember our drive here, how Kendall looked me straight in the eye and said, *One day I'm going to give you a compliment and you're going to believe me.* I don't know if I believe him, exactly, but I still want to acknowledge this victory. I found this clue on my own. I followed my instincts and it paid off, so why can't there be a world where everything else works out for me, too?

Kendall turns the flash drive over so he can read the words scrawled onto the side. "Well," he says. "Are we going to crack it open?"

I glance toward the concierge and wonder if it'll ever get

easier to ask complete strangers to commandeer their work computers. Something tells me Candy might not be as open to the idea as Dani was. That girl was hungry. Candy looks content. But before I can ask, before I can even think of how to phrase the question, Candy extends a hand. She has jewels pressed into each nail and her voice is almost reverent as she asks, "You want to open that file?"

She grins like we're the only two people in on a secret, and her fingers are soft against mine as I hand over the flash drive. She slides it into the base of her computer with absolutely no hesitation as the other concierge shifts in his seat.

"That's definitely not allowed, Candace," he whispers, glancing over his shoulder. "Someone could see you."

Candy rolls her eyes. "I've worked here since before you were born, Jeremy. What are they going to do? *Fire* me?"

Jeremy looks like he thinks they should do just that, but I see the subtle shift in his position as Candy clicks into the file—how he inches forward, pulled by the same relentless curiosity still driving me across state lines. That's Decklee Cassel's magic, I think. The fact that even Jeremy the Concierge, who has probably never broken a rule in his life, is willing to risk it all for a few minutes of music. Candy grins, painted lips splitting wide, and then she clicks play.

The new song is the opposite of this morning's wild anthem. It's soft and lilting, like a quiet afternoon on Carla's porch. It makes me think of weekends with Emily and Madison, curling up with Mom on the couch to watch *SNL* reruns, and Kendall holding me outside the Brentwood House. *Home*. It's like that moment in the courtyard where everything felt clear, and without even meaning to, I think I know where this song is leading me next.

It's the last place I ever thought Decklee would go, the last place *I* want to go, but maybe this quest has always been circular for me. Maybe I was always supposed to end up right back where I started.

I lean into Kendall's shoulder, savoring the solid feeling of him against me. We might be as temporary and fleeting as this song. We might be fundamentally incompatible, but I would go back to Mayberry with him right now, if he asked. I would go almost anywhere. He slides a hand around the curve of my hip and leans down to whisper in my ear.

"You know where to go?"

I shiver, letting him pull me closer. "I didn't say that."

"But you do. I can tell."

Maybe there's something beautiful to being known like this. Maybe being seen isn't a curse. For all the time I've spent learning about Mayberry, I don't think I've taken the time to let anyone truly know me. Emily and Madison and I have been friends for so long that I can't remember how we became a unit. We just did, and even now there are pieces of myself I haven't shared with them. But I could see myself telling Kendall one day. I might tell him now, if he asked.

What do you want, Darren?

The same question that's been haunting me all week. I turn to face Kendall, still half-pressed into his side, and blurt, "I'm good at this."

His eyebrows lift. "Yeah?"

"Yes." I nod. "This is what I want to do. Forever, I think. Find stories, track them down, figure them out. I think I'm good at it."

Kendall grins. "You are. You're really good at it."

The song comes to an end, the last twangy guitar chord fading into silence, and Candy sighs, the echo of a breath I think we've been holding since Decklee's time capsule turned up empty. I pull out of Kendall's grip and brace my elbows on the desk, trying to mirror his relaxed, confident posture from earlier. "You said you've worked here awhile?"

Candy blinks, like she's just now remembering Kendall and I are here. "Yes ma'am."

"Were you here the night Decklee started her tour? For the after-party?"

"Of course. It was my first week on the job."

Jeremy the Concierge practically falls out of his seat. "*What?*"

"Oh, I never told you?" Candy shrugs. "It was wild—they had all those buses parked out front, everyone was here. Fans, reporters, police. That friend of hers almost got arrested."

I straighten. "Wait, who?"

"I never remember her name. Short woman. Dark hair?"

"*Mickenlee Hooper* almost got arrested? Here? Why?"

Candy shrugs. "Not sure. Some altercation with the police? I was on turndown service back then, but we all heard the shouting."

"Damn." Kendall shakes his head. "Good for her. You should put that in your story, Purchase."

I'm still trying to wrap my head around the idea of perfect, poised Mickenlee Hooper getting into an altercation with anyone. She had always been so careful not to be seen or draw attention to herself.

"Could I talk to you more about it sometime?" I ask Candy. "I'm a journalist back home and I'm sort of working on a story about, well . . ." I wave a hand around the hotel lobby. "*This*. Do you have a card?"

"She's really good," Kendall interjects. "Best writer I know."

I'm pretty sure I'm the only writer he knows, but I appreciate the support.

"Sure." Candy shuffles around until she finds a crumpled business card. "This is my desk number. You can give me a call anytime."

I take it and slide it into the back of my phone case, right next to Dani's. "Thanks."

"Good luck." Candy holds up the flash drive. "Do you want this back?"

I hesitate. The lobby is empty, no one to document that we've found the clue. I could take it with me, keep it as close as possible until we finish this, but that doesn't seem right anymore. I shake my head.

"You keep it. Give it to the next reporter who comes in. They can break the story and let the estate take it from there." I reach for Kendall's hand, savoring the feeling of his fingers slipping through mine. When I look up at him, he's already grinning. "Let's go home."

TWENTY-FOUR

Decklee
Los Angeles, 1978

The night I win my first Oscar, I look like midnight and magic wrapped in dark silk.

All these years later and I'm still not sure how Markell does it. He's always made me dangerous in a subtle, delicate sort of way. He's always made sure I turn heads, and tonight he put me in blue—an inky, sequined gown with a slit halfway up the right thigh. It keeps the cameras on me all night, turning heads at an award show that shouldn't even be mine to take.

Mickenlee and I are the Hollywood newcomers—two country girls who somehow lucked our way into an Academy Award nomination for Best Original Song. We're hardly supposed to be here and we're definitely not supposed to win, but the West Coast hasn't learned the very important lesson people down South have had years to unpack: don't underestimate Decklee Cassel.

You can barely turn on a radio without hearing my voice, but

California is a different, mythic beast. I remember thinking the same thing about New York years ago, how the entire city was wild and untamable, but Los Angeles is rough. I feel its claws locked around my throat even now, a beckoning challenge. The people here either love me or don't know I exist. I don't care. Tonight is another chance to get a brand-new audience to love me, and Markell makes me shine even from the opposite side of the country. He left me a piece of jewelry, of course, a Fansworth original brooch in the shape of a rose. I have it pinned right inside the zipper, next to the old silver cat, but as I turn to walk the carpet, I wish more than anything he was here.

Tonight, it's just me and James, another chapter in our on-again, off-again relationship. It's something of a joke now, a point of conversation every time people see us together. They ask me why I keep coming back, ask James why he hasn't locked me down yet, and always find some twisted, obnoxious way to make me the villain. *Cold, flighty, selfish Decklee Cassel, who doesn't stop to think about her partner's feelings before jetting off on another tour.* Sometimes I want to tell them the truth, just to give everyone something else to gossip about.

The Nashville reporters and I have a routine now. They know what to ask. I'll smile and squeeze James's arm and act like everything they say isn't wildly insulting before we pivot back to my music and they let me go inside. But here, under a bright California sky, no one is familiar with the bit. When a reporter who obviously learns who I am seconds before opening his mouth asks how long we're going to last this time, it takes everything in me not to throttle him on the spot.

Ask me about my nomination, I think. *Ask me about the movie or my music or the thousands of other things I could do if you let me.*

Out loud, I laugh and look up at James from under my eyelashes. "I have a good feeling about this one. Probably because he looks so handsome tonight. James is wearing Markell Fansworth, too, can you tell? He's the absolute genius designer behind this dress."

Maybe it's the thought of Markell that makes me feel bitter and jagged, because when the same reporter asks, "So, do you think you're taking home a ring tonight?" I don't respond with my usual joke.

Instead, I snap, "What I'm taking home is a gold statue," before turning on my heel and marching inside.

Ricky always knew I wanted to write for film. I told him I wanted big ones, box office hits, something that would make me a star. What I got instead was a low-budget independent project called *Sacred Sin*. Tonight, the film's only other Academy nod is for its lead actress, Kiara Howard, who's as fresh in Hollywood as I am. I don't know why I'm surprised. All these years later and Ricky still thinks he can get away with handing me nothing. I wonder if part of him hates it, the fact that everything I touch turns to gold without his help. I wonder if he'll ever get tired of taking credit for my success when it does.

"You look beautiful."

Mickenlee's voice is low in my ear, so quiet I don't hear it until I find my seat next to her. I let my fingers brush hers as I sit and wish I could take her hand completely.

"Big crowd tonight, don't you think?" I say. "Feels different than Nashville."

"It feels richer."

Mickenlee grins and I think of a boy in a Memphis hotel room who told me he wanted to make clothes for exactly this kind of rich person. *You in the market?* he had asked me, one eyebrow lifting. I had thrust my chin out, all sharp edges and unrefined ambition, and said, *To be rich? Always.*

That's how I watch the ceremony now—through a screen of old, hazy memories, constantly glancing over my shoulder for someone who's not here. When it's time for me to change for my performance, Mickenlee squeezes my hand once. "I'm proud of you, Cleo," she whispers. "Go prove them wrong."

Not "good luck," never "good luck."

She knows I don't need it.

Mickenlee and I wrote "Bring It In" together, just the two of us. Two names on the credit line where most nominees have dozens. We wrote it for a specific moment in the film, but I feel Mickenlee in every word—the part of her that longs and wishes and aches. The part that thinks, for some wonderfully naive reason, that there might be a chance for us somewhere.

She wrote it for me. I know that. So when I sit down at the enormous piano in the middle of the stage, when I spread my fingers against the smooth, ivory keys and play, it's not Markell I see behind my eyelids. It's her. The way her hair curls around the nape of her neck, the freckles in dotted constellations across the bridge of her nose, the way she feels wrapped around me in the dark. The way I sometimes wish we met in a different place, a different time, so that when red-carpet reporters ask too many nosy questions, I could pull her out of the crowd and say, *Here, this is who I love. This is who I want and nothing you say will make me ashamed.*

They've turned the lights down onstage tonight, lit me from above with a single spotlight that catches in the crystals sewn into my train. This dress is another Markell creation, a cream-colored gown that spills to the floor behind me. I told him last year I wanted to look like a star, like someone reached up and pulled me off the edge of a spiral galaxy, and he did it. He makes me burn.

I love the character of Decklee Cassel, the one built from sequined boots and statement pieces and wigs, who smiles and banters with every reporter. I love the makeup and the songs and all the things that make me special, but I don't think I mind this version either. It feels like long dirt backroads and warm summer nights. It feels a little more like Cleo Patrick.

There has never really been a way for me to have both, but *damn*, does Markell try.

It takes several seconds after I finish to finally hear the applause. My fingers tremble on the keys, uncertain for the first time all night, but then I look up and catch a glimpse of myself on-screen out of the corner of my eye. *Radiant.* It's the word Ricky likes to use, and tonight it's true.

There's a rush to award shows, a flow you can't disrupt. Because of how late I perform, I'm barely back in my seat before they announce our category. Mickenlee straightens, and again I instinctively glance over her shoulder before remembering Markell isn't here. James tries to take my hand and I very obviously pretend to ignore him, reaching for Mickenlee instead. Her fingers are viselike around mine as the room falls silent.

When I sat down after my performance, Mickenlee looked like she had been crying. But when we win, she actually *does* cry, just claps a hand over her mouth like she can't quite believe this is real.

The theater erupts into cheers and I hug them all—Ricky, who didn't give me the movie I deserved but has to watch me fly anyway, the producers who know me by how much money I make them, even James. And then, because no one's telling me not to, I turn and throw my arms around Mickenlee so hard we both stumble. She laughs, strangled and breathy in my ear, and hugs me back in front of everyone.

And no one cares. Because we *won.*

I try to take her onstage with me, but she shakes her head, motioning me forward, so I walk up alone. Then they hand me the statue and I almost forget how to breathe. I have a lot of awards by now, but this one feels earned. It was the hard one, the one that demanded sacrifice after sacrifice.

"I have a lot of people to thank for this," I say. It's the practiced speech, the one that makes me sound flustered and wild and happy. Humble, when that's never been a shade for me. "First to Ricky Grasso, for signing a sixteen-year-old girl at a Memphis open mic. To my family," I say, because that's what they all expect me to say even though I haven't had a family for years. "Thank you for all the support. Thank you to the

Academy for having us, and to Marty and Anne, who made the most beautiful film I've ever seen. And to Kiara." I lift my statue in her direction. "You really are the best actress of our generation. You deserve all this and more."

Kiara shakes her head and blows a kiss back to me on the stage as the audience claps for her, too. I find Mickenlee in the audience, glowing brighter than any star, and I clutch my Oscar to my chest in a vain attempt to calm my racing heart. I don't have this next part planned, but looking at her now, I'm not sure how I thought I could say anything else.

"And I wouldn't be on this stage tonight without Mickenlee Hooper," I say. "Her talent is truly unparalleled, and I couldn't ask for a better partner in this industry. They told us a long time ago that two women don't sell records, that we were a risk and a liability. Well." I lift an eyebrow, making sure I'm looking right at Ricky when I say, "These two women produced an Oscar-winning song. How do y'all feel about that?"

I remember the rest of that night in a series of wine-soaked snapshots and images. I don't know whose house we end up in, just that it's rich and wonderful and everyone around us is very drunk. I drink champagne straight from the bottle, pausing only to dip pieces of fruit in an enormous chocolate fountain. Ricky hugs Mickenlee, people I don't know hug me, and Kiara toasts us all, holding her own Oscar up for everyone to see. We're all laughing, standing at the top of this mountain we climbed, and I pull Mickenlee into my arms for a brief passing second. I unfasten Markell's brooch and pin it to her dress with shaky fingers. She always looked better in red, and when she looks up at me through long, delicate lashes, I wish more than anything I could kiss her right now.

That night, the only thing people talk about is my win.

The next morning, they talk about my speech. They talk about Mickenlee's hand on my waist at the after-party, mine on her arm, and the way I didn't look at James once. They talk about all the things they believe us to be in a way that twists it so completely I don't even recognize the accusations.

How Close Is Too Close?
"Just Friends," Says Source
near the Country Singer

The headlines feel like ripping back a curtain. I read them over and over until my eyes blur, until my brain stops and I think, *This is it.* Here is the thing that ruins me. It's not a bad album, it's not a botched tour. It's the thing Ricky warned me about years ago, something true and real. Something I wish I didn't have to deny.

But you will.

Of course I will. Because for a minute last night, I was on that summit. I stood under the lights with a statue in my hand and knew that absolutely everyone in that room loved me. And when you have the world like that in the palm of your hand, ready and waiting and eager for more, you don't let it go. You can't. You pay the cost, whatever it is, and you keep moving forward step after unsteady step. One song at a time.

TWENTY-FIVE

Darren

Mom calls an hour into our drive to Mayberry.

"Hi." I press the phone to my ear, like it'll somehow close the distance between us. "We're on our way back now. How are you?"

Kendall and I are still about five hours out and the gas station we're currently stopped at doesn't have the best reception. I watch him outside my window, hands braced on his hips as he fills up the tank.

"I'm fine," Mom says. "I miss you. How are things going? You both behaving yourselves?"

"Oh my god." I slide down in my seat. "Yes, obviously." Then, because I want to talk about literally anything else, I add, "Have you been watching the news?"

I launch into an abbreviated version of the last two days, and I practically feel Mom relax as I work my way through the story. I tell her about the Rainbow Wall and Top Cat and Dani's big break. I tell her about that first, pulse-pounding moment when I saw the Nashville skyline, and how, for the rest of my life, I will hold a personal grudge against content creator/noted insurrection enthusiast Mike Fratt. I conveniently leave out the part where Kendall snuck me into a bar and I defaced a historic landmark, but when I reach the end of the story, Mom is laughing along with me.

"Wow. That sounds like quite a weekend."

"It was," I say, still breathless. "And I've been trying to write something about Decklee all week, but I think this whole thing is more of a Mickenlee Hooper story. I mean, no one's seen her in decades, but she wrote all these new songs. Why?"

"I've been wondering the same thing," Mom says. "She's obviously still out there. You could find her."

I still don't know if I could, but hearing Mom say it releases the last bit of tension in my chest. "I think the time capsule is in Mayberry. Isn't that weird?"

"Why would it be weird?"

"Because." I twirl the cord of Kendall's phone charger around my finger. "Decklee never came back. I didn't think she'd hide something that important in town, but it fits the last part of the rhyme."

"Right," Mom says. *"One for the money, two for the show, three to get ready—"*

"—and four to go. That was on the last flash drive."

Last week, I might have second-guessed myself. I might have circled back through the song again and again, overthinking every message or insisting it had to be somewhere else. But I've been trying something new without even realizing it—throwing myself forward, trusting my instincts, and hoping other people trust me enough to follow.

Static crackles down the line again and I straighten. "Hey, can I call you when we get close? The signal isn't great, and we need to get back on the road."

"Sure," Mom says. "Be safe. And tell Kendall hello for me."

"Will do. Love you."

"Love you, too."

The phone goes silent in my hand and I drop it into a cup holder, next to where Kendall's orange soda is dripping condensation onto the gear shift. It's too hot to sit in the car alone, but when I open the door, the humidity is just as bad. The air is thick in my lungs as I watch Kendall dock the gas nozzle and turn toward me.

"Was that Carla?" he asks.

I shake my head. "No, it was my mom. She said to tell you hi, by the way, so I think you're back in her good graces."

"Thank god. I didn't know how I was going to face her."

I grin, folding my arms as I let my feet swing back and forth in the open air. I know it's a little thing, Kendall wanting to impress Mom. It's the bare minimum, really, but I've never had someone care about me in this way. I wonder if this is what Carla meant when she told me I'd know when someone liked me.

"So," Kendall says, mirroring my posture as he turns to face me. "How did you know we were heading back to Mayberry, anyway? I've listened to all those new songs, you know. I've played them multiple times and I can never figure out how you know."

I shrug. "It's mostly the rhyme from the flash drive—*four to go*. It's the end of the trail, but it also feels like it's about Mayberry. I've listened to every single Decklee Cassel song, Kendall. I know the themes. I know what she writes about, and she *never* writes about home."

"Really?" Kendall asks. "Never?"

"No. Not in the literal sense, anyway. She's written songs about Nashville and Memphis and New York, songs about all the people in her life who feel like home, but she never wrote about Mayberry. She never even talked about it."

But she wrote about it now, in the new song that sits in some thorny, complicated cavern in my chest.

Kendall tilts his head. "So how do you know she's talking about Mayberry now? Couldn't that new song also be metaphorical, or something?"

I open my mouth, unsure of how to explain it. "It's just different. There's a lyric near the end—*You were the one I meant to lose, try to shake you, never do*. I think that's what I would write about Mayberry, if I had to."

There's a line forming between Kendall's eyebrows. I want to reach up and smooth it away. We're close enough that I could do it if I wanted, just close the distance between us and see what happens next. "That's a good lyric," he says.

I nod, throat suddenly very dry. "It's Mickenlee's for sure. The way she wrote about the South was magical. It almost makes you want to stay."

"What do you mean 'almost'?"

"I mean..." Again, I struggle for words. "I mean that I'm going to college next year. I don't know where, but the minute people find out I'm from Arkansas, they're going to have this idea about what that means and what I stand for. It's going to be a *thing*."

"That happens everywhere," Kendall says. "To everyone. Their opinion isn't your problem."

"But it's different. People will hear my accent and just assume I voted a certain way or that I'm uneducated or that I, like, accidentally endorsed a political insurrection on the internet."

Kendall rolls his eyes. "That is the whitest thing I've ever heard, Purchase. Full offense. You've lived in Arkansas your entire life. How do you not know all of that is just thinly veiled classism from people who want to feel superior? You really want to look at me and tell me everyone out here is a flag-waving bigot?"

"No," I say. "Of course not."

"Exactly. Because I live here. My family and friends are here, and you don't get to lump me in with Mike Fratt because you feel sorry for yourself."

"I know!" I cry. "Of course I know that, Kendall. That's why it makes me so angry when other people think that way."

"It makes you angry because you *love* it here."

I open my mouth, but nothing comes out. Kendall is standing right in front of me now, close enough for me to watch the muscle tense in his jaw, and all I want is to tell him he's wrong. I've never loved this place. I've wanted to leave since the moment I knew it was an option. But he doesn't give me a chance.

"I've read your stories," he says. "Someone who hates Mayberry couldn't write about it the way you do. You really care about those people and what they have to say. It reminds me of those songs we've been finding—like you're writing about home."

I let out a choked laugh. I appreciate the compliment, but I'm nothing like Mickenlee Hooper.

"I'm serious, Darren," Kendall protests. "I'm not kidding."

For a second, he sounds genuinely distressed, and I realize this might be the first time he's used my first name. I shake my head. "I know. I'm sorry, it's just . . . I've wanted to write like her for as long as I can remember. Her songs are art, Kendall."

He shrugs. "So are your stories."

I grip the passenger seat behind me in a vain attempt to steady my thundering pulse. It's another minute before I can speak again. "I meant what I said last night, you know. I don't hate you. I don't even hate Mayberry, but most of the time I feel like things would be different if I grew up somewhere else. I'd have more opportunities, better college options, more career connections. I could have done summer internships, I could have traveled. I feel stuck here."

Kendall braces one hand against the truck. "I think that's just how life works. I feel like that, sometimes."

"You do?"

"Of course. Like, where would I be if I kept playing tennis? What if I took that scholarship and left?" Questions like that tend to bury me, but Kendall continues like nothing is wrong.

"I think everything seems more enticing from the outside, but I like what I have in Mayberry. I like knowing you."

Again, I wonder how long I've been sitting in the dark, so focused on getting out of Mayberry that I never noticed the boy right in front of me. I slide out of the car slowly, carefully, because I don't want him to pull away. "I like knowing you, too," I say. "I'm, like, really, *really* glad to know you."

I recognize the irony, of course. Me, the writer, suddenly lost for words when it comes to telling Kendall how I feel. I think he gets it, though, because he reaches up and tucks a loose strand of hair back behind my ear. His hand lingers, right at the nape of my neck, and it's like every nerve in my body comes alive. I want him to kiss me. I've wanted it for a long time now, I think.

But when he leans in, closing the space between us, something like panic shoots up my spine. I pull away, and before I fully process what I'm about to say, I blurt, "I like girls."

Kendall stops, one hand still braced against the half-open door. "I . . . what?"

I want to close my eyes. I want to sink back into the safety of the truck, but I force myself to meet his gaze. "I like girls," I repeat. "I like boys, too, I mean. I like *you*, but . . . I don't know. It feels like something you should be aware of?"

"Okay." Kendall nods solemnly. "Sure. And I just like girls. As far as I know, anyway. Is that helpful for you at all?"

I let out a choked, breathy laugh. "That's not what I mean."

"Isn't it? I don't want to steal your thunder, Purchase, but I know. You have, like, four ear piercings, your phone background is currently a picture of Santana Lopez, and you talked to me at *length* last year about how Jo March was a lesbian. You couldn't be more stereotypically bisexual if you tried."

Bisexual. I look down at my feet still sandwiched between Kendall's. I've thought it plenty of times, but I've never said the word out loud. It makes me think of the pin on Dani's bag, how she was confident enough to display it to the world. I don't know if I feel like that yet.

"Whatever," I mutter. "Jo March *is* a lesbian."

Kendall laughs and I hate that I can't even pretend to be mad at him for dramatic effect. "That's debatable," he says. "But thanks for telling me. I'm sure it wasn't easy."

But it was easy. Everything is easy with him. I didn't realize how heavy this part of me had become until I shared it. I relax against the car. "Thanks for listening. I don't know what it means, exactly, but—" I stop. Kendall is staring at me so intently I actually feel the weight of his gaze on my skin. "What?"

"Nothing! Sorry!" He blinks, shaking his head like he's trying to clear it. "But can I still kiss you? Or is that moment gone?"

I laugh again, and this time, it's real. I reach up, wrap both arms around Kendall's neck, and finally, *finally* kiss him. Before this weekend, I thought I knew everything there was to know about Kendall Wilkinson. Each time I found something new, I was sure I'd discovered it all, pried everything out of him into the open. But when Kendall tilts his head, one arm locking around my waist as he deepens the kiss, I realize I'm sorely mistaken.

There's no way I ever could have anticipated this.

The want hits me like a truck on a Tennessee highway, tearing every thought out of my head. I want him. I want *this*. I've driven hundreds of miles this weekend searching for something I still don't know exists, but here's Kendall—hand tangled in my hair, lips parting for mine, skin hot under my hands. Here's something I never thought I'd find in Mayberry, and in this moment, I don't ever want to leave.

TWENTY-SIX

Decklee
Los Angeles, 1978

"I don't understand what the big deal is, Mick. It's one date."

We're in my hotel room, fifty floors above LA's bustling downtown strip, and Mickenlee is pacing—back and forth across the patterned carpet with her hands on her hips. Ricky leans against the wall, watching her move. I've seen him in damage-control mode for countless others, people who do reckless things because they think they're unsinkable, who tear apart every opportunity they've been offered, just to feel something. People who aren't me.

And I'm sitting on the bed, legs folded beneath me, with my Oscar in my lap. *This is the prize*, I think, running a finger over one gilded edge. *This is what makes it worth it.*

"One date?" Mickenlee's face is a frigid mask. "You think that's going to make this go away?"

"It might. People are easily distracted."

"And what if I don't want to go?"

I look up as she turns on her heel and stalks back across the carpet. "You think I wanted to take James to every red carpet?" I ask. "You think I wanted them to write those things about us? They just need a different story."

Mickenlee scoffs. "I'm not their story. I never wanted to be."

"Maybe. But it's not my fault they wrote what they did."

She finally stops in front of the bed, glaring down at me with last night's makeup still smudged under both eyes. "Why do they have to write anything at all? Why can't we just *be*?"

"Because, Miss Hooper," Ricky says, expression carefully blank, "I think you'd both like to keep your jobs."

Mickenlee's jaw tenses and I know what she wants to say. That she doesn't care about the job. That we could quit, leave this town and everything we've built together. It's the same thing she whispers to me in the dark, the same fantasy I wish I could believe.

"Decklee has a point," Ricky continues. He taps a pen against the palm of his other hand, the weathered professional even now. "I can book you a later flight home, set you up with Don Hasselhoff this afternoon. It'll be public. Lots of people would see."

Mickenlee wrinkles her nose. "Don Hasselhoff."

She says it like it's an insult, like the name burns her tongue.

Ricky shrugs. "He's expressed interest in seeing you."

"Yes, I'm well aware."

Don Hasselhoff is the kind of man who gets what he wants, who has directed so many blockbuster films he's lost the art of subtlety. He expects the world to turn over for him, to *give* him things, and Mickenlee would have a terrible time with him.

I would have a terrible time just thinking about it, but these are the sacrifices we make.

I'm silent for too long. I know I am, because when I look up, I feel Mickenlee slip that much further away. If Ricky weren't here, I would take it back. I could tear down her walls, take her into my arms, and whisper every secret, scandalous thing I can't say out loud. That I love her. That I wish it wasn't like this. That I would date a thousand Don Hasselhoffs before I let anyone learn the truth.

Markell made me look like a star last night, but this morning I feel like a comet—a fiery remnant burning through everything I have left.

"It's one date, Mick," I say. "I do it all the time."

"I know you do," she says. "That's what I'm worried about."

"Don't be. Everyone will forget in a few days if you give them something to talk about."

Mickenlee's eyes flutter closed. She takes a deep breath and I watch her roll out her shoulders, smooth back her hair. Mickenlee Hooper has been playing this game as long as I have. She knows what we have to lose.

"Fine." Her voice is clipped. "*One* date. Tell Don I'll meet him in an hour and if he says *one word* to me about his lifetime achievement award, I will leave him in that restaurant."

She stalks out of the room without saying goodbye, but I don't care. She can hate me all she wants today if it means this will go away tomorrow. Ricky nods slowly and puts away his pen. "This is the right move," he says. "Let's not blow it, okay?"

Then he shuts the door behind him.

I used to think Ricky was the one who made me this way—cold and selfish and calculating. It used to be the only way to make him pay attention, but now I'm not so sure that's true. Maybe this has been a part of me all along, the Decklee Cassel who always knew who her collateral damage would be.

I grip my Oscar so tight my knuckles ache. "You're worth it," I say out loud.

But no one answers. I am alone. And the room stays empty and quiet and cold.

TWENTY-SEVEN

Darren

"**N**o, Kendall, there's no way out. You have to pick."

We're driving along the empty, wooded stretch of state road right outside Mayberry, five minutes from the county line and twenty minutes from civilization. The world is dark, flying by outside my window, but I feel lighter than I have in weeks.

Kendall grimaces, eyes stubbornly fixed on the road. "You're asking a really loaded question, Purchase."

"I'm not." I hold up the three CDs from his glove compartment. "Fuck, marry, kill your terrible music taste."

He exhales, looking resigned to the worst. "I feel like I have to marry the cast of *Mamma Mia*. They seem like a lot of fun, and I think we'd have a long and happy life together."

"Excellent." I put one CD down. "Great choice. Next."

"But this is where it gets tricky, you see."

"No! I don't see! And the fact you aren't immediately killing *Cats* (2019) is more than a little concerning!"

Kendall laughs and the sound slides over me in the dark. We've spent the last several hours playing various versions of this game. *Pick a dream job no one would ever let you do. What's your favorite pet that's not legally supposed to be a pet? If you could go anywhere in the world, where would you go?*

Now, cradled between familiar backroads, the Tupelo sun feels a lifetime away. So does the drive through Mississippi, the sunset over the trees, and the dinner break when we finally crossed back into Arkansas. Mayberry is nothing like Nashville or Memphis, but something inside me relaxes at the familiar curve of the dusky pavement. I can handle this town. I've done it for years.

"Are you still thinking about the time capsule?" Kendall asks. "Or are you thinking about *Cats* (2019)?"

I run a hand over my face. "I need you to know that I have never willingly thought about *Cats* (2019). So, yes, I'm thinking about the time capsule. I don't know where to look."

"That's okay, we'll figure it out." Kendall keeps his eyes on the road, but I can feel him grinning. "I trust you."

There it is again. *Trust.* Like it's guaranteed. Like he has no reason not to. Again, I wonder what Kendall and I are going to do when we get home, when he pulls into my driveway and we stop being *us*. Maybe it's bold of me to assume there's an *us* to begin with. I'm about to ask him what he's thinking when my phone buzzes in my lap.

I haven't been ignoring my friends all weekend, exactly, but I definitely haven't been responding to every message. When Emily texts me now, I assume it's something that can wait. Instead, it's a single message that says Shit, Darren, I'm sorry, followed by a Twitter link. Anxiety prickles up my spine and I'm about to tap into it when I get another text from Madison and a third from Mom. They both send me the same link.

Kendall glances over at me. "What is it?"

I shake my head. There's a strange dread building in my chest, the same feeling I had back in Nashville when I thought everything was about to go wrong. I tap on the link, turning up my volume as a grainy video fills the screen. I recognize Mike Fratt immediately, standing outside a corporate-looking building on a dark, unfamiliar street. I recognize the group around him, too, cameras held aloft to capture every detail, and, worst of all, I recognize the box he's holding between both hands. As I watch, Mike turns toward the camera, flashes a peace sign, and cries, "Shout-out to the boys and shout-out to the fans. I couldn't have found this without you! Tune in tomorrow for an exclusive Fratt Baby giveaway—we're three million dollars richer!"

Kendall taps the brakes a little too hard. I lurch forward, caught between the seat belt and my own plummeting stomach. *No.* I swipe out of the video, scrolling for some confirmation this is a hoax, but all the replies are the same.

Wooo, congrats Mike! Proud to be a part of this victory!

Lol I can't believe it was in Nashville the whole time, you should have just stayed in town.

Bro, when do you get the money??

It's like someone ripped the road out from under me. For a minute, I let myself believe that this is all social media speculation or bot accounts. But then I see the articles: every valid, reputable news outlet in the country reporting on a victory that's not mine.

> **Content creator and influencer Mike Fratt (@FrattTown) has found the Decklee Cassel Memorial Time Capsule at 10:37 p.m. CST in Nashville, Tenn. The box was buried in front of the DCR Records Executive Office on 16th Street.**

I let out a strangled laugh, nails digging into my thighs. "He found it. They found it in *Nashville.*"

There's something terribly comforting about coming back down to earth, about knowing that no matter how long I run or how far I stretch, I'm always going to be the girl from Mayberry. I'm never going to leave. The time capsule isn't here. It never was. I was delusional, looking for clues in places they didn't exist because I wanted to feel special.

Kendall's hand lands on my arm. "Darren—"

"Pull over."

He hesitates, still driving toward home, and I wonder what

it'll feel like to shatter. I wonder if I'll take him down with me. "Pull *over*, Kendall. Please."

When we finally come to a stop, it's in the corner of Bob's parking lot. *Right back where we started.* I throw the door open and jump to the pavement. Loose gravel crunches under my shoes and then I'm walking away from the car, scrolling through story after story in a vain attempt to find one that tells me I'm right.

"Darren, wait!"

I hear Kendall behind me, but I don't look back. I can't. It's like this morning, when I realized that I hadn't just lost my own way out, I lost his dream, too. He catches my arm right as I reach the edge of the parking lot.

"Stop. You can't just leave."

I let out another low, humorless laugh. "Why not? It's over, isn't it? I was wrong about the last clue. We lost and it's my fault."

"What? No." Kendall's grip tightens. "You think I care about the clue? That's not why I'm here."

The wind tugs at the bottom of his shirt, illuminated from behind by the distant glow of Bob's sign. Thunder rumbles overhead and I shiver at the first touch of cold wind. I know exactly why he's here. For his restaurant. For his family. He's here because he trusted me, and he should be angry, too, furious at me for losing the thing that was supposed to save us both. *What do you want, Darren?*

"I wanted to find that time capsule."

I don't realize I say it out loud until the wind steals the words from my lips. I did everything right. I solved every puzzle, de-coded every lyric, pored over the jewelry case at the Brentwood House like it was all connected, and I still lost. Someone else dug it up. Someone else looked through the things Decklee left behind and someone else is getting that money.

"He found it," I snap when Kendall doesn't move. "Mike Fratt found all of it. Do you even care?"

It's an unfair judgment to hurl at the boy who's repeatedly shown me he does, but I'm not feeling particularly fair right now. Kendall's eyebrows lift and I know he's about to talk me down. He's about to say something sweet and wonderful and I can't hear it. I pull out of his grip as thunder rumbles overhead.

"Don't. We were *this* close and I couldn't do it. There's no money, no prize."

Something flickers across Kendall's face, too quick for me to catch in the dark. "You think I care that much about the money, Darren? Really? Is that the only reason you went? What about finding those new songs or writing your story?"

"Of course it was about the money!" I cry. "The rest of it doesn't matter if I'm stuck in this town. There's nothing for me here, Kendall. You know that."

The wind picks up, but not before I hear Kendall's sharp in-hale. "Really?" he asks. "There's nothing for you here?"

His voice is calm and measured, but that response slices me to the bone. The hurt is clear on his face, but right now, I don't care. Right now, *I'm* hurt, and I want to make sure he feels it, too.

"No," I say, forcing as much venom as I can into the single syllable. "I hate this place. There's no reason for me to stay."

I recognize what this is the second I say it—the nail in the coffin between us. I'm not going to stay in Mayberry. Kendall's not going to leave. It's an impasse neither one of us can overcome.

I don't know how long we stand at the edge of the parking lot. Behind us is Bob's, glowing and warm. To our left, a road. At our backs, a field filled with tall, swaying grass. I know every inch of this town, could walk home with my eyes closed.

My throat aches as I watch Kendall seal himself up. "Come on," he mutters. "Let me take you home."

"I'll walk."

I walk home from work all the time, he knows that. There's no reason for him to offer, but still, he tries again. "Darren—"

"I said it's fine, Kendall." I step back across the grass. "I just want to go home."

Home. Because that's what Mayberry is now. Because home is a place you're not supposed to leave. The first cold drop of rain catches in my hair as I turn toward the road, and this time, when I go, Kendall doesn't stop me.

TWENTY-EIGHT

Decklee
Nashville, 1986

I write a song in the hour before dawn, when the sky is still black and the weight of everything I carry grows too heavy to bear.

Mickenlee is in bed, curled up in one of my old T-shirts. I watch her breathe from my spot at the window, slow and steady. We have a routine now. Whenever anyone gets too nosy or makes an accusation that's a little too accurate, we go out. I let James kiss me in a place that's not exactly private and Mickenlee picks a man at random. We're photographed apart. We're seen holding hands with other people. Everyone makes their jokes about me, and the rumors die.

I'm allowed to be cold, flighty, selfish Decklee Cassel in public as long as I keep making records. New girls show up in this city every day, guitar in hand, music in their blood, and they're allowed to be ambitious. They're allowed to fight. They look to me as an example and I let them.

They don't know yet what this city will demand, all the pieces of them it'll chip away. They don't know it's impossible to have all the things they want.

Mickenlee stirs when I crawl back into bed. "You okay?" she asks.

I nod and pull her close, tucking her into my empty spaces. "Just needed to write something down."

She nods, eyelashes a soft brush against my neck. I feel her settle against me, fingers knotting into the fabric of my shirt as she breathes, "I love you."

It's soft in the dark, a dangerous confession. I press my lips to her hair and whisper it back, stuck between reality and that strange, dreamy state where anything is possible. "I love you."

Everything, I think as I close my eyes. *I can still have everything.*

♪ ♪ ♪

THERE'S ONLY SO long you can play a game like this before somebody figures out the rules.

In our case, it's an up-and-coming reporter from *The Tennessean* who lays out exactly who I've been dating for the last two decades—when I see James, how long the relationship lasts, how often Mickenlee Hooper's car is parked in front of my house. It's detailed, it's concise, and it's compelling as hell. It keeps Ricky on the phone day after day, watching me like I'm about to combust and take his whole empire down with me.

"This is ridiculous," Mickenlee says one morning, throwing

aside another magazine. I catch a glimpse of the headline as it slides across the kitchen table. It's about me. Us. "They need to stop speculating, Ricky is going to tear you apart."

He already has. I don't tell her that, though. I don't tell her about the meetings where Ricky walks me through, in excruciating detail, exactly how much we stand to lose. Contracts, record sales, tour venues. Everything I do depends on people liking me, on not being a liability, and I can't guarantee either when I'm with her.

I pick up the discarded magazine. "They're saying your car is parked outside my house almost every night."

"Well, yes, that's because it is."

"So maybe we should stop for a bit."

Mickenlee stands, pushing back her chair until it skids across the floor. "I don't want to stop, Decklee. We shouldn't have to."

Of course we shouldn't, but that isn't my fault. Mickenlee has known exactly who I am from the moment she knocked on my door in the rain. She knows what I want, and she knows it comes with a price. I'm always going to love her; there's not a world where I don't. Most days it feels like we were made for each other, but if I have to let her go to keep us safe, I'll do it. Just for a little while.

"Other people live like this, you know." Mickenlee turns back to the stove, flipping a pancake with more force than necessary. "There are places for us, communities that wouldn't tear apart every aspect of your life. Markell does it. He and Derrick are happy."

I resist the urge to point out that Markell has been blacklisted from every runway in the country for telling the world who he loves. "I know. I'm happy for him, but I can't do that."

"You *could*," Mickenlee snaps. "You could stop caring and we could live. Exactly like we are now."

It's not the first time she's said this, but it's the kind of idea only people like Mickenlee Hooper can entertain. She's never had to share a motel bathroom or play the same set over and over or claw her way out of a town that wanted to bury her. She would be fine if she left this industry. Her life might be better, even, but mine would be over.

"No," I say. "I can't. We'd lose everything."

"We wouldn't—"

"We *would*, Mick." I toss the magazine aside. "It doesn't matter what I want—there are real, powerful people out there who wouldn't let it happen."

Mickenlee scowls. "You're one of the most famous people in the country, Decklee, I think you'd be fine."

"No, they'd make an example of us. Maybe things would be different if I was some young, edgy, new artist, but I know my audience."

"Your audience loves you."

But they don't. They love the idea of me, this kind, generous, talented person I've carefully crafted for the last several decades, and that's not something I want to lose. But Mickenlee is looking at me with such raw optimism that for a minute, I desperately want to believe her, too. She takes my hand, winds her fingers through mine, and says, "Tell me what we should do, then. Tell me what the plan is, because I can't live like this forever."

I shake my head. "It's not that simple."

"It could be, though."

"But it's not. You want the truth, Mick? You want them to leave us alone? Get married."

She flinches, dropping my hand like I've slapped her. "What? No."

"You wanted a plan," I say. "There it is. Move in with someone else, throw a big, fancy wedding. They'll forget all about me."

I'm surprised the words come out at all, like the idea doesn't bottom out my stomach. Mickenlee's face is a mask of icy disgust. "That's horrible, Decklee. That's the opposite of what I'm asking for."

"It doesn't matter. You're asking for something that can't happen. We can't be together like that in public. We can't announce it to the world and expect things to be normal."

"I don't want normal." She rubs a hand down her face and across the back of her neck. "I just want you. This isn't . . . Who would I even ask?"

The answer comes so quickly I'm surprised I haven't thought of it before. "James," I say. "You could marry James."

"*Your* James?"

My face twists in involuntary disgust. "He's not mine."

Mickenlee turns her back on me, hands braced against the counter, but the more I think about it, the more it makes sense. James and I have been on and off for years. Mickenlee is supposed to be my best friend; it's only natural for them to fall for each other. I know James only puts up with me because he gets a raise every time we go out. I wonder how much Ricky would pay to get Mickenlee out of the public eye completely, to make her someone else's problem.

"It could work," I say. "If he could get everyone to leave us alone for a while, we can figure something else out."

Mickenlee's knuckles whiten on the counter. I know she hates the suggestion, but I hate it more—the thought of her on someone else's arm, in someone else's bed, whispering secrets to them in the dark. I set her up, poised her to take the fall, and still, I resent her for it. I come around the table to stand next to her and take her face in my hands. Her eyes widen ever so slightly and I remember wanting to fall into them the first time we met, to know what it was like to swim in her. I trace my thumb over her cheekbone once, twice.

"You know I love you, right?" I ask. "I would never hurt you. And I would never ask you to consider this if I thought there was another choice." I watch her lips part, waiting until she's unsteady and trembling under my hands before leaning in. "Do you love me?"

Mickenlee's eyelids flutter. Her brow furrows and she nods, just like I knew she would.

"Then *trust me*, Mick. This would fix everything. No one would question it, no one would question *us*. Please," I add with a quiet desperation I know will break her. "Please think about it and I'll never ask you for anything again."

My fingers catch in her hair, and I remember pulling pins

from her curls at the Grammys years ago. I remember her coming undone in my arms.

"Never?" Her voice catches, and when I kiss her, I feel her hesitation die on her lips. She fists a hand in the front of my shirt, pulling me against her, and I know I've won before we break apart.

"Never," I say.

This time, I know she believes me. I've learned to twist the truth in subtle, intangible ways and find all the vulnerable places no one thinks to guard. I learned it from her—trick after trick plucked from Mickenlee Hooper's brilliant lyrical repertoire. Because we're special. Because I don't have a choice.

Because I think this is the only way for me to truly have everything.

TWENTY-NINE

Darren

¶ cry on the walk home, just tuck my chin into my collar and let every piece of anger and frustration go. The tears are hot on my cheeks, damp as the summer rain. When I turn into my driveway, I try very hard to pretend I haven't noticed Kendall trailing me the entire way home.

I know he lingers in the street as I yank open the front door. I know he rolls down his window and tries to say something else, but I ignore him. It was wrong to yell at him like that, to blame him for all the selfish, broken parts of me, but I want to live in this anger a little longer. I want to see if it consumes me this time. So instead of looking over my shoulder or reaching out, I just slip inside and slam the front door behind me.

The rest of the weekend passes in a slow, relentless crawl as the last week of summer draws to a close.

I sleep through most of the next afternoon, only waking when Mom sets a plate of scrambled eggs on my bedside table.

She spends the rest of the day cleaning, vigorously scrubbing dishes and mopping the floors so she doesn't have to think about Monday's appointment. I know she's trying to stay positive, but without the time capsule to look forward to or the promise of a prize, it's hard for me to think about anything else.

On Monday, we drive to the hospital together. I hold her hand the entire way back and we spend the rest of the day orbiting through the house in tense, nervous silence. When Dr. Vij finally calls to tell us the tumor is benign, it's like the world tilts under my feet. I throw myself into Mom's arms with so much force she almost drops the phone.

"This is unnecessary!" she groans. But I inhale the familiar scent of her strawberry shampoo, I feel her heartbeat through her worn T-shirt, strong and steady and *alive*, and I think this is the most necessary thing in the world.

We're both half crying, half laughing when we break apart, and for a single, spellbinding minute, I don't remember what was so important about this weekend.

That night almost feels like old times. Mom cracks open a six-dollar bottle of wine and turns on "Whiskey Red" so loud I feel the bass reverberating in my rib cage. But when she holds out a spatula, motioning for me to sing along, the words don't come. Because even though I'm here with her, I'm still thinking about Kendall onstage at The Bridge, how he made everyone sing that song for me. I'm thinking of the flash drives scattered across the South, an unfinished rhyme I still don't completely understand, and the single missing brooch from the museum collection.

I'm thinking about how, even though someone found the time capsule, we still haven't heard those new songs.

I see Mike Fratt when Mom turns on the news later and it's a testament to my self-control that I don't chuck the bottle of wine at the screen. He's smiling through a mouth of too-white teeth, hands settled lazily on his hips as he talks to a reporter. The headline stamped across the bottom of the screen reads UNIVERSITY OF ALABAMA SENIOR FINDS DECKLEE CASSEL TIME CAPSULE, WINS THREE MILLION DOLLARS.

"Good for him," Mom says, kicking her feet up on the coffee table. "I'm glad someone found it."

I scowl at the TV. "*He* didn't find it. His fans did."

It's been almost two days since Mike Fratt won and he has yet to release anything off the new album. I keep expecting the estate to do it eventually, to drop something big now that the quest is over, but they've gone silent, too.

Mom glances toward me as I cross my arms, still resisting the urge to put my fist through Mike Fratt's spray-tanned face. "Well, I bet you had more fun," she says. "When are you going to tell me about it? I'm dying to know."

I shrug, gaze fixed stubbornly ahead. "It was fine. We didn't win."

Even now that her appointment has passed, I can't fully articulate all the things I felt on that trip. Maybe Mike Fratt didn't deserve to win, but I sure as hell don't either.

A few days later, I go back to work at Bob's. I usually ask him to cut my hours in August so I can get ready for school, but now I'm wondering if I can afford to. I can't put off my applications much longer, but there are so many things to pay for—tuition, housing, meals, books. It's too much.

Kendall isn't on the schedule at all that day. I force myself to ignore the empty place behind the register where he usually sits, but when Bob comes back from lunch and accidentally knocks over the boxes I'd meticulously stacked in the back, I glance instinctively over my shoulder for Kendall. He should be here now, biting back a grin as Bob steps over the mess and carries on like nothing happened. He should be shaking his head and pointing out that we don't get paid enough for this before kneeling down to help me pick up.

But he's not here, of course. I spend the rest of my shift with Bob in awkward, heavy silence, resisting the urge to text Kendall a debrief of everything that happened since we last spoke.

I know I was wrong to push him away. I try to tell myself it's fine, that I shouldn't have gotten that close in the first place, but the guilt sits like a stone in the pit of my stomach. I don't know how to unwind this tangled mess of feelings. I don't know how I would begin to explain all the things that led me to that moment in the parking lot, and I don't know if I deserve to have Kendall listen.

I spend the rest of the week working, trying to pull together a feature for the new year. Usually I'd ask Carla for help, just sit myself on her porch until we found the heart of the story together, but I've hardly seen her since getting home. Sometimes I catch a glimpse of her in the garden or coming home from running errands and wonder if she's avoiding me, too.

My only distraction is my *Mayberry Unpublished* account. I

call Emily as soon as she gets back to town and ask if she wants to do a photo shoot behind the library. There's less pressure to be perfect here, in the confines of a very imperfect social media platform, so I don't feel the weight of every crushing expectation as I jot down notes on my way across town.

"I feel like I should be the one interviewing you," Emily says after I finish staging the shots. She piles her hair on top of her head with one hand and scrolls through the photos with the other. "You're the one who had this big, life-changing adventure."

Emily's grandparents are the only people I know who own property outside of Mayberry. She always comes back from Lake Michigan tan and blond and bursting at the seams with stories far more interesting than this place ever allows. This year is the only time I might have her beat.

I shake my head. "I wouldn't call it life-changing. I'm still here, aren't I?"

Emily shrugs. I'm close enough to catch a whiff of her vanilla perfume, to feel the warmth of her bare arm inches from mine, and for a second, I feel something stir in my stomach. An old, rusty whisper of a suggestion. But the idea of her doesn't ache as much as it used to. It doesn't consume me like thoughts of Kendall do, winding their way into my dreams until I wake up heavy with guilt and reaching for him.

I want to find him. I want to apologize, but I'm still not quite sure how to put everything I'm feeling into words. What happens if I confess all the terrible, selfish thoughts tucked deep inside my chest? What happens if he can't forgive them? I'm slowly accepting the fact that I'm not getting out of Mayberry anytime soon, but I can't stand the thought of losing Kendall, too.

I pass the high school on my walk home, a flat brick building set against a dusty football field and a faded country road. Someone is mowing the lawn up front, but there are no cars in the parking lot. It's just me. I look over both shoulders once before slipping in the back door.

The hallway smells clean, freshly waxed and so different than the usual mixture of sweat, rubber, and cafeteria food that it takes me a second to orient myself. There's my old locker, down the first hallway, right next to Emily's. There's the gym. There's the Mayberry County High School notable graduates wall, two lonely pictures hanging above my head.

I know which photo they have of Decklee; I've walked by it every day for the last three years. She's fourteen, grinning and wild beneath a mane of flyaway curls. Her smile is wide, unabashed, and gap-toothed, and I wonder how anyone could have looked at that girl and thought she belonged here.

"What was the point?"

I don't mean to say it out loud, but I don't know who else to ask. Why create this quest? Why trick me into coming back here, empty-handed and alone? Hiding two clues in Nashville doesn't make sense, and even though I've listened to that last song time and time again, analyzed every lyric, I still don't know how it would lead anyone to DCR Records. Again, I think of that last flash drive, buried in the dirt in Tupelo. *Four to go.*

I have to be missing something. The piece that brings the story together, the tie that binds all my loose ends. Or maybe

I'm not. I lost, didn't I? I failed. And now I'm here again, stuck in the same place I was at the beginning of this summer. Such is the loop of Mayberry.

Such is my fate.

♫♪♫

CARLA IS BAKING something with chocolate. I smell it from the sidewalk as I turn into my driveway, but I hesitate before opening the front door. Mom is stuck in an admin meeting for the rest of the afternoon. Madison is still at camp. Emily is baby-sitting her younger brothers, and the idea of being alone in this house crawls over my skin.

I sit down on the front step, ignoring the burn of hot cement against my thighs, and pull out my phone. There's only one person I want to call right now. It's been almost a week since I've seen Kendall. He's been suspiciously absent from Bob's, leaving me to work through the hottest, most exhausting week of summer alone. I would have been more annoyed if I didn't absolutely deserve it. But that also means I've had a lot of time to think about what I want to say, and even though I don't entirely know how to say it yet, I know I want to try.

Summer is drawing to a close. My senior year starts in a few weeks. I might never be able to pull myself out of this town completely, but if I really am stuck here, I know exactly who I want at my side.

When I finally build up the courage to call, the phone rings for so long I'm afraid he's not going to pick up. But then there's a click at the end of the line and Kendall's voice is soft in my ear.

"Hi."

That's it, a single word, but I sag against the porch. "Hi," I say. Silence follows, Kendall clearly waiting for me to elaborate. I take a deep breath and, before this moment of clarity fades, blurt, "Are you around? I missed you at work this week and I'd really like to see you. I want . . ." I trail off before finding my voice again. "I want to apologize for all the things I said."

"Oh." Kendall hesitates, and for a second, I think he's going to tell me no. I think I would deserve it. Then he exhales and says, "Sure. Are you going to come in?"

I look up. "Come in where?"

Carla's door creaks open and there's Kendall, standing on the porch with his phone pressed to his ear. "Over here, obviously."

"What the hell?" I stand and pick my way across the yard. "What are you doing?"

"Testing a new recipe. I told you she likes me."

He stands back to let me through the front door. The smell of chocolate only grows stronger as I follow Kendall down the hall and into the kitchen. Carla straightens when we enter, muffin tin clutched in one hand. She's in a pink dress today, cream-colored cardigan hanging casually from one shoulder.

"Darren," she says. "I haven't seen you all week. Do you want some tea?"

I shake my head, resisting the urge to point out that I'm not entirely responsible for our lack of contact. I clasp my hands behind my back and watch Kendall slide into his seat at the kitchen table, unsure of where to begin.

"So," he says, like he's reading my mind. "You want to apologize."

"Um, yes." I swallow over the lump of nerves in my throat and glance at Carla, who's still measuring flour for another batch of muffins.

"Oh, don't mind me," she says. "I'm not even here."

Kendall nods in agreement. "Anything you have to say, you can say in front of my friend Carla."

"Oh my god." I drag a hand down my face. "Okay, fine. You want the truth? I did start that quest for the money. That was always the goal. I wanted to hear the new songs, sure, but I wanted three million dollars more. I was going to use it to pay Mom's medical bills and get out of Mayberry, and the whole weekend, I felt like I was getting sign after sign that I was on the right track. I was confident. I knew where to go, things kept working out, and I was trusting myself for the first time in . . . ever? Maybe? So when I was wrong at the end and the time capsule wasn't here, it just made me wonder about all the other things I was so sure about that weekend and how I was probably wrong about them, too."

It just keeps coming, one truth after the other. I feel Carla watching me over my shoulder as Kendall leans forward in his seat and decide it's now or never.

"It just feels so black-and-white sometimes," I continue. "Like, I can either have the career I want, or I can be from Mayberry. I don't think there's a way for me to have everything, but I also think you're right. I wouldn't be who I am if I didn't grow up here. I wouldn't have my friends or my life or you, and that's not something I want to be ashamed of. I always said when I got to college, I would just tell everyone I was from Vermont or something, because what does it matter? It's not like they'd care about this place. But I think I care about it, actually. Like, yes, this town is slow and monotonous and *frustrating*, but I missed you this week. I missed doing inventory and throwing Cheetos at the birds by the dumpsters, and that's not something I could do in Vermont. That's something I like about here."

Kendall opens his mouth to speak, but I hold up a hand. I can't stop now. I have to get everything out before I lose my nerve or give in to the tears forming in the back of my throat.

"I still want to leave," I say. "I still want to go to college and see the world and learn about things outside this town. Maybe I won't get to go next year. Or maybe I'll go to a state school or take online classes and figure it out. I could be okay with that, I think, but I'm not okay with hurting you, or making you feel like you aren't just as important to me. I've spent my entire life getting ready to leave. I didn't even really know you before this weekend and we've been friends for years. How fucked up is that? So I'm sorry for pushing you away last weekend and I'm sorry for not calling you sooner. You're not nothing, Kendall. If I'm stuck in Mayberry for the rest of my life, you're, like, the only person I'd want here with me."

I let out a small, shaky breath and wonder if he can tell how much my hands are trembling behind my back. "Okay. That's all, I think."

There's a second where no one moves, every word hanging

in the air between us. Then Kendall stands, coming around the side of the table until we're face-to-face, and I barely have time to look up before he pulls me into his chest. I bury my face in the soft fabric of his shirt and exhale a choked, relieved sob.

"I'm sorry," I say again. "I was so focused on getting out, I thought I could be Decklee Cassel or something."

Kendall runs a hand over my hair. "I'll say this a thousand times, Purchase, but I don't think Decklee Cassel is a very good role model."

"Why? Because she left?"

"No. Because according to you, everyone left *her*, and I don't care what you say, I don't think you want to do this alone."

When Kendall releases me, it's like a weight lifts from my shoulders. He's right. We built something solid last weekend—a home that's not exactly physical but still as much a part of me as the worn bricks of my own house.

"Well." Carla sets a folded dish towel on the counter. "That was very dramatic."

I pull away and swipe the back of my hand across my face. I almost forgot she was still here. She's standing with one hip braced against the counter, eyebrows lifted, and for a second, something about the expression sticks in my memory. The feeling vanishes as soon as it comes, and I sink into the open chair next to Kendall as he pours himself another cup of tea.

Despite our closure, there's still a loose thread here, some part of the puzzle I can't figure out. I try to sort through it as Carla slides a tin of freshly baked muffins in front of us.

"Are you two staying for lunch?" she asks, shrugging out of

her cardigan and tossing it over the back of a chair. "When is your mother home, Darren?"

"Not until later," I say. "I was going to—"

I stop as Carla turns back toward the table. Without the cardigan, I can see the rest of her dress clearly—the smooth pink fabric, the cap sleeves, the rounded neckline. I've seen her wear it dozens of times on dozens of different occasions, but the thing that catches my eye now isn't the dress at all. It's the brooch pinned to her collar, a ruby-encrusted pin in the shape of a single, blooming rose.

I clutch Kendall's forearm as my stomach bottoms out. *The brooch.* The same one Decklee wore to the 1976 Oscars, immortalized in that photo at the Brentwood House. The same one missing from the museum display, the one I assumed was lost to time. But it's not lost. It's hers.

Carla lifts an eyebrow, still waiting for an answer, but I can't speak. I see it now that I know what I'm looking for. It's impossible not to. The high cheekbones, the piercing blue eyes, the mischievous tilt to her small mouth. The face that was only ever captured halfway—behind a hand, under a hat, turned away from the camera.

"Oh my god," I whisper, voice hoarse. "You're Mickenlee Hooper."

THIRTY

Decklee
Indianapolis, 1986

The day we fall apart, I'm in Indianapolis, running a sound check for the opening night of my latest tour.

It's supposed to be a party, a celebration of the last year of hard work, but all I'm thinking about is how Mickenlee isn't here. How she's probably downtown right now, watching James Brody get down on one knee in front of a few conveniently placed cameras. I know she's doing it for me. I know she's doing it *because* of me, but that doesn't stop jealousy from sinking claws into my skin the longer I think about it.

That feeling drives me through the rest of the sound check, and when I finish the last song, I look down to find Markell waving at me from the track. He's wearing something too bright and too clean for a Midwest fairground, but I don't care. I fling myself into his arms the second I get offstage, ignoring the stagehands still attempting to unwind my mic.

"Hi," I whisper. "I'm so glad you're here. Thank you for coming."

Markell hugs me back, tight. "Yes, well. I'm famously un-employable at the moment thanks to Ronald Reagan."

"Ronald Reagan can go fuck himself." I tug off my mic and hand it to one of the hovering stagehands. Then I take Markell's arm and together we wander down the track.

The fair doesn't officially open until tomorrow, but I can hear the steady hum of people setting up booths on the other side of the fence and the sounds of livestock getting unloaded from trailers. The stands are empty except for a few lone light-ing designers making last-minute checks before the show.

"How's Derrick?" I ask Markell as we come to a stop halfway down the track.

"Good. How's Mickenlee? Where is she, by the way?"

There's the jealousy again, a low pang in the pit of my stom-ach. "She's fine. She'll be back soon, she's just out getting proposed to."

Markell's brow furrows. "What?"

"She didn't tell you?"

That's strange. We both tell Markell everything. But I've also had plenty of opportunity to tell him our plan and still kept it to myself. I try to keep walking, but Markell holds out a hand.

"I'm sorry, who is proposing?"

I shrug as casually as I can, trying to keep my voice light. "James Brody."

"James from your label?"

"Mm-hmm."

Markell stops, heels digging into the dirt track as his eyes narrow on me. "And whose idea was that, Decklee?"

I hate how he's looking at me, like after everything, I'm still the villain. *Cold, flighty, selfish Decklee Cassel.* I toss my hair over one shoulder and keep walking. "Don't say it like that. She wants to."

"No," Markell says. "She loves you. There's a difference."

"Shh!" I look over both shoulders before grabbing his sleeve and hauling him off the track, into the shaded tunnel that cuts through the stands. Dust still clings to the walls, but at least it's empty in here, away from prying eyes. "I'm not making her do anything."

But Markell just shakes his head, continuing like I haven't spoken. "How would that even work? Is he just supposed to be okay with a payout? Is she still going to write your love songs? I mean, what is the plan here?"

"I don't *know!*" My voice is too loud, echoing off the walls. I drag a trembling hand down my face. "I don't know. I have a show tomorrow. I leave on tour after that. Everyone is watching me right now and I am trying to protect her."

"No, you're protecting yourself."

"So what if I am, that's not a crime! I have wanted this my entire life, Markell. Everything I've ever done has been so I can have *this*. You don't understand, I would lose everything."

I so rarely see Markell angry that it takes a second for me to recognize it now. He lets out a cold, hollow laugh. "I already lost everything," he says. "All my clients, all my shows. No one's hiring me—of course I understand."

"But you chose that." I'm pacing now, back and forth in the cramped tunnel, unable to keep still. "You chose to make your show into some political statement, and you chose to make yourself a target."

"I have been a target my entire life, Decklee!" he cries. "If it wasn't this, they would have found something else. I know you worked hard. I know they weren't always fair to you, but we are *not* the same."

We both come to a halt on opposite sides of the tunnel, breathing hard. "Then what am I supposed to do?" I ask. "I can't just—" My voice cracks and I bite down on the inside of my cheek. "This will work. It'll be fine."

Markell is still looking at me like I'm a stranger, like we haven't spent our entire lives chasing the same thing. "No one is saying you have to make a big statement," he says. "But you can't ask Mickenlee to fight those battles for you either. That's not a relationship."

"Oh, you find a partner and now you know everything about relationships?"

"No, of course not. But I know you and you're wrong about this."

Maybe I am, but I don't need a lecture. He has no idea what I'm dealing with. I smooth back my hair and straighten, forcing my breathing to steady as I stare him down across the tunnel. "That's none of your business. I hired you to design this show, not tell me what to do."

His lip curls. "Fuck you."

But I'm already stalking out of the tunnel, heading backstage. "If you can't do your job, I'll find someone who can."

By the time I stumble into my dressing room, my feet ache from my new suede boots and the tears I swallowed earlier threaten to reappear. What the hell does Markell know? He can hate me all he wants, he can cast silent judgments on my life and my relationship, but I don't need his opinion. I've never needed anyone.

I slam the door behind me and I'm about to collapse in my chair when I see it's already occupied by Mickenlee. "Oh!" I sag against the wall, relieved to see her back, and tug off one boot. "How did it go? Let me see the ring."

I know she sees me in the mirror, but she doesn't move. She just sits in my chair, eyes fixed on her clasped hands, and it's another minute before she whispers, "I couldn't do it."

I tug off the other boot and toss it into the corner. "Couldn't do what?"

"Marry him." Mickenlee looks at me then, and there's ice creeping across her expression. "I thought I could, for you. I know we talked about it, but then he asked me and I realized all the things he'd expect and all the roles I'd have to play and I just couldn't. I'm sorry."

"I . . ." It takes me a minute to fully process. "Okay. Does Ricky know?"

Mickenlee shakes her head. "I came straight here. James might have called him. I don't know, he was . . . not happy."

Of course he's not. We've dragged James around for years, made him the other half of my joke. I know he takes Ricky's money. I know he gets more attention when he's with me, but this was supposed to be something permanent. I wonder, briefly, if James's pride would be hurt enough for him to end this entirely, to run straight to the papers and tell them everything he knows. It would sell well, I think.

People love destruction when it isn't happening to them.

"Okay," I say again. "It's fine, I'll talk to him. We'll figure something out."

A sad smile flits across Mickenlee's face as she watches herself in the mirror. "Do you love me, Cleo?"

I flinch. That's the kind of question that has claws, a double-edged truth I never know how to navigate. "Yes. Of course."

"Would you leave with me if I asked you to? Would you take a break?"

I laugh. "Sure, as long as I'm back in time for tour."

"That's not what I'm asking."

"Then tell me what you're asking, Mick. I can't read your mind." I shrug off my jacket, careful not to wrinkle any of the feathers carefully sewn along the back. "I have a show tomorrow night. We have an album to finish. Where do you think we're going?"

"I don't know." She's so still she could be a statue, one of the shiny, gilded awards that lives on my mantel. "But I can't do this anymore."

"You can't do what? The tour? Fine! Take a break if you need to. Go home. No one expects you to be here the whole time."

There's a tear in the left sleeve of my jacket; I'll need to get Markell to fix it later. It's another thing to add to my list, another thing to think about, and I'm annoyed Mickenlee is choosing now to panic. We had a solution. We had a way out and she said no.

"I'm not talking about the tour, Cleo," Mickenlee says. "I'm talking about us."

That makes me pause. I look up from the jacket in my lap, and for the first time, I notice how tired she looks. There are dark circles stamped under her eyes and her usually tailored dress hangs too loose off her shoulders. Hollow. That's a better word for it, like someone reached inside and scooped her out.

"Are you . . . ?" I can hardly get the words out. "What are you saying?"

"I'm saying you could come with me." Mickenlee turns away from the mirror at last. "We could go anywhere, Cleo."

"Don't call me that."

"But aren't you *tired*?"

Am I? I haven't stopped moving since I crept out of my bedroom window and hitchhiked to Texarkana. I haven't wanted to. Staying still gets you killed in this industry. Complacency doesn't work. The only reason I have a career at all is because I haven't stopped, and I'm not sure what will happen if I let myself now. I don't know who I am without this.

"No," I whisper. "I'm not. I can't leave."

Mickenlee's hands are cold, fingers desperately winding through mine. "Please, Cleo, I am begging you—"

"That is *not* my name!" I yank my hand from hers. "I'm about to leave on tour. We've been planning this for over a year and we have another album due in October. What the hell am I supposed to do with this? Seriously, what do you want me to say?"

"That you love me! That you care about something other than *this*."

"And what if I don't? This is my life, Mick, you know that!"

It comes out harsher than I mean it to. I watch the words hit her square in the chest, but I don't take it back. I do love her. I do care, but Mickenlee Hooper grew up in the Nashville suburbs. She went to Ivy League schools and bought designer dresses and had her uncle nepotism her into this career. It doesn't negate her talent or drive, but she doesn't know what it's like to be nothing and no one, or to have every door slam in her face because of it.

The silence stretches too long before Mickenlee stands. I feel it hang in the air between us, ready to shatter, as she tucks her hair behind her ears and grabs her purse from the ground. "Is that really how you feel?"

I turn back to my jacket, running a finger across the tear in the fabric. "It doesn't matter how I feel. I can't leave."

"And what if I don't need you to come with me?"

"Then go." I wave a dismissive hand over my shoulder. "Just close the door on the way out. I have things to do."

Mickenlee won't actually leave, I know it. We've fought before and each time she ends up back in my bed, trembling and breathless and swearing this is *the last time*. I don't think we could exist without each other at this point. We've grown together in too many ways, torn each other up from the inside out. She's a part of me, a beating heart right in the center of my chest, so I know when she walks toward the door that this fight isn't permanent either.

"You won't always have this, you know," she says. "You won't always have them."

I can never look at her when she's like this. I shake my head and go back to sorting through my station, cataloging the costumes for this weekend. "I'll see you tomorrow, Mick."

She lets out a small, breathy laugh. "No, you won't."

She doesn't come to my room that night. It takes me hours to fall asleep, alone in the dark, but I don't think anything of it until she misses sound check the next morning. She's not in the stands, not on the buses, not in my dressing room. I search the entire fairgrounds before giving in and calling her. When she doesn't answer, I call Ricky, and when he doesn't know either, I get mad.

So this is what she wants to do? She wants to play games and make me come to her? Fine.

I borrow a car that morning and drive five hours south, straight through Kentucky, until I hit Nashville. I storm inside the house, calling for her in every room, but Mickenlee isn't there. It's empty and dark, no sign that she's been here since we both left last week. Dread curls in my stomach as I get back in the car and reverse the trip, a sinking, swallowing feeling that consumes every thought. By the time I get back, my show is about to start and people are frantic.

I am, too.

Markell is backstage, steaming my first costume, and I'm so relieved to see him still here that I have to press a hand against the wall for support. "Markell!"

"Whoa." He holds out a hand as I stumble into him. "Where

the hell have you been? Everyone's looking for you."

He tries to hand me the costume, but I brush it aside. "Where's Mickenlee? She's not here. She's not at home."

Markell blinks, eyes widening at the realization. "You . . . drove to Tennessee?"

Of course I did. Because Mickenlee's gone. Because she's playing games I don't have time for. Because I need her with me now. I knock the steamer out of Markell's hand and step closer. "Where is she?"

"I don't know."

"Liar." I've known Markell most of my life. I've lived with him, fought with him, worked with him. I love him in the same fierce, twisted way I love Mickenlee, which is how I know with absolute certainty that he is lying to me now. "Where is she?" I repeat. "Where did she go?"

Something tightens around my chest, pulling the air out of the room. I can't get enough of it. I don't remember how. Mickenlee would never leave without telling Markell where she was going. She would never leave him like this, and if she told him and not me . . .

I stumble forward, gripping Markell's shoulders as my knees give out. He catches me before I hit the ground, but I can't move. I can't breathe. My pulse is a relentless, rapid drumbeat in my ears, panic flooding my veins with each traitorous heartbeat. Maybe this is the final breaking point, one sacrifice too many, one step too far.

"Please," I gasp. It's the only thing I can say, over and over, pressed into Markell's chest. "Please, you have to tell me."

There are people gathering behind me; I hear the rushed, frantic conversations like they're coming from very far away.

"Decklee?"

"There she is."

"She's on in ten, why isn't she dressed?"

"Stop!" I feel Markell wave someone away. "Does it look like she's going onstage right now? Just give us a minute."

But the sound of his voice snaps me back to reality. I realize I'm crying as I lift my head and inhale a shuddering gasp. "I have a show."

"No." Markell's hands tighten around my shoulders. "You don't have to, Decklee. Just breathe."

But I want to. That's what he and Mickenlee will never understand. I can hear the crowd now, a relentless roar filling the stands, thunder through my veins. It's what I practiced for. It's what I worked for and it's why Mickenlee left. I push Markell away and wipe my face with both hands. "Get out."

"Decklee . . ." He reaches for me, face stricken. I don't care.

"Get *out*," I say again. "You're fired, Markell. I don't want you here."

I turn and snatch my costume from the floor. Someone helps me into it in the wings. Someone hands me a microphone and wipes the last of my tears and swipes on some lipstick. I don't know who. I don't care. I curl my hands into fists and march toward the stage. My feet ache in the new boots, yesterday's blisters reopening as I walk. I wonder if this is what winning feels like.

One more step and I'm there, standing under the lights. I

pick up my guitar from a stand in the back and nod at the band already waiting for me. Then I smile into the microphone and hold my head high.

"Are y'all ready for a show?"

Are you ready to love me?

I give the best performance of my career that night, to a screaming fairground in the dusty Indiana heat, to a crowd of people who want nothing more than to drink me in. When I finish and stumble offstage in another pair of beautiful, glamorous boots, Markell is gone. Back to Paris, probably, or New York. Somewhere far away and far from me. Mickenlee is gone, too, and there's nothing left to prove she existed. She's the ghost in my photographs, the voice in my songs, the constant shadow at my back.

She's gone, and I think, for the first time, that I don't know how to do any of this alone.

THIRTY-ONE

Darren

I t's never quiet in Carla's house. There's always something—the beep of the oven timer, the swell of the radio, the rustle of dry wind through her garden outside. It's always undeniably alive, but now the silence presses in on me from all sides as that one phrase echoes in my head again and again. *You're Mickenlee Hooper.*

I know I'm right. It's the same bone-deep certainty I felt all last weekend. I point across the kitchen toward Carla with one trembling finger. "That brooch," I say. "It's part of the Fansworth collection, isn't it? It's the only one missing from the museum."

Carla looks down. I watch her throat bob, a sharp up and down, but when she looks at me, her expression is blank. "I don't know what you mean."

"Are you being serious?"

I want to laugh. I want to scream. There are two images of her in my head right now, a double-vision blur I can't make sense of. There's Mickenlee Hooper, Vanderbilt graduate, Harvard Law School dropout, Grammy Award–winning lyricist. And then there's Carla, my neighbor. Carla, my *friend*, who bakes us scones and helped me through Mom's chemo and gardens in the middle of hot Arkansas summers.

Who I thought I knew.

I shake my head and try again. "Who are you?"

Carla's chin lifts and I see the flash of it again—the woman sprawled on the grass with Decklee in Memphis, sitting cross-legged next to her in an old porch swing. "My name," she says simply, "is Carla Krenik."

"That's not what I'm asking."

"I know exactly what you're asking, Darren. It's none of your business."

I'm gripping the table so hard my fingers ache, and I'm surprised to find that underneath the disbelief and incredulity is something that feels like betrayal. I tell Carla everything. I trust her as much as I trust Mom, more than I trust myself, and I'm just now realizing that I don't know her at all. She's looking at me with thinly veiled suspicion, like I'm a stranger instead of the same girl who spends most afternoons sipping homemade iced tea on her porch. It's not fair. There are so many things I want to ask, but the only question that comes out is "How?"

Carla rolls her eyes. I've seen her do that a hundred times, when I complain about a grade on a paper, when I talk about leaving Mayberry, but this time it feels pointed. It feels mean. She turns her back on us and picks up the tray of muffins. "Have you never heard of a stage name?"

"You have to know that's not the part of this I'm focused on."

I glance over my shoulder at Kendall for backup, but he looks just as surprised as I feel. "Okay," he says, pushing himself out of his seat. "Let me get this straight. You"—he points at Carla— "live here. You're Darren's neighbor, and, not going to lie, I kind of thought we were friends, so I'm a little offended that you never said something before. But you're telling me that the reason you're secretly loaded is because you wrote all those songs? You were the one in the papers? You have a *Grammy*?"

"I have fifteen." Carla picks up the tray of muffins and shoves it under Kendall's nose. "Do you want one?"

"What? No?" Kendall swats it away. "What the hell is going on?"

I have no idea. I run a hand through my hair, rings catching in a tangle near the back. *Here's your story.* The thought snags in my brain as I yank my hand free. This is what I'd been chasing on the road last weekend. This is the story I wanted to tell and now it's here, sitting in my lap. Finding Mickenlee Hooper decades after her disappearance? Forget Decklee's time capsule, people would want to read about *this*.

It's a story that might get me out.

"Why are you here?" I ask, unable to keep the bitter edge from my voice. "You're from Nashville. You have absolutely no connection to this town, but you've been here for . . . what? The last thirty years?"

Why would anyone choose this? Why would one of the most talented, beloved writers of the last fifty years just give that all up?

"You don't know how long I've been here," Carla says. "*Hand Me My Heart* didn't come out until '95. I was still working."

"Yes, but those weren't your songs. Your name was on that record and on *All the Colors* because of your contract, I'm assuming, but you didn't write them. I can tell. You and Decklee stopped working together years before everyone thought you did. Why?"

Carla turns away and the sun streaming through the kitchen window catches in her hair. It outlines her profile in stark, purposeful lines, and again I wonder how I missed it. How I stared at those pictures for so long without making the connection. "What do you want, Darren?" she asks. "What are you trying to do here?"

Again, I think of the story. I think what it would be like to know every detail of what happened between her and Decklee, how they came together, how they wrote the way they did, how they fell apart. I think about writing it down, crafting it into the perfect pitch, and sending it into the world. Something like that would change my life. It would absolutely ruin Carla's.

"Nothing," I say. "I'm not trying to do anything. I just want to understand."

I step forward, but she flinches away, back into the shadows. Her face is like steel—cold and unforgiving—and I wonder if, despite everything, she never really expected to be found out. I hold up both hands and try again. "You wrote those new songs, I know you did. Did you set up the time capsule hunt, too? Did you and Decklee do it together?"

"You think Decklee Cassel created that quest for anyone but

herself?" Carla sets the muffin tin down with a little too much force. "She doesn't work with anyone. She does whatever she wants exactly when she wants to do it. I had no idea what she was planning."

"But you still went back to her," I say. "You were the one who left, but you still agreed to write that new album. Why? What was the point?"

Kendall is standing between us now, shifting from foot to foot like he's anticipating a fight. He might get one. Carla has listened to me and Mom talk about Decklee Cassel and Mickenlee Hooper for years. She's seen us singing in the car, crying along to "Whiskey Red," and she never once said a single word. It makes me second-guess everything she's ever told me.

Carla doesn't answer. She just folds her arms and levels me with a frigid, piercing stare. "What do you want?"

It's the same question I've been asking myself for months, the same one I thought I figured out last weekend. Images of her and Decklee flash through my mind. Two girls pressed together without a care in the world, grinning under a wide Tennessee sky. Sitting side by side at the Grammys as the whole theater cheered. The headlines after the Oscars and all the implications the two of them avoided for years. *Here it is*, I think. The real reason I wanted to find Mickenlee Hooper. The real question I've wanted to ask since the day I heard the longing ache behind "Whiskey Red."

"I was right," I say, half to myself. "You went back to her for the same reason you left. Because you loved her."

I look up, but Carla's expression is unreadable. She feels

like ice, the corners of her mouth turned down, and when she speaks again, there's a carefully contained fury pulsing under every word.

"I think it's time for you both to leave."

"What?" I reach out, trying to catch her arm. "Carla—"

"I'm not a story, Darren." She herds us toward the door with surprising ferocity for someone who'd be two inches shorter than me without heels. "I'm not one of your leads. You want answers? Fine. I came to this town because it's the last place anybody would look for me. *Especially* Decklee Cassel. I like it here. I built a life, and you don't get to take that from me for your fifteen minutes of fame."

Kendall's hand is on my arm, pulling me back, but I'm frozen in the hall, unable to move as the words crash over me. Is that really what she thinks? Is that how she's always seen me—rash and careless and totally destructive? *You are*, whispers a voice in the back of my head, *you always have been*. Even now, my first thought had been about my story, about all the different ways I could use this revelation to get the things I want.

I shake my head, trying desperately to clear it. "You're my friend, Carla. I wouldn't—"

"Wouldn't you?" she snaps. "Wouldn't you do anything to get out of here, Darren? Haven't you told me that for years?"

She flings open the front door and practically shoves me and Kendall onto the porch. "Please," I try again. "I'm sorry, I shouldn't have said that. I'm just trying to understand what's going on."

"You and everybody else."

She starts to close the door and my patience snaps. "I'm not Decklee Cassel, Carla!"

The world around us goes very still. I hear Kendall suck in a breath through his teeth, feel the hot blaze of the sun at my back, but I don't move. Standing in the doorway like this, Carla looks like a picture, like a clipping of a girl from the past, like everything I've been chasing for the last seventeen years. She gives us both one last dismissive look. "Have a good summer, Darren."

And she slams the door in my face.

THIRTY-TWO

Decklee
Nashville, 2022

I write a song in the waiting room of the Vanderbilt University Medical Center, and this time, the words don't come.

I know the quiet that accompanies news like this—the lowered voices, the kind eyes. I saw it with Ricky years ago when the doctors read him his diagnosis. He laughed in their faces and died a week later, so when they tell me mine, I know what to do. I sit, I listen, I thank them for their time. I fold my hands in the back of the car on the way home, and then, when I'm alone in that vast empty house, I shatter every dish in the cabinet, throwing them against the wall over and over until there's nothing left.

Not fair. This isn't fair.

I gave up everything for this. I did everything right. I lost people, I pushed them away, I learned to live without the other halves of my heart because this is what I wanted. I climbed every mountain they put in front of me, conquered every single obstacle, and this is how it ends? With me spluttering out? Fading?

I think I've always been afraid of this, of leaving a legacy that can't stand the test of time. Ricky's funeral was grand—rich and wonderful and packed with every important person the music industry had to offer. Because he was *Ricky Grasso* and he made you a star. But that was two years ago. People don't talk about him anymore, because there are younger, better managers in town, ones with résumés twice as long. He was a flash. He was lightning. And I want to burn forever.

I clutch the phone to my chest for a long time before dialing. It's entirely possible Markell won't pick up. I certainly wouldn't if our situations were reversed. I cut him out after that show in Indianapolis, unable to look at him without seeing her. Now my assistants go through his assistants to order new costumes and red-carpet gowns and we see each other once or twice a year in passing. I can't think about it too long without feeling like my heart is going to squeeze out of my chest. I can't face how much of our situation is my fault, so when the ringing finally stops and someone on the other end of the line says, "Hello?" I almost don't believe it's real.

"Markell." I slide down the wall until I'm sitting amid the shattered contents of my kitchen. "Hi."

I don't know how long he'll stay with me. I don't know why he even answered, so I tuck my knees into my chest and tell him everything. It pours out of me, this vicious, raging fountain of past regrets, and by the time I'm done, I'm breathless and angry and wishing, for the hundredth time, that I wasn't so completely alone.

"I'm sorry," I say when I finish. "I don't know why I'm telling you this, but I'm . . . I wondered if you were in town."

I hear him inhale on the other end of the line. I want to reach through the phone and grab the sound, clutch it close to my chest to remember when he hangs up. "I'm in New York right now," he says. "We're about to go upstate for our daughter's birthday."

"Oh. Right." Because Markell has a real family. He has people who love him the way he deserves to be loved and he hasn't thought of me in years. I squeeze my fist around a jagged piece of glass, ignoring the bloody sting in my palm. "That sounds like fun. How's Derrick?"

"He's good. Thank you for the wedding gift, by the way," he adds. "It's the best espresso machine we've ever had."

I let out a choked laugh. "It better be, seeing what I paid for it."

Markell laughs, too, and for a minute, I can trick myself into thinking that he's here with me. That he never left. "I can come down this week," he says.

"No." I'm immediately embarrassed I asked. "It's okay, I just . . . I didn't want to be alone. But it's fine, honestly. I feel better."

He's silent for a minute and I wonder if he expects me to cry. I wonder if I *should* cry. I haven't been able to since that night in Indianapolis, and even now, with time dripping through my fingers, I don't feel anything other than comfortably numb.

"Okay," he says. "Do you have someone else who can come by tonight?"

"Of course," I lie. "Have fun upstate."

"I will."

Neither of us know how to end this. There aren't words to describe what we are to each other now. I hang up first before throwing my phone across the kitchen.

I try to write a song that night, surrounded by broken glass and shattered promises, but the words stick in my throat. I used to think I could live forever, that whatever legacy I left behind would transcend myself. Now I wonder if that was a lie, too.

I spend the rest of the week like that, trying to put myself into words, and when the doorbell rings after days of solitude, I'm not thinking about Markell or our phone call. But he's there when I open the door, carry-on suitcase at his side, and for a brief, terrible second, I think I'm hallucinating. They told me this would happen eventually, that I'd start to see things that aren't there.

I grip the door with one hand. "Hi."

"Hi." He looks me up and down, taking me in from head to toe. "You look good."

That's not true. I look terrible. I look like I've spent the last week on my kitchen floor, tearing page after page out of my notebook and trying not to step on glass. I look like someone who's been told they're going to die. "Why are you here?" I ask.

Markell shrugs out of his jacket. "Because you needed me."

"But . . . why?" It doesn't make sense. "I never did that for you."

"I know," he says. "Good thing I'm not you."

I let out a choked laugh, and when I look up at him again, my throat tightens painfully. My next inhale comes as a hitched sob, and then I'm finally crying, tears streaming down my face as I grip the doorframe.

Markell drops his suitcase and pulls me into his chest, right there on the front porch. There are still cameras out here sometimes, people who like to drive these winding roads in search of a story, but right now, I don't care. I wrap my arms around his neck and suddenly I'm fifteen again, curled next to him on a dingy motel mattress. We're sitting together on the bus out of Memphis, silver cat pin pressed into my palm. He's fluffing my dress at the Grammys. I'm watching him leave. I used to think hearts were like glass—shiny and sharp and so very breakable. Now I think the only person I was terrified of breaking was me.

We sit together on the couch with mugs of tea steaming in our laps. There are too many things to apologize for, too much lost time to rewind in a single afternoon, but I still try. He shows me pictures of his daughter, Dani, and tells me how she's going to college in Memphis next year. She wants to be a reporter and I laugh, remembering all the times reporters tore our lives apart looking for something scandalous. He tells me about how Derrick took up art in retirement, how he sells landscape paintings out of their garage now. When he's done, he looks at me with blazing sincerity and says, "You're not going to die, Decklee. I don't think you know how."

I wish more than anything I could believe him.

By the time we fall silent, the sun is sinking below the horizon outside. I take his hand, reveling at how it still feels the same, all these years later.

"Have you called her?" Markell asks.

I know immediately what he means. I shake my head. "She doesn't want to see me."

That's the truth. I'm going to spend however long I have left trying to make things up to Markell, but there's no world where I have enough time to start with her. She's gone, vanished without a trace, and even now, years later, I have no idea where to find her. I look for her in every city, I think I see her face in every crowd, but whenever I look over my shoulder, it's always a trick of the light.

"It doesn't matter," I whisper. "I couldn't even if I wanted to. I don't know where she is."

Markell is silent for a long time. He runs his thumb over the back of my hand and exhales. "I know," he says. "But I do."

THIRTY-THREE

Darren

"Happy first day of senior year!"

I look up from my locker just in time for Madison to throw herself into my arms and send us both stumbling into the flow of first-period foot traffic. Her collection of beaded camp bracelets digs into my spine as she hugs me tight.

"How was camp?" I ask when she releases me. "Was that cute counselor back?"

"No, he actually got arrested for fraud."

"Fun!" I sling my backpack over one shoulder and the two of us head down the hall. We say hi to Emily coming back from gym, pointedly ignore Benton and Mary Kelly, who are aggressively making out in the middle of the senior hallway, and wave to everyone else as we pass. The hallways are bursting with noise and light and all the strange, wonderful anticipation that comes with the first day of school. Madison is happily chatting about the *other* cute counselor who has, conveniently, not been arrested for anything, and I stay quiet. I haven't told her or Emily the details from my summer road trip with Kendall or anything about what happened with Carla. They don't feel like things you can slip into a casual conversation, especially when I'm not sure I fully understand them myself.

Beneath the buzz of conversation is a familiar sepia-toned nostalgia. I feel it everywhere now. Last year, the idea of living in Mayberry was stifling. Now it's like an inevitability. Maybe this is why everyone in town moves so slowly, takes their time. When you don't have anywhere to go, there's no point in hurrying.

When the bell rings at the end of the day, I'm still staring at the same blank notebook I'd started on Carla's porch the day Decklee's announcement came over the radio. The page is empty except for the words scrawled at the top. *Fall feature story about . . .*

I never did figure that out, did I?

I shove everything in my backpack and fall into the crowd heading out to the parking lot. Madison stays after school for cross-country, so Emily and I walk home alone, shoulder to shoulder, until we reach the fork where she turns left and I continue straight.

"How's Kendall?" she asks.

I look up, surprised at the question. "What do you mean?"

"I mean you two are dating, right? That's the vibe I'm getting?"

My cheeks burn. Kendall and I haven't exactly had a conversation about what we're doing now that we're home, but we talk every day. He texted me this morning to wish me good luck on the first day of class and just remembering it now makes my chest flutter with excitement.

"I knew it!" Emily points at me triumphantly. "Finally."

I hold up my hands. "I didn't say anything!"

"Please, you're smiling at the *idea* of dating him. One time I asked you about Benton and you literally gagged."

"Yes, well. That's because Benton is horrible."

We stand at our intersection a minute longer, Emily grinning up at me through her freshly chopped bangs. There's this warm, giddy light spreading through my chest, and when she turns toward home, waving at me over her shoulder, I think I'm glad I'm here for this. I'm glad I'm able to enjoy these little slices of home.

The rest of the walk is short, but I call Kendall anyway, desperate to hear his voice after all day inside.

"I hate working without you," he says when he picks up. "Please, drop out of school so I don't have to organize the breakroom by myself."

I grin. "Tempting. Do you think I'll get a raise?"

"Oh, never. Bob would sell the place before promoting either of us."

I'm sweating by the time I turn onto my street. The only thing Mayberry High School hates more than my articles are girls in tank tops, which is why I'm dressed like a seventeenth-century nun despite the fact it's over a hundred degrees. I find myself longing for Bob's frigid air-conditioning as Kendall runs through his day at work. He might be stuck organizing the breakroom, but at least he isn't outside. Even Carla's roses are wilting, and my stomach gives a low pang at the sight of them.

I peer into her garden, hoping to find her on the porch, but of course she's nowhere to be seen. I miss the easy familiarity of our conversations over the fence. I miss having tea on her porch, gossiping about everyone in town, and doing homework at her kitchen table. Last year, I could have burst through the front door with my complaints about the dress code and Carla would have nodded sagely and drawn up a plan to sue the administration into the ground.

But the last few weeks have been a guessing game. Would she be outside? How long could I avoid her? Would she ever want to see me again? I can't take a whole year of this. I hate that she ever thought I'd choose my own self-serving interests over her feelings, and I hate myself for even considering the possibility. And I miss her.

It's another minute before I realize Kendall has stopped speaking. He's just there on the other end of the line, letting me walk and think in silence. "Hey, Kendall?"

"Yeah?"

"Can I call you back? I have something I need to do."

I know he understands what I mean. "Sure thing," he says. "But if I don't hear from you by tonight, I'm going to assume she murdered you."

I laugh. "That might be a good call."

There's a brief pause where I wonder how we're supposed to end phone calls now. In the end I hang up first, deciding that's a conversation for another day. Then I take a deep breath and turn up Carla's driveway. I know she's home the second I knock on the door, because I can smell cinnamon from all the way out here.

"Carla, it's me."

When she doesn't respond, I knock again, louder this time. "Hello?"

Nothing.

I roll my eyes and slam the heel of my palm into the door again and again. "You can't ignore me forever! I'm not—"

The door swings open and I almost fall, catching myself on the doorframe just in time.

"Darren." Carla says my name like it's the last word she wants in her mouth. "To what do I owe the pleasure?"

I straighten and toss my hair out of my face. "It's the first day of school," I say pointedly. "I always come over after the first day to tell you which teachers grew facial hair and who broke up with who."

One of her eyebrows lifts, ever so slightly. "So, who broke up with who?"

I scowl. "*Not* Benton and Mary Kelly."

Carla stands in the doorway so long I think she's going to shut me out. I think she's going to leave me on the porch and pretend I don't exist. Then she shakes her head and steps back to let me into the hall. "I don't know what you ever saw in that boy."

Relief sweeps through me as I follow her toward the kitchen, relaxing into the familiar pattern of conversation.

"Where's Mr. Wilkinson?" Carla asks. She grabs a pitcher of

lemonade off the counter and pours a glass instinctively. "Is he coming?"

I shake my head. "No, he's at work. But he'll be thrilled you asked about him. It'll be a completely unnecessary boost to his ego."

She almost laughs; I see it in the way her mouth twitches. She almost lets me in. I lean against the counter, gaze falling on the half-finished crossword in the corner. "It's 'amputated,'" I say.

"What?"

I wave a hand at the puzzle. "Twelve down, 'surgically removed.'"

That's how I feel now, standing in her kitchen with all this anger between us—like a very important, very vital part of myself has been yanked out.

"I did want to write your story," I blurt. "When I left on that quest, I wanted to find something I could sell to get me out of here. And when I heard those new songs, it felt like a sign. I wanted to find Mickenlee Hooper and tell the world what happened. But that doesn't matter to me, Carla. I don't care. I would never use you like that. I just want to know what happened. I want to understand."

I know it's risky to bring up the same subject that made her kick me out in the first place, but I need Carla to know the truth, at least. Slowly, she lifts her own glass of lemonade and takes a sip. It's not an answer, it's not an agreement, but I take it as permission to continue.

"So here's what I think," I say. "You never set out to be famous. You didn't want to be onstage, or in press photos. That was Decklee's job and even though you were credited, most people saw that music as hers. Her songs, her lyrics, her stories, but I think you liked it that way." I'm spinning this story for myself mostly, watching it unfold in the warm, sweet-smelling space of the kitchen. "Kendall said something when we were on the road, you know. That Decklee was . . . not necessarily a good person. I think she was dedicated and ambitious and probably left a lot of broken pieces for other people to pick up."

A muscle twitches in Carla's jaw. I watch her expression harden, and again, I shiver at just how cold she feels. This next part is harder, more personal than anything I've shared before, but I don't think I can ask her to trust me if I don't also acknowledge my own secrets, the truth I've kept tucked in the dark for years.

"I don't want to pretend to know how things were," I say carefully, unable to meet Carla's gaze. "But freshman year, there was this girl, Miranda Song. One day, she kissed me behind the bleachers. It was my first kiss actually, and at the time I didn't even think about the fact that she was a girl. I just thought about how cool it had been to kiss her and how excited I was to see her again. But the next day, she acted like I didn't exist. She only ever kissed me behind the bleachers or at night after football games when no one could see."

Even now, I can still feel Miranda's hands on my hips, her lips on my neck. When I finally got up the nerve to ask what we were, she had shrugged and said, *Nothing. This isn't something you tell people about, it's just something you do.*

"Anyway," I continue. "I didn't really think about what that meant for me until later. And then I spent weeks googling a bunch of different 'Am I Gay?' quizzes and convincing myself it was 'just for research.' But it turns out straight people don't spend night after night taking quizzes to confirm if they are, in fact, straight, so. Joke's on me, I guess."

Carla stares at me a long time, painted fingers tapping against her side. Her silhouette in the afternoon sun so familiar that I have no idea how I never put it together. "And this is news for you?" she asks. "That you like girls?"

"Yeah." I nod. "I mean, no, the feeling was always there, obviously, but it's definitely a new—" I break off. "Wait, is it not news to you?"

Carla shrugs. "I just assumed you knew and weren't telling anyone."

"I . . . what?" I shake my head, realization locking in a second too late. "Wait, could you *tell*? Is there, like, a *vibe*?"

"You're asking me if you have a gay vibe?" Carla asks, completely deadpan. "Is that a real question?"

"Oh my god." I bury my face in my hands. "Okay, never mind, that's not the point. The *point* is that I know it's, like, okay to be out in some places, but it still doesn't feel okay for two girls to kiss in Mayberry. Gay people exist here, obviously. They exist everywhere, but that doesn't mean it's easy."

Carla looks down, gaze coming to rest somewhere between my feet. "I know," she says softly. "It's easier when people aren't looking, but we didn't really have that luxury."

"The headlines after the Oscars," I say. "I've seen them."

"Yes, everyone did. But it didn't start there. People had been talking about us for years."

"How did it start, then?" I ask. I feel Carla start to hesitate, so I offer up, "For me, it was my friend Emily. I don't know how long I had feelings for her, but I remember the exact moment I thought about kissing her and the exact moment I made myself stop. That's why I started dating Benton last year. Because Emily was someone dangerous and real who I cared about very much, and I thought I could make those feelings go away."

I realize I've never said that out loud before, never put the feeling into words. I've always thought vocalizing it would break me, or change everything somehow, but nothing happens. The world keeps turning and I exhale, pressing my palms against my thighs.

Across from me, I hear Carla do the same. "We were together for years before the Oscars. Honestly, we were together from the day we met. It was always going to happen eventually, but that was the first time it was a big enough story. The first time we got scared."

"She was dating someone," I remember. "Some guy from her label."

Carla laughs softly. "No, she was never dating him."

Of course, I figured as much, but this is where the story goes cold for me, where I'm unable to keep grasping at straws because there's nothing left to grasp. "So what made you leave? Did you just want to start a new life?"

"No." Carla leans back against the counter. "I left because Decklee Cassel was a selfish coward, Darren, and I loved her too much to stay." I must look shocked because she lets out a hollow laugh. "Mr. Wilkinson's a good judge of character. You should keep him."

I nod, turning the words over in my mind. It's a harsh truth, the exact opposite of everything I thought I knew about Decklee Cassel, and still, I don't think I'm surprised. "How long did you know that about her?" I ask. "If you were together for so long—"

"There was always a scandal, always a story. I was . . ." Carla falters, and I notice, for the first time, how hard she's gripping her glass—fingers white-knuckled and trembling.

"I'm sorry," I say. "You don't have to—"

"You'll make a lousy reporter if you apologize for every question," she snaps. "I told Decklee I would give it all up—the money, the music, the career we built. I told her I didn't care, that I'd leave with her, and she told me that wasn't an option. She wanted me to get married, to sacrifice myself to build her up, and that was it, I think. That was when I realized she would always love herself more."

This isn't something you tell people about, this is just something you do.

Those words had always stuck with me, shame under my skin. The Decklee Cassel who fled Mayberry would never risk going back, even if it meant keeping the people she loved in the dark.

"I can't even blame her," Carla adds. "If I worked my way out of here, I'd feel the same, but I also couldn't stay with her after that. I mailed her lyrics for the next record because I had to, but she didn't use them. I don't think she ever looked at them. I just knew she'd never find me here. She hated this town almost as much as you do."

I flinch, pulling away from the comparison. At the beginning of the summer, I would have welcomed it. I would have made that single compliment my entire personality, but now I don't think I hate this town. Decklee wanted to make it go away. I want to make it better. When I try to speak again, the words stick in my throat. "I don't think I want to be like her."

"I know," Carla says. "You're not, I'm sorry. She would have never apologized the way you did to Kendall. She would have never admitted she was wrong."

A small comfort, but I take it. "So why go back?" I ask. "Why go back to record those new songs, after everything you went through to leave?"

"I didn't," Carla says. "She found me. She told me she was dying and wanted to write one more album."

"And you did?"

She rolls her eyes and it's such a Carla response that I almost laugh. "Of course I did. I loved her. Even then, all those years later. We made the album, she made me all sorts of promises, and then she left. I never saw or heard from her again until that radio announcement."

Oh. I remember Carla on the porch that day, how she'd retreated inside the second the announcement was over. I thought it was because she wasn't interested, that she didn't care about Decklee's music the same way Mom and I do, but no. It was always something deeper. "I don't understand. Why would she do that?"

Carla sighs, a weary exhale I feel deep in my bones. "You don't understand Decklee Cassel, Darren. No one does. But you can survive her, if you're lucky."

I run a hand over the table, following the imaginary time-line. Decklee's diagnosis. Finding Carla in Mayberry. Writing new songs, new lyrics. "I thought the fourth clue was leading me here," I say, half to myself. "I thought the time capsule was buried in Mayberry. It was the perfect song, the perfect setup. There's no reason for it to loop back to Nashville."

But maybe there was no reason for any of it. I had set out on the quest thinking it was for me, for the fans. I believed every clue had meaning, every answer was leading me somewhere new, but maybe Decklee only ever built it for herself. Maybe there was no strategy, no reason, just another way to keep her legacy alive for a little bit longer. I hate that I'll never know for sure. This isn't a smooth ending tied up with a neat ribbon like I'd been anticipating, because Decklee wasn't either. In the end, she was a girl just like me, who let her fear of all the wrong things drive her over the edge.

"I'm glad you went," Carla says. "I'm glad you found what you were looking for, even if it wasn't a story."

She runs a hand across her face, and I realize I've never seen her cry. She must have, of course, behind closed doors or into her pillow. Decklee had walked back into her life, used her up, and disappeared. I can't turn on the radio without hearing Decklee Cassel's name. What must it be like for Carla to go through this alone?

I set down my cup and cross the kitchen in two quick strides.

Usually, Carla tolerates my hugs. Today, she practically falls into it. "Are you okay?" I whisper into her shoulder. "Are you going to be okay?"

She's silent for a long time, just standing there with her arms wrapped around me. Eventually, she sighs and pulls back. "I'm tired, Darren."

It's not an answer, but I feel the truth of it echo through me. I meant what I said earlier. I don't want her story, but I think this moment right here would make a good one. People connected by grief and time. Singular moments that fall through the cracks. I've spent my entire life chasing Decklee Cassel, wanting her courage and her drive. But that sort of destructive star power isn't sustainable.

"It's kind of disappointing, isn't it?" I say. "All that work and I still ended up back here. I never even heard that new album."

Carla's eyes narrow. "Really?"

"Yeah. Mike Fratt has it. Which is just, like, a wild thing to say out loud. He's doing a livestream premiere next week, but if he thinks I'm logging on to his channel for any reason, he's delusional."

The corner of Carla's mouth lifts, and for the first time all afternoon, I think she might actually smile. "Well, we can't have that."

She pulls herself out of my grip and walks over to the desk. After a minute of rummaging through the drawers, she turns, something clutched in one fist. Another flash drive, this one clear of cryptic rhymes and shining in the midafternoon sun.

My heart leaps into my throat. "Carla."

"Yes?"

"What is that?"

She glances at the flash drive in her hand. "This," she says, "is a pretty spectacular album, if I do say so myself."

"Oh my god." I lurch forward. "You *have* it?"

"I literally wrote it, Darren."

"Oh my god." It's the only thing I can say, the only thing that feels adequate for a situation like this. I take the flash drive with trembling fingers. "Can we . . . ? Can I listen to it? Is that weird? I don't want to . . . ?"

"For heaven's sake." Carla rolls her eyes, but she's smiling, really smiling now. "Come on."

I call Mom and Kendall as Carla brings another pitcher of lemonade out to the porch. They show up within minutes of each other, sweating and breathless and demanding an explanation I don't give. Instead, I slide the flash drive into my laptop and open the screen. Carla takes her usual seat, Mom sinks down in one of the rocking chairs, and I sit cross-legged on the floor next to Kendall, back braced against the railing.

I remember thinking once that moments like this were special—me and Mom and Carla sitting on her porch, enjoying the afternoon. And even though Carla's right, even though it *is* a truly spectacular album, I don't think it's what I'll remember. Instead, I'll remember Kendall's arm around me. I'll remember leaning into his shoulder as the first chorus kicks in, I'll remember Mom, blinking back tears, and I'll remember Carla, watching us all with her face tilted toward the sun.

She reaches over to pat my shoulder and I grab her hand

before she can pull away. I want to commit this moment to memory now, memorize every detail so that when I go to college next year and people ask me where I'm from, I can say *here*. I can tell them I'm from Mayberry, that I love it almost as much as I wanted to leave, and that every single one of those people has a special place in my heart. Because they do. Because they're a part of me. And right now, sitting on the porch with my favorite people in the world, I can't believe it's something I was ever ashamed of.

THIRTY-FOUR

Decklee
Mayberry, 2024

¶ t's raining the day I drive to Mayberry.

I'm not supposed to drive by myself anymore. A week ago, a doctor in a long white coat told me that could be dangerous, but I don't care. I'm Decklee Cassel. And I don't take orders from anybody.

I practiced what I would say on the way over. I had something prepared, I think, but when she opens the door and I see her for the first time since the last time, I forget how to breathe. I forget why I'm here and I forget why I didn't come sooner. Her eyes widen, lips parting, and I know beyond a shadow of a doubt that she never thought I'd find her.

I'm still the surprise no one sees coming, the girl at the Oscars in the blue dress.

It takes her a minute to speak, and when she does, it's as familiar as breathing. "What are you doing here?"

She's smart for choosing this place. I didn't believe Markell when he told me that night. I thought he was lying, but the truth is unavoidable. "I'm not here for you," I blurt, too quick to be true.

Her eyebrows lift and there's the Mickenlee Hooper I know, the one I missed like a heartbeat. "No," she says. "Of course not."

The rain is still falling, pinging off the railing at our backs. I wonder if she sees this moment the way I do—a split-screen hazy memory. Me, on her porch in a town that's not quite ours. Her, on a different porch in a different city, demanding I let her in and give her a chance.

"I'm dying, Mick."

A shadow flits across her face. "I know."

"No, I'm actually dying. As in—"

"I *know*, Decklee." Her jaw is set. "Is that all?"

It's not enough. Of course it's not, I've been dead to Mickenlee Hooper for years. But I didn't drive all this way for nothing. I lean in, force her to look up at me through the rain. "I want to do it again."

"Do what?"

"Record. I want to write with you. I want to make something new, something for after—" I break off. That's uncharted territory. I swallow and try again. "I haven't put out an album in eight years. I don't want to fade like that. I want to know someone will remember me."

You won't always have this. That's what Mickenlee said the day she left. She had been correct then and she has every right to throw it back in my face now. But she just folds her arms and says, "You're not easy to forget."

She still has constellations of freckles on her cheeks. I want to reach up and trace the cluster on the side of her jaw. "That's not what I mean," I say. "I don't want people to be able to forget. I don't want them to have a choice."

Mickenlee nods, a slow realization. "Right. Because you came here for them."

Them. The fans. The industry. The life I chose. I nod. "Yes."

"And why would I want to come back for that?"

I reach into my pocket and pull out a piece of old sheet music. "Whiskey Red"—battered and worn, ripped from the number of times I've opened it, read it, then folded it again. Maybe we would never have this kind of magic again, but right now, this paper is proof that it was ours once.

"Because this was the best song you ever wrote, Mick. I think of you every time I hear it because it's brilliant and wonderful, and I don't think we're done."

Because I'm here now, begging, and I know I didn't listen when you asked me. I know I didn't go with you, but you were always a better person than me.

That's what I count on now. That Mickenlee Hooper is still a better person than I deserve. That maybe, *maybe*, she wants this as much as I do.

We stand like that for a long time, her in the doorway, me on the porch. She looks down. "You have no right to be here."

"I know."

"You're the one who ruined this, not me. You're the reason we're like this."

"I know."

"You don't deserve my help." Her voice cracks. "You don't deserve anything."

She's right. She's always right. I step forward anyway. "I know."

There are tears caught in her lashes and I hold out a hand. I didn't think about what I'd do if she said no. I didn't think about where I'd go. Back home to an empty house, to a city that's forgetting about me. To nothing and no one. Despite everything, that's where I ended up, caught in the loop of a town just like this one. *You won't always have this.*

But here is my hand, open and trembling, hanging in empty space. Here is what's left of my heart. All these years later and I'm still reaching, still clawing and fighting for something I don't deserve. Mickenlee takes a breath. I watch her shoulders rise and fall.

Then, like she still can't quite believe this is where we ended up, she reaches back.

THIRTY-FIVE

Darren
One Year Later

"**D**arren Purchase! I thought you weren't getting back until tomorrow!"

Kendall throws his arms around me the second I walk through the door, squeezes me so tight my feet lift off the ground. I shiver when he whispers, "I missed you," into my hair.

The gas station on Hawthorne is completely unrecognizable from the nights of midnight tarot readings and seances. Now it's bustling, alive and cleared of cobwebs and phallic graffiti. Kendall knocked out the entire south wall when he bought the place to make room for more windows, and everything's painted a bright, vibrant yellow. I can smell bay leaf, cinnamon, and ginger wafting from the kitchen, and the food steaming on the tables around me looks delicious.

"This is incredible," I say, still taking in the new additions as Kendall reaches over to hug Emily and Madison as they come in behind me.

"Smells great, too," Emily adds. "You got a table open?"

"Oh, you haven't heard?" Kendall folds his arms. "We're Arkansas's newest 'Must Try.' We don't seat just anyone."

"It's okay," I say. "I actually know the owner, I'm sure he could put in a good word."

Kendall pretends to consider. "I'll see what I can do. Want me to get anything started before we go?"

"I'm good," I say. "We should be back for dessert."

Kendall glances over his shoulder. I can see his staff flying back and forth inside the kitchen, calling out order numbers, dodging plates, while his father stands behind the counter, talking a group of middle school girls into buying an entire coconut cake. I know Kendall's swamped, but I also know that he understands why I need him now. He nods and unties his apron. "I think they can handle themselves for a few hours."

I steer Emily and Madison to their table and tell them we'll be back soon. It's an empty promise, one I don't know if I can keep, but it feels better than nothing. We're supposed to be celebrating our last weeks of summer before heading off to college and it's not their fault I need to do this next part alone.

The parking lot outside is packed, cars lining either side of the state road, waiting for available tables. Kendall reaches for his keys, but I shake my head. "Nope. It's my turn."

He laughs. "You get *one* car and you're a new person, Purchase. All that money did go to your head."

"Shut up." But I'm smiling as we climb into my hand-me-down Subaru and pull out of the parking lot, back toward the center of Mayberry.

"How have you been?" he asks after a few minutes of silence. "I feel like I've hardly seen you this summer."

"Not entirely my fault," I say. "You were opening a restaurant."

"And you moved to campus early," he shoots back. "How does it feel to be a college girl now?"

I bite my lip, remembering the overwhelming maze of buildings and lawns. "Like I'll never live up to all the things people think I can do?"

"You will." He says it with so much certainty that it's hard not to believe him.

I blush and stare pointedly out over the road. "How's business? All that fancy grant money really worked in your favor. You have more customers than the McDonald's in Ashdown."

"Well, we both know who I have to thank for the fancy grant money."

I do. That's what makes this next part so hard.

I park in front of my old house, on the side of a road that doesn't quite feel like mine anymore. I haven't lived here since June, but the familiar blue tile and sun-drenched driveway are the same. The only thing that gives away its emptiness is the SOLD sign stamped into the front yard.

It hasn't stopped being weird.

"Your mom found a place, right?" Kendall asks.

I nod. "Thirty minutes outside of Nashville. You wouldn't believe how funded those suburbs schools are."

Mom's pay raise is great for her, and the whole situation is great for me because she's close enough to let me borrow her washing machine and still far enough away for me to pretend to be a normal Vanderbilt student. But we're not here for me. We're not here for my old house.

I reach for Kendall's hand and we walk together up Carla's porch. I try, really try, not to look at the wilted roses, overgrown bushes, and unmowed lawn. That's on me, I suppose. I haven't been around to take care of the place.

"Have you been inside yet?" Kendall asks, voice low and close to my ear.

I shiver. "Not since she left."

Left. It's too light a word. One day Carla was here, tending to her garden and talking to Mom over the fence. The next, the house was empty, quiet, and cold. Carla Krenik vanished into the night, no more than a whisper. I suppose I shouldn't have been surprised; she was always good at disappearing. I just didn't think it would happen like this.

"It feels weird, doesn't it?" I say as I pull the door open.

Kendall shrugs. "It shouldn't. This place is yours now."

Another chill creeps through me as we step into the hall. It's true. Carla left me everything—all the things she didn't need, all the things she couldn't take. It's overwhelming and wild and so unexpected that it's taken me five whole months to come back here. I don't know Mayberry without Carla.

Maybe that's part of the reason I can't stay.

"Okay," I say, more to myself than to Kendall. "Let's take an hour or two tonight and get a feel for what we're working with, and then come back tomorrow and finish up. Or I can come back," I add. "I know you're busy."

"Trying to get rid of me." Kendall squeezes my hand. "How

many times do I have to tell you, Purchase? I'd only do this for you."

The same thing he said when I finally asked him on a real date last year.

The same thing he said when I told him I loved him and he pretended to consider before scooping me into his lap and kissing me breathless in the bed of his truck.

The same thing he said when we broke up after graduation, when I told him I was leaving and didn't want him to follow.

I've been desperately trying to imagine a future without Kendall, trying to make it feel real and normal before I leave for good next week. Long distance won't work. It's something we both agreed on long ago, but the rapidly approaching expiration date didn't make things easier.

I swallow over the sudden lump in my throat. I've actually been doing a great job of holding it together this summer. I've bounced around from newspaper boot camp, to orientation, to a vacation with Madison and Mom at Virginia Beach. I haven't had time to think about Kendall or, more accurately, my lack of Kendall.

I blame Carla's creepy, empty house for bringing him back now.

"Where does she keep everything?" Kendall asks, glancing around the bare living room. "Bedroom? Closet?"

"Over here." I motion him toward a door set off from the kitchen. "She showed me once, but I haven't seen it all."

I flick on the light, illuminating a rickety set of stairs, descending into the dark.

"Oh." I hear Kendall audibly gulp over my shoulder. "It's a murder basement. I get it."

After I turn on the light at the bottom of the stairs, it becomes significantly less murder-y and significantly more overwhelming. There are shelves upon shelves of boxes, bins overflowing with handwritten sheet music, baskets of photo albums, wardrobes trailing sequined gowns across the dusty floor. Everything smells like mothballs and dirt, and even our shoes leave imprints on the dusty cement under our feet.

"Okay," I say, trying to survey the room as objectively as possible. "Let's think. We need a pile for museum donations, one for the Brentwood House, and one for the Smithsonian exhibit. And then we need a pile for the scholarship auction."

Kendall nods. "That was a great idea, by the way. Really. You're going to change a lot of people's lives with that."

I make the mistake of looking at him then, catching his grin in the dim light. I straighten my shoulders and turn away. "Let's get started."

It's easier said than done. The first box I open is stuffed to the brim with notebooks and I recognize Carla's handwriting right away. There's a lyric on the first page from the bridge of "Whiskey Red," another toward the middle that inspired the ending of "Times Are Changing." Piles and piles of lyrics overflowing in my lap. She wrote like she knew her time with Decklee was limited, like she had to get every ounce of herself onto the page.

"Oh my god," Kendall says. At first, I think he's as entranced as I am by the sheer number of songs in my lap. Then I turn and find him kneeling on the cold cement, an Oscar clasped in both hands. "I'd like to thank not only God, but Jesus," he begins.

"Kendall."

"And the Academy, for this amazing opportunity. As you all know, I am the *best* actor of our time, and this award is only more proof that I . . ." He trails off, eye catching on something over my shoulder. "Holy shit, there are *more*?"

Of course there are. There are shelves upon shelves stacked with gold statues. Grammys. CMAs. Radio awards. I don't know what Mike Fratt ever did with his winnings. I don't care enough to find out, but Decklee Cassel's time capsule is *nothing* compared to this.

"Thanks for doing this with me," I say as Kendall rubs the dust off an AMA statue. "I know you're busy, but it felt weird to come here without you."

"I'm glad you asked." He shakes his head. "I can't believe all this has just been here the whole time."

I nod. And now it's mine. We both know it's Carla who got Kendall the grant for his restaurant, even though it came from the estate. The Decklee Cassel Memorial Entrepreneurial Grant, a five-hundred-thousand-dollar gift to get a new idea off the ground.

"I didn't apply for this," Kendall said one afternoon when we were both sitting on her porch. "I can't . . . This is so much."

"It's not something you apply for, Mr. Wilkinson," Carla said. "It's a new award. You need to be nominated."

"Okay," he said, reading through the letter again and again. "Okay, so who nominated me?"

Carla looked at him for a long time before saying, "Me," and that was the end of the conversation.

Just like that, Kendall had his restaurant. He had a way to pay for night classes at the community college and a new transmission for the truck. And I had a letter of recommendation written by Mickenlee Hooper herself. Even though Carla says my application is the reason I got my scholarship to Vanderbilt, I don't think it hurt having her on my side. But then she left me this house. She left me everything, and I don't know what to do with it.

"It's quiet in here, don't you think?" Kendall asks.

I know what he means. The house is alive with ghosts. If I close my eyes, I can almost see Carla in the stairwell, in her favorite yellow dress and heels, apron tied around her waist. I see Mickenlee Hooper as she was in the seventies, slamming a new contract on Ricky Grasso's desk.

And maybe one day I'll tell Kendall about the phone number Carla slipped between the pages of my notebook that last day on her porch. Maybe one day I'll tell him about the letter she sent me from California, the polaroid of her and Markell Fansworth tucked in the back, and the note at the bottom that said *Visit soon!* Maybe I'll tell him about how, for the first time in decades, she's no longer alone.

"Here." I dig an old record player from under a pile of silk dresses. "Play something."

"What are you in the mood for?" Kendall flips through the records, turning them over as I lean back on my hands.

"Something good."

He knows what I mean. There are a few seconds of staticky silence before the song pours through the speakers. "Whiskey Red" sounds different on a record player. It sounds like how it was meant to be played, old and crooning and slow.

"Damn, this really is a good song." Kendall's nodding along to the beat. Then, without warning, he extends a hand in my direction. "Come here."

"Kendall . . ."

"Please, Darren? I came to the murder basement in the ghost house for you."

I let him pull me across the dusty floor until I'm pressed into his side and my arms wind their way around his neck instinctually. He rests his chin on top of my hair as I exhale, settling into the familiar way we fit together. He smells like ginger, like the kitchen of his restaurant, but also like something deep and familiar and so utterly Mayberry.

It hits me for the first time then that I'm really leaving. This isn't the kind of town you come back to. There's no reason for me to visit. Mom is gone, the nearest hotel is miles away, and even though we both knew this was coming, it didn't stop Kendall and me from crying and fighting and trying to make it work. But the truth never changed.

Kendall isn't leaving Mayberry. I'm not going to stay.

"Are you scared?" he asks.

I know what he means immediately and press my face into his shoulder. "Yes."

There's no point in trying to hide it. It's not the same as I was last summer—afraid of letting everyone down, afraid of failing, afraid of *myself*. Those fears still linger, of course, but they're different now. They're more in check.

"I've never lived anywhere else," I say, voice muffled by his shirt. "I don't know how."

Kendall tightens his grip on me. "You're going to Vanderbilt," he says. "You're doing the thing you've wanted to do your entire life. You'll figure it out."

"But what if I never come back?"

The question slips out before I can stop it, but Kendall doesn't hesitate. "You were always bigger than this town. You were always going to change the world. But *shit*, I'm really going to miss you."

I pull back and his eyes are as bright as mine. "This sucks," I say. "Really. I hate this."

"Me too."

But maybe this is what life is. You form communities, you grow roots, you let places and towns and people work their way under your skin. I'm going to rip myself up next week when I drive to Nashville, and I'm going to feel every second of it. Maybe everyone has little roots inside them, curled up clippings of different eras, different lives, different loves. Even if the Mayberry part of me shrivels up and dies, I'm certain Kendall will still be here, decades later, right in the center of my heart.

The chorus of "Whiskey Red" kicks back in and I feel it like a hook inside my rib cage. The same words I've heard thousands of times, cutting me open, fraying my edges. When I open my eyes, I see Carla, standing next to the pile of notebooks I'd been flipping through. Her hair is loose, flowing around her shoulders, and she's smiling at me, swaying back and forth to the music. I blink and she's gone.

Kendall wipes the back of his hand across his face and stands. "Dance with me."

The same way we did in a Nashville bar, in the sticky summer heat. The same way we have all year. And now I find myself reaching for him one last time, pushing myself to my feet to take his hand. "I'd only do this for you, Wilkinson."

Then we dance, the final chorus of "Whiskey Red" echoing off the dusty basement walls.

And Kendall and I are the only two people in the world.

Acknowledgments

People told me that my second book would be harder to write, but what they all failed to realize is that I am simply Built Different because this book has always sort of been my happy place. I wrote it before I even queried *Made of Stars*, so I've spent a lot of time staring at the original Google doc and secretly hoping it would find its way into the world one day. I don't really believe in having a "book of your soul," but I do feel very lucky that this one exists and incredibly grateful for all the people who helped make it a reality.

To Claire Friedman, agent of my dreams. I remember being so nervous to send you this book after you'd just signed a sci-fi. I didn't even know if it was something I could pull off, but you've been the best, most supportive advocate of this story (and me) since day one. I never thought I'd find someone who so clearly gets what I want my books to say, and I feel very fortunate to have you in my corner. You are, unfortunately, stuck with me!

To my editor, Maggie Rosenthal. This book is so special to me, and to have you treat it with such enthusiasm and thoughtfulness has meant the world. Thank you for understanding the heart of this story from the beginning and for believing I could tell it. I've always known I was in good hands, but after this one, I really feel like I ended up in the best.

Publishing is such a team sport, and this book exists mostly because of all the people working behind the scenes. A huge thank-you to everyone at Viking and Penguin Teen for putting this book in the hands of readers everywhere and an extra-special shout-out to Louisa Cannell and Kristie Radwilowicz for giving me the best yeehaw cover imaginable!

The fact that I'm writing acknowledgments for my second book is a testament to how many people have literally picked me up off the ground along the way. To my AMM critique group and to Andy specifically, who read an early draft of this book and texted me "this Carla bitch is suspicious" before she was even halfway done (I know you love being right, so here's a public acknowledgment that you were onto something). To Mary E. Roach and Brit—publishing really bonds people and so does getting stung by Chesapeake Bay jellyfish. Since we've lived through both, I think this means we'll be together forever, which is fine with me because I already have an entire shelf dedicated to housing every book you write. And to Serena Kaylor. I'm forever grateful for the day we slid into each other's inboxes because I couldn't imagine doing this with anyone else.

To Emma Benshoff, Emily Van, Victoria Hendersen, SJ Whitby, Phoebe Rowen, and everyone who read an early draft of this book in whatever iteration. Your kind words and encouragement meant more to me than you know.

To Sophia DeRise. You've read every version of this book since the time it was a single-POV fetus in a Google doc, and you've owned unofficial Decklee Cassel fan art since 2020, when the idea of me publishing anything was still a wild, unimaginable dream. You really deserve an entire book of thanks, but I hope this is enough for now. Thank you for pushing me through multiple late-night revisions, for always responding to my ten-minute-long voice notes, and for texting me "I think we need to acknowledge the implications that 'Losing You' by Taylor Swift has on the Mickenlee Hooper Cinematic Universe" seconds after the song leaked. You were right, of course. The implications are life-changing.

To Sasha Smith for always being down to drink wine and eavesdrop on Emissary first dates with me. Thank you for being the perfect confidant, the most supportive cheerleader, and the best Dollywood road trip partner.

To the real-life Ricky Grasso, tour director extraordinaire. I'm sorry I didn't give you a better character, but in my defense, I didn't think this book would ever see the light of day when I wrote it, and you have a cool name! Just know that I do actually adore you and am constantly counting the days until we are reunited.

To my family, who never misses an opportunity to promote my books. Your support means the world whether it's from the opposite coast or from a boat in the middle of the ocean.

To Caysi, Alexis, Carissa, Chelsea, and Maria. We stumbled into each other's lives a decade ago, and I'm so glad we never left. Your encouragement, extensive grassroots marketing campaigns, and ability to answer every random question I have is such a big part of why I'm able to do this at all. And to Chelsea specifically—I know we both kind of laughed when you told me about Dolly Parton's Dream Box and I said, "omg what if they open it and it's empty?" but here we are. Your silly little fun fact inspired an entire book, and if I had to pick anyone to be my musical cross-country road trip partner, it would be you.

To Maria (again). You get your own paragraph because we moved in together the week I got my first agent offer, and now there are two (!!) books on our unofficial Jenna Voris bookshelf. Thank you for being the best Nashville guide, for driving me around your ex-boyfriend's neighborhood until I found the perfect Brentwood House, and for telling me that Kendall finding street parking on Broadway was totally un-realistic. I didn't change the scene, but I do appreciate the commitment to detail. Again, you know way too many pub-lishing secrets to ever be allowed to leave me, and I wouldn't let you even if you tried. And of course, special shout-out to the Rapisardas for lending me their guest room every time I came to town and to Eli for answering all my Vanderbilt/ Nashville history questions. My timeline can't thank you enough.

To Sarina Allison. I know I say this all the time, but I'm a bet-ter person for knowing you. I didn't realize how personal this book would become or how much of it would unintentionally mirror our own journeys, but please know that it exists in part because your courage and commitment to being yourself gave me the strength to do the same.

And a final thank-you to anyone who picked up this book. The first time I heard the word "bisexual" was in an episode of *Glee*, which is arguably one of the worst places to have a nu-anced conversation about identity, but when I was a teenager, access to queer stories was limited. I didn't fully unpack the implications of that particular episode until later, but I did try to write the story my teenage self would have wanted—something messy and dramatic and larger than life but something that is, ultimately, hopeful.